Praise for Riddle of the Haunted Hoard

"Pucci is revealed to be a sharp, smart, witty, and likable detective on a fun, and sometimes scary, adventure... The protagonist only becomes more endearing as the story goes on, and it has a carefree energy that readers will enjoy. A simple but entertaining supernatural thriller with an appealing main character." —*Kirkus Reviews*

Five Star Reviews from *Reader's Choice*

Author L. J. Aldon brings a fresh voice to paranormal mystery through a clever blend of supernatural elements and traditional sleuthing, and I loved every second of this high-stakes adventure that had a unique mood and feel to it. The story combines elements of traditional mystery with paranormal intrigue, creating a fresh take on the genre while maintaining the satisfaction of classic detective work.

I would enthusiastically recommend The Riddle of the Haunted Hoard to readers who enjoy mysteries that successfully blend supernatural elements with traditional detective work. —K.C. Finn for Readers' Favorite

Gripping, entertaining, and filled with unexpected twists, The Riddle of the Haunted Hoard will leave you eagerly awaiting the next installment. This novel is enjoyable, with smooth pacing that never lags. L. J. Aldon is especially skilled at writing character dialogue and can spin a story into an intriguing and intricate mystery. — Ibrahim Aslan for Readers' Favorite

L. J. Aldon has a true knack for the atmospheric in The Riddle of the Haunted Hoard, mixing the supernatural with a classic whodunit. Aldon does well in engulfing readers in a whirlwind of paranormal energy that, quite literally, surrounds Pucci as she is pulled further into helping JD. I loved the turbulent peeling away of what has transpired and felt that Pucci was a totally relatable, likable, and capable character who is absolutely worthy of a series.

Aldon's prose is sharp and comfortably marries Pucci's psychic abilities with the procedural elements of the investigation. Fans of paranormal mysteries will relish the deft storytelling, multi-layered characters, and all the seen and unseen forces at work. Very highly recommended. — Jamie Michele for Readers' Favorite

Pucci displays a respect for the supernatural, the rituals of engaging with spirits, and compassion for the newly deceased. The writer conveys much detail about her with simple yet effective descriptions. The mystery components in the novel are gripping and well-written, taking the reader on a winding journey to unmask the killer. — K. T. Bowes for Readers' Favorite

More from The Sager Group

The Swamp: Deceit and Corruption in the CIA
An Elizabeth Petrov Thriller (Book 1)
by Jeff Grant

Eat Wheaties: A Novel
by Michael Kun

#MeAsWell: A Novel
by Peter Mehlman

Death Came Swiftly: Novel About the Tay Bridge Disaster of 1879
by Bill Abrams

High Tolerance: A Novel of Sex, Race, Celebrity, Murder... and Marijuana
by Mike Sager

Miss Havilland: A Novel
by Gay Daly

The Orphan's Daughter: A Novel
by Jan Cherubin

Lifeboat No. 8: Surviving the Titanic
by Elizabeth Kaye

Into the River of Angels: A Novel
by George R. Wolfe

Goodbye, Sweetberry Park: A Novel of City Life,
Creeping Gentrification and Flesh-eating Snakes
by Josh Green

See our entire library at TheSagerGroup.net

Riddle of the Jeweled Cipher

L.J. Aldon

A PUCCI RIDDLE MYSTERY

Riddle of the Jeweled Cipher
(A Pucci Riddle Mystery Book 2)

Copyright © 2025 L.J. Aldon

All rights reserved.

No part of this publication may be reproduced, stored in a retrieval system, or transmitted, in any form or by any means, electronic, mechanical, photocopying, recording, or otherwise, without the prior written permission of the publisher.

Published in the United States of America.

Cover and interior designed by Siori Kitajima, PatternBased.com

Cataloging-in-publication data for this book is available from the Library of Congress

ISBN-13
eBook: 978-1-958861-56-1
Paperback: 978-1-958861-55-4

Published by The Sager Group LLC
(TheSagerGroup.net)

Riddle of the Jeweled Cipher

L.J. Aldon

A PUCCI RIDDLE MYSTERY

THE SAGER GROUP
Artifex Te Adiuva

This is a work of fiction. Unless otherwise indicated, all the names, characters, businesses, places, events and incidents in this book are either the product of the author's imagination or used in a fictitious manner. Any resemblance to actual persons, living or dead, or actual events is purely coincidental.

For the Pucci's – Barb, Jena, Annie and Carolyn

And to all of you who read the first book and took the time to share how much you loved it and couldn't wait for the next—this is for you.

From my heart to yours, thank you.

Acknowledgements

Once again, I'd like to thank my editor extraordinaire, Pam Nettleton, for believing in Pucci. Also, my publisher Mike Sager for his continued belief in me.

My sister, Lauryann, for her unwavering support, encouragement, and promotion of the Pucci series.

My deepest gratitude to Harry Palmer for creating the Avatar® tools, which not only helped me overcome limiting beliefs about my writing but also allowed me to create with free attention.

And to my husband, Roy—for his love and for creating a safe space to create.

Contents

Acknowledgements xi
Prologue xv

Chapter 1 1
Chapter 2 7
Chapter 3 9
Chapter 4 11
Chapter 5 15
Chapter 6 23
Chapter 7 29
Chapter 8 39
Chapter 9 43
Chapter 10 47
Chapter 11 53
Chapter 12 57
Chapter 13 67
Chapter 14 73
Chapter 15 77
Chapter 16 83
Chapter 17 87
Chapter 18 95
Chapter 19 101
Chapter 20 109
Chapter 21 115
Chapter 22 121
Chapter 23 127
Chapter 24 131
Chapter 25 139
Chapter 26 143
Chapter 27 149
Chapter 28 153

Chapter 29 159
Chapter 30 165
Chapter 31 173
Chapter 32 177
Chapter 33 183
Chapter 34 187
Chapter 35 199
Chapter 36 205
Chapter 37 209
Chapter 38 215
Chapter 39 219
Chapter 40 221
Chapter 41 227
Chapter 42 231
Chapter 43 235
Chapter 44 239
Chapter 45 245
Chapter 46 249
Chapter 47 253
Chapter 48 259
Chapter 49 265
Chapter 50 271
Chapter 51 277
Chapter 52 283
Chapter 53 287
Chapter 54 293

Author's Note 297
About the Author 300
About the Publisher 301

Prologue

Georgetown, Grand Cayman, 2006

Blood pounded in his head, sweat poured down his temples. His trembling hands slowly lowered the binoculars from his bloodshot eyes. The bullet wound in his neck pulsed with pain as he scratched around the bandage that covered it. The low branches brushed against the wrinkled, scaly scar below his left eye.

"Bloody hell," he muttered to himself, "they have it. They found the cipher." He leaned against the tree for support, still weak from the loss of blood. The branches swayed gently in the warm, tropical breeze. He looked around for Anya. Something about her he didn't trust. Had she gotten too close to the women? His head was spinning. No matter, once he recovered the cipher, she was no use to him. No loose ends.

He watched as the inspector walked away from the table and out of the restaurant. The Riddle woman stayed. He watched her study the cipher. A server came by and blocked his view.

"Now what?" he put his question to the tree.

A disembodied voice hissed in reply. "You know what you need to do." Fear surged as he spun around too quickly. All went black.

Chapter 1

San Diego, California, One Year Later

Pucci repacked for the fifth time that day. She just knew that one last sweater should fit somehow in the already overstuffed suitcase. She had splurged for this trip and bought a high-end, navy-blue suitcase that was reinforced on all sides. It also came with upgraded zippers. "I'm going to need those zippers to hold!" she exclaimed, sitting on the suitcase, grunting as she began zipping.

"Who goes to Scotland in the winter, anyway?" her friend, Jamie, called out from the kitchen.

"Apparently I do," Pucci said, closing the zipper. She remained still for a few moments, fearing an explosion.

"Well, I just heard it's crazy cold there in the winter, and dark at like 3 p.m. in the afternoon, so why bother going this time of year?" Jamie said, coming into Pucci's bedroom. She looked at the overstuffed suitcase and started laughing. "Where are you going to put my gifts that you're buying for me?"

"Oh, damn, good point, Jamie. I guess I'll just have to buy small ones and pack them in another carry-on or something. I'll figure it out as I go. Plus, it stays light in Scotland till 4 p.m."

Jamie rolled her eyes. "You are the only person I know who would literally wing it on a trip like this. You have no reservations anywhere, you're not renting a car, and you have no idea where you're going to be and when. In a foreign country, for goodness' sake!"

"Only partially true. I got a great deal on a first-class ticket to London and then a train to Edinburgh. Booked a room in a castle too! I love going to visit places when they're not overrun by tourists. December in Scotland will be beautiful. And, my pilgrimage to Rosslyn Chapel will be a magical moment. I've been wanting to go to all these places for years. I have felt an energetic pull, especially to Rosslyn ever since I can remember after reading about it as a child. So going there for work to visit the distilleries on Islay is just icing on the cake! Islay is where all the great peaty Scotch whiskies are made."

Jamie pulled a face. "How can you drink that? I much prefer a good margarita."

Pucci chuckled. "Oh, and I ended up buying that rail pass. That's pretty good for me!" Pucci said, grunting as she lifted her suitcase to check the weight. "And I think I told you, when Randi found out I was going to be in Edinburgh, she asked for my support to help bury her great aunt. Do you remember Randi?"

Jamie nodded and smiled, "I remember Randi. I think we met at your birthday party last year. What a cool life she leads, sailing all over the world."

Pucci looked up at Jamie. "That's right. That was a fun party! By the way, Jamie, thank you, my friend, for house-sitting for me. It's such a comfort for me to know that you'll be here."

"A month's free lodging in San Diego? Are you kidding? You're doing me a favor!" Jamie said. "Come get some food before you go. I just make some quesadillas with New Mexico Hatch green chili peppers."

"Yum! Give me a minute, I need to pack all the electrical converters," she said as Jamie walked out of the room. Pucci looked up from her packing when she felt a familiar sensation in her stomach. David, Jamie's recently deceased husband, was suddenly standing in front of her. "David, I don't have time for another chat. I need to finish packing and get to the airport."

The apparition before her was one of the most solid she had ever encountered, which sometimes unnerved her about David's appearances. His features—a thin face with a rather large nose and thin lips—rested atop a semitranslucent body, still clad in a flannel shirt and baggy jeans.

"Could you just get one more message to her?" he asked in a forlorn voice. "Please tell her I'm sorry about the pink bunny underwear I got for her last Christmas."

"What? You gave your wife pink bunny underwear?" Pucci chuckled.

"I thought it was a sweet gift at the time," David said. "Could you just please tell her I'm sorry for that gift?"

"Well, OK, if it's that important to you." She turned to the door and yelled out. "Hey Jamie, can you come in here for a min?"

Jamie walked back to the bedroom, cinching up her green-chili-stained apron. "What's up?"

"David wants to apologize to you for giving you bunny underwear the last Christmas you were together," Pucci said in a kind voice. She knew how sensitive Jamie still was about David. Pucci had relayed some previous messages from him. Jamie always listened, but Pucci knew she didn't quite believe that Pucci was actually talking to her deceased husband.

"I don't know who you're talking to, Pucci, but David never gave me any bunny underwear," she said, turned on her heal and left the room.

"That didn't go over too well." Pucci said to David. "Are you sure you're remembering correctly?"

"She said she thought they were silly and for a little girl. I felt awful." He looked startled as Jamie suddenly walked back into the room.

"Pucci? What color were they?"

"He said they were pink."

Jamie felt faint and reached for a wall to lean on. "Oh my, oh my, I remember them now. I told him they looked like they were made . . . "

"For a little girl," all three said together, even though only Pucci could hear David.

She stared at Pucci, tears welling up in her eyes. "My God, you really have been talking to him all this time?"

"Yes, my friend, I wouldn't put you through any of it if it wasn't true and important to David," Pucci said gently, walking over to her. They hugged. Pucci let her cry. "He's always near you, Jamie. He loved you so much."

"David was my one and only. God, I miss him," she said, drying her tears. "Thank you, Pucci. You have no idea how much this means to me. When I go home, I'll look in my drawer. Hopefully I still have that pink bunny underwear!"

Pucci heard a sniff from down the hall as she smiled at David, mouthing a thank you as he vanished back to wherever it was he came from.

Pucci needed to bring one more important item. She reached for an antique puzzle box her grandmother had given Pucci as a child—a place for her to store all her secrets. There was a hidden drawer that could only be accessed by placing both hands and fingers in the correct positions; otherwise, it remained inaccessible. Pucci gently pushed in the specific spots with her fingers, and the drawer opened with a click revealing a magnificent sight—an antique, exquisite piece of jewelry, the jeweled cipher.

Light fractured through the seventeen flawless diamonds, each one cut with astonishing precision and held fast by gold foil settings that shimmered like trapped fire. Fourteen smaller stones created an elongated ring, precisely framing three larger diamonds arranged in a straight, commanding row. The symmetry, the elegance—it was more than stunning; it was intentional, purposeful, a puzzle waiting to be solved.

Pucci's fingers hovered over the intricate design, her pulse quickening. This jeweled cipher wasn't merely decorative—it was a treasure shrouded in secrets. Some ciphers revealed hidden messages when deciphered, others were engraved with initials or symbols, and a few, like this one, functioned as puzzles built into jewelry, requiring assembly to unlock their meaning. The tiny tabs along its edges weren't ornamental; they were functional markers, meant to connect this piece to others, forming a larger pendant—a remnant made to conceal codes and mysteries. These artifacts were incredibly rare, whispers of them appearing in historical studies and riddles she had poured over for years. And now, one lay before her.

This was the other reason she was going to Scotland. Detective Chief Inspector Olan Lathen of Scotland Yard and Pucci had discovered this piece about a year ago on Grand Cayman when they worked together on a case to find a missing hoard of valuable jewels. When Olan and Pucci found the hoard of stolen jewels—the Cheapside Hoard—she and Olan had discovered this piece sequestered in a reliquary pendant. The pendant, designed specifically to hold sacred items, was among the artifacts of the hoard. But this one came with a ghost.

They found the cipher, but before they could really discuss it, Olan had to suddenly leave for the airport back to London and Scotland Yard. Pucci stayed at the restaurant to savor her rum. A ghost materialized, cloaked in white with a red cross stitched onto the chest of the garment. The ends of the bars of the cross flared outward. Pucci recognized the iconic outfit of the Knights Templar. He told her that another key piece connected to the cipher was hidden in Rosslyn Chapel in Scotland. She must go before the evil gets there first. And then he was gone.

Chapter 2

Standing in the security line in the San Diego Airport, Pucci breathed a sigh of relief. Her nightmare of forgetting her passport, still fresh in her mind. She reached into her zippered compartment in her purse once again, gripping it with her fingers while still in place. Her rapid heartbeat slowed slightly. There it was, in the same place as it was the last time she checked, five minutes ago. She left her finger on it as she moved through the line, just in case.

If you're going to be like this for the next month, you're going to be exhausted, she thought. She made her way through security, to the gate and sat down. Taking out her passport, she looked at the recent photo. The unsmiling, teal-eyed woman with short brown hair—her bangs were slightly longer now—stared back at her. She chuckled at her thin lips; not much lipstick was wasted on her. She closed the passport, tucking it safely back in its designated compartment and zipping it up in her purse. The monitor showed an on time departure, first stopping in Chicago, then on to London.

Pucci loved to people watch yet deliberately avoided making eye contact with the ghosts that accompanied live humans. As she watched a family hurrying to their gate with a grandmother ghost traveling with them, she thought back to her conversation with her dear friend Varvada a few weeks ago. Varv, as Pucci affectionately called her, had been an extraordinary friend and confidant to Pucci during the Grand Cayman trip. That trip had involved ghosts, treasure, murder, and Olan. She sighed. Olan, Chief Inspector Olan Lathen, her detective from Scotland Yard. In fact, he wasn't really her detective. They hadn't spoken in quite a while. Their last conversation was brief and he seemed emotionless. The phone call had left her feeling empty and sad, so she'd called Varv. The connection reignited the excitement of the mystery they had solved last year, helping her forget the hole in her heart for a moment.

Varv probably couldn't meet in Scotland as she had an interior design commission in Cardiff, but she'd try. Maybe they could meet up in London, she suggested. Pucci wanted to make that happen. They had hung up with Pucci promising Varv to take pictures of those gorgeous men in kilts!

An announcement came over the loudspeaker, letting folks know that the first-class ticket holders could now board at their leisure. Pucci got up and walked right onto the plane, stowing her carry-on and her purse at her feet. She thought to herself, *Wow, look at all this room!* The flight attendant came by and offered a glass of champagne. Pucci accepted with a giggle. *Now this is the way to travel!*

Pucci picked up her phone to send a quick text to Randi. They had plans to meet in Edinburgh in a few days for the funeral, and while Pucci secretly hoped Randi might join her at the castle afterward, she didn't want to impose. She typed out a message, letting Randi know that her flight to London was on time and promising to stay in touch as their meeting day approached.

She settled into her book just as the doors were being secured. The seat next to her was empty, so no one to tell her life story to in the time from San Diego to Chicago. She was a little disappointed. But exhaustion took over as she had been up late every night preparing for the trip. As soon as they passed over Albuquerque, New Mexico, she fell asleep.

Chapter 3

"**I** better get going, my dear. I need tae go sell my castle."

"Said no one . . . ever," Katie said, pulling a face at her father.

He laughed as he bent down to put his computer in his briefcase. "Sounds funny tae say, too. It's going to break my heart to sell the ol' girl," he said, glancing at a flyer, recently faxed over from the realtor in Edinburgh, Scotland. "We have 21 acres, did ye ken?"

"Dad, how do you not know your facts about your ancestral home?" she said as she glanced at the property information and photograph on the fax. "Pretty photo of the grounds. The falconry lesson going on in the background is a nice touch. I wish I could come back with you."

"Aye, I wish ye could too, Katie. I'd like the help and moral support. But you need to stay in the States and finish your degree. Besides, I need to stop in London to handle some other business before I fly home. I'll come back to Chicago as soon as I can, love. And quit calling me Dad!" He chuckled, emphasizing the last "d" as he hugged her close. "Oh, my wee bairn."

"I am not a child anymore, Da!" A tear came to her eye. "I'll miss you."

He pulled away and looked out the window. "Och, looks like my taxi is here. I'll call when I get home to the castle," he called out, as he picked up his carry-on and headed for the door.

"Don't forget your passport, Da!" she called back, picking it up off the kitchen table and running it out to him. "Some Earl of Strathhammond you are! You'd forget your head if it wasn't attached!" She reached up and gently kissed his cheek in a last farewell as a light snow was falling. She waved as the taxi made its way to Chicago's O'Hare International Airport.

He weaved his way through the crowded airport to the gate just as the last people were boarding the nonstop flight to London. He handed his ticket to the gate attendant.

"Good evening, Mr. MacNevin. Let me take you to your first-class seat," the tall, pretty flight attendant said in a slight Scottish accent. She recognized the name and the man as one of the most eligible bachelors in Scotland.

"Nay bother, but thank you," he smiled back, his posh accent back in place. He walked down the Jetway into the plane, put his suitcase in the overhead, and sat down next to a small, brown-haired woman who was gently snoring.

Chapter 4

"I was hoping to have coffee with you in the morning." He smiled his charming, crooked smile.

Pucci blushed as she turned to leave. He reached out and caught her. He slowly brought her close. She turned and looked up into his moonstone eyes as he gathered her up into his arms. His energy felt like a welcoming cocoon. She felt safe in his arms, her head against his warm chest. She heard his heart gently beating. She moved slightly away, still cradled in his embrace. He leaned down, their lips almost touching. . . .

Way off in the distance, Pucci heard a voice.

"Excuse me, miss." The voice got louder. "Miss?"

Pucci started awake, unaware of her surroundings for a moment. She turned to see the kind face of a young pretty woman in a uniform staring down at her. As her vision focused, the woman said, "You need to put on your seatbelt, ma'am, we'll be landing in London soon."

Pucci turned and looked out the window. She could see a large city coming into view. How she could have slept all the way to London?

A deep voice with kindness in its delivery asked from the seat next to her. "Are you alright lass?" His sky-blue moonstone eyes showing concern.

Pucci, trying not to gape at the man, closed her mouth and said, "Oh, ah, yes, I'm quite alright, thank you. Just a little disoriented." She kept staring. Here was the man she had just seen in her dream state. Same eyes, same crooked, charming smile. *That was a dream?* She searched her mind, still feeling the heat of his hands on her waist, his musky scent still lingering. Fighting the desire to lean over and bury her nose in his collared shirt to breathe him in, Pucci reached for her purse. She desperately wanted to see what she looked like. Or not. Cringing at what she might see in the mirror.

"You were sleeping soundly there for the entire trip. I can imagine you feel a wee bit out of sorts." He put his book into his briefcase.

"Yes," she said in a small voice, not wanting to look at him again. The mirror she held displayed her messy hair. "*Oy*," she said to herself.

"Do you live in London? Or just coming for a visit?" he asked, with a refined Scottish accent.

"Just visiting, I live in California. I'm actually on my way to Scotland but need to stop in London for a few days," Pucci answered, still feeling flustered.

"Oh, aye. Me as well. I live in Scotland, outside of Edinburgh, looking forward to going home after some business in London."

Pucci felt his energy change when he mentioned his home. She felt a fondness and a sadness. Not wanting to pry, she gently asked, "Have you always lived in Scotland?"

"Aye, and all of my ancestors, going back centuries," he replied. "So what brings you to Scotland this time of year? We dinnae get a lot of tourists in winter," letting his refinement slip slightly.

"That's actually why I'm coming now. I'm not a big tourist person and love to learn from the locals. I am going to Islay to the distilleries. I write a blog about spirits, the alcohol kind, not the other, not that there is the other, I mean . . . " she stammered, blushing.

He tilted his head slightly, the sexy crooked smile returning. "Oh, aye," is all he said.

Pucci decided not to clarify. She wasn't very smooth in the company of exceedingly handsome men with Scottish accents, or any handsome men, for that matter. She turned and looked out the window and asked, "I wonder why we haven't landed yet?"

"We've been circling for quite some time, have ye not noticed?" he said.

"Oh, ah, of course. I noticed, just wondering why," she said, stumbling over her words. What was wrong with her? *Just because he could be on the cover of GQ magazine doesn't mean you have to act like a teenager.*

The flight attendant walked by again and paused in their row. "Mr. MacNevin, we'll be landing soon. Please make sure your seatbelt is fastened. Can I get you anything else? My phone number, perhaps?" she said, clearly flirting with him.

Pucci looked at Mr. MacNevin, then at the flight attendant, wondering how he was going to respond. Pucci felt his slight embarrassment. She liked him even more. "Nae, thank you, but this young lady might need something?" he said, turning to Pucci.

"Oh yes . . . ma'am?" she said, turning to Pucci, slightly annoyed.

"Could I have one of those hot towels? I think I missed them when I was asleep," she asked. She wanted to get her money's worth in first class before landing. The flight attendant walked away and hurried back with towels for Pucci and Mr. MacNevin.

"Good idea, thank you," he said to Pucci, not the flight attendant.

"Mr. MacNevin. I'm sorry I didn't have time to talk to you more." Pucci said, smiling as the plane touched down.

"You have me at a disadvantage. You ken my name, but I dinnae ken yours," he said, leaning close to her.

She felt heat rise in her. Hot flash? Hormones dancing the jig? Embarrassment? He waited for her reply. She breathed. "Pucci. My name is Pucci Riddle. It's nice to meet you, Mr. MacNevin. And, may I ask what ken means?"

"Och, sorry, it means 'know.' And, please, call me Braden. And very nice to meet you, Pucci. If you have time in your busy schedule sampling our peaty whisky, here is my card. Call, I'd love to take you for dinner. Or, at least I'm hoping to have coffee with you."

Pucci's breath caught.

She watched as he hurried out of the plane. She saw him amongst the crowds as she headed for the luggage carousels. He went the other way, out the front doors. There was something intriguing about him, a subtle energy that seemed both familiar and mysterious.

Chapter 5

After navigating her way through Heathrow and deciphering the train schedules, Pucci secured a reasonably priced hotel in the Cheapside area of London. The thought of staying near the location where the Cheapside Hoard was discovered fascinated her. The hoard—over 400 pieces of Elizabethan-period, late 16th- to early 17th-century gems and jewelry—was unearthed beneath a cellar in Cheapside in 1912 and earned its name from the neighborhood itself. Recognized as the most extraordinary find of gems and jewelry in the world, it was transferred to the Museum of London and made its public debut in 1914. After the exhibition was dismantled, the hoard remained secured in the museum's archives for decades until, about four years ago, it was stolen by a gang of thieves.

The stolen treasure eventually found its way to Georgetown, Grand Cayman, only to meet its fate with Hurricane Ivan off the coast. There it lay as sunken treasure until it was accidentally discovered by JD Langer. Solving the mystery of JD Langer's murder ultimately led Pucci to locate and recover the hoard. She thought back to that moment months ago in the graveyard, vividly recalling the overwhelming feeling when she unearthed the stolen treasure. The memory of the antique pieces glinting in the light flooded her senses once more.

Despite the absence of the original buildings where the hoard had been discovered, Pucci felt a deep connection to the place. Now, a modern high-rise apartment complex with mirrored windows dominated the area. St. Paul's Cathedral loomed in the skyline, its iconic dome reflected in the sleek glass façade of the contemporary building—a striking juxtaposition of London's rich history and its evolving urban landscape.

Since the hoard was returned, the Museum of London was in the process of developing a newly designed exhibit for the Cheapside Hoard, slated to open "soon." Pucci had kept in touch with Brent Nash, a gemologist and jeweler she had befriended during her time in Georgetown. Brent had been instrumental in helping Scotland Yard identify pieces of the hoard. The museum, grateful for his expertise, enlisted his continued assistance in researching and cataloging the artifacts for the upcoming display. During their last conversation, Brent had shared his excitement about the exhibit, though he admitted that progress was slower than anticipated.

***

In the process of solving JD's murder just over a year ago, Pucci faced the most harrowing moment of her life—staring down the barrel of a gun held by the head of the notorious gang of thieves that stole the Cheapside Hoard, a man known only as Pirate. Though DCI Lathen had fired a shot that seemingly ended Pirate's reign, his body was never recovered. While the world assumed he was dead, Pucci couldn't shake the suffocating weight of his presence. His dark, malevolent energy still haunted her dreams, an unrelenting shadow that terrified her. She knew she had to find him before he found her—and threatened everyone she held dear.

One of Pirate's gang members, Valerie Baine—also known as Charlene—had died during the museum heist that led to the theft of the Cheapside Hoard. The three other gang members perished as well when their boat went down, taking the treasure with it, during Hurricane Ivan. Their remains had yet to be identified.

Scotland Yard had already interviewed Valerie's parents but uncovered nothing useful about the elusive ringleader. Pucci, however, wasn't ready to give up. While in London, she decided to visit Valerie's parents herself, hoping to piece together more about Pirate's identity and his sinister motives.

Pucci woke the next morning jet lagged, but at least she had gotten some good rest. Tea was first on the agenda. When in Rome and all that. She made herself a cup from the tea set up in her hotel room.

Her next order of business was to visit Valerie's parents. After Valerie's body had been identified through dental records, Olan had provided Pucci information about her. Since Pucci had previously assisted Scotland Yard—and solved the Cheapside Hoard mystery—Olan gladly shared what he knew at the time.

Valerie's recovery from the Thames had left little doubt about the tragic circumstances of her death. Pucci hoped her parents might be able to fill in the missing pieces about Valerie's life, especially regarding who had employed her.

The grieving parents had shared little with Scotland Yard, only that their daughter had fallen in with bad people but had seemed to turn her life around after securing an internship at the Museum of London four years ago. Valerie had maintained contact with her parents while working at the museum, but three years ago, the communication suddenly stopped. The news of her death had been a devastating shock.

Pucci caught the train down to the Docklands, Valerie's last known address, her parents' home in Poplar. Looking out the window of the train, she marveled at the amount of giant cranes erecting high-rises—modernity rising at the cost of old London falling.

The train station was confusing to navigate. She took a few wrong turns before finally seeing an exit toward the direction she desired, away from the river. The neighborhood around the train station showed signs of ongoing renovations of old warehouses and the arrival of upscale restaurants near the Dockland location of the Museum of London.

As Pucci walked away from the area being gentrified, the neighborhoods became sketchier and more run down. Trash, discarded broken toys, and broken-down cars filled the tiny fenced in front yards. She turned down a street walking past old, neglected houses, all a mundane worn-out brown color. The generic front doors gave off an energy of unwelcome.

She found the Baine's door and knocked. A woman with a cigarette dangling precariously from her lips yanked the door open yelling, "What?"

Pucci, slightly startled, backed away from the door. "Hello, I'm sorry to bother you, but I'm with Scotland Yard," she said, stretching the truth. "I'd like to talk with you about your daughter."

The woman took the cigarette from her lips, looked Pucci up and down and opened the door so she could enter. The woman spoke with a gravelly voice, probably from years of smoking. "Why are you here? We answered all your questions months ago." She shut the door, blocking out the light and fresh air.

Pucci contained a cough. "I'm what some might call a specialist in personality behaviors. I tend to see things that others would miss," she said, feeling clever creating this explanation. She hoped Valerie might make an appearance in her spirit form while Pucci was here. "Could I please ask you a few more questions? And, if you wouldn't mind, I'd like to see her room as well? I assume you were her mother, Mrs. Baines?"

The woman snubbed out the cigarette in an overflowing ashtray and nodded her head, her eyes squinting as the last exhale traveled past them.

"I don't know what we're going to do without our Valerie. Her father hasn't been able to talk about it at all, and I have no one to talk to," she said practically tearing up. "She was so ungrateful!" Mrs. Baines cried out, angrily, spitting her words in Pucci's face.

Pucci didn't understand the sudden turn of emotion as she backed away. She felt the woman's energy. It was chaotic and fragmented. *This poor woman*, Pucci thought. *It feels like she's losing it. I'm going to need to tread very carefully.*

"Mrs. Baines, I don't want to take too much of your time. Would you mind if I see Valerie's room?"

Mrs. Baines shrugged. "Suit yourself, it's upstairs, to the right." She said as she walked into the living room and turned on the telly.

Pucci watched the mother of the dead girl completely disengage from life as she stared at the screen and lit another cigarette. Pucci started up the stairs. The hallway at the top was dimly lit. She found a door to the right and walked in.

The room looked untouched since their daughter moved out a long time ago and certainly hadn't been disturbed since her death a few years ago. It still looked like a little girl's room. She picked up a photograph of two teenagers laughing.

"That's me best friend," the ghost said.

Pucci dropped the photo and whipped around. There was Valerie—well, the ghost of Valerie—standing in the middle of the room, next to her old bed with the pink and baby blue bedspread cascading down the sides.

"Valerie!?" Pucci said. The ghost nodded. "Wow, you scared me."

"Me mum isn't doing too good. She doesn't even realize me da left her a few weeks ago. Thinks he's going to walk in any minute. I don't know what to do," Valerie said, reaching for the photograph she was unable to pick up.

"I'll try to get her some help." She paused, feeling the ghost's distress. "Valerie, I really need your help. Do you remember anything about your death? Can you remember anything about the leader of the gang you were working for when you stole the Cheapside Hoard?"

"Who are you?" the ghost asked.

"My name is Pucci. I help earthbound spirits, like you, find peace so you can cross over. I'm also being followed and threatened by whomever you were working for. A very evil and dangerous man. Please Valerie, please, do you remember anything? He's the one that ordered you killed. He's trying to kill me and my friends."

Valerie's form wavered and faded slightly. She turned away. Pucci could feel her sadness.

"No, I don't know who he is. I never met him. I was dealing with two other men. They worked for a man they called Pirate."

"Do you know anything about him?"

"Well," her form floated over to her dresser. "I followed the two men one day. I overheard them talking to Pirate. They said something that really scared me. I don't remember what it was, but I remember I wanted to find out more."

Suddenly her mother opened the door. "What are you doing in my daughter's room? Who are you? I'm calling the police!" she screamed.

Pucci started to answer, but Mrs. Baines rapidly thumped down the stairs, coming out of one of her old worn slippers. She was heading for the phone.

"I have a diary, in my top drawer," Valerie said. "Take that, it might help. And please, get help for me ma." And with that, she followed her mother down the stairs.

Pucci dug in the top drawer. Beneath underwear and bras, she found a small red diary sequestered in some red panties. She crammed the diary into her purse, shut the drawer, and ran down the stairs. She heard Mrs. Baines on the phone to the police and decided not to bid Mrs. Baines goodbye.

As she quickly walked toward the docks, Pucci found a pub. She loved old pubs, and this one hadn't been renovated. It's low lighting, fireplace along one wall, and small wooden tables were welcoming.

She sat down by the fire and removed her coat just as the server walked up. "What can I get you, love?"

"I'll have a beer," Pucci answered, glancing over at the bar where the bartender was pulling on large, tall handles "I've seen those big pumps in other countries. For dispensing ale, I believe? We don't have a lot of those in America."

"I don't think you have real ale in America, either. That's what comes out of those here in England, real ale. You'll be wanting a cold brew then from the keg," she said, smiling. "Those are the smaller handles."

Pucci, warm from her speed walking episode, replied, "That would be great, thanks," chuckling at the barb about American ale.

She pulled the small diary out of her purse, wondering how the police missed it. It was tucked into some underwear, but come on, still pretty obvious. Maybe the person searching didn't want to fondle the panties. Their loss.

Luckily, it wasn't locked with a silly key girls sometimes wore as a necklace. She opened it up to the first page just as her beer was set down in front of her. She read out loud, "Property of Valerie, leave alone." She sipped her beer. The server came back around. Pucci, realizing she hadn't eaten anything, asked, "Excuse me, do you have any chips?"

"We don't serve food," she replied.

"Not even a bag of potato chips?" Pucci asked.

"Oh, you mean crisps, yes, we have those, I'll bring you a bag.... Americans," she said, chuckling to herself.

Pucci chuckled as well. Chips were French fries here—got it. She skimmed the disparate journal entries, looking for anything written regarding the heist. Coming to the last entry, she sat up in her chair. Here was the break she was looking for.

"Atta girl, Valerie. We're going to Oxford."

Chapter 6

Anya

As Pucci's plane touched down in London, Anya was having a hell of a day in Edinburgh, Scotland. Getting that nutcase, Pirate, back to Edinburgh from Grand Cayman undetected by the authorities was no mean feat, let alone keeping him alive after he had been shot in the neck. Over oceans, countries, and cities, they were finally back with the rest of their outfit. It had taken months.

The blue diamond smuggling operation, which originally took her to Grand Cayman to receive a shipment from South Africa, was still running in Edinburgh. It had continued seamlessly while she and Pirate were in Cayman and during their return. Coming back empty-handed—without the blue diamonds and without the stolen jewels from the Cheapside Hoard—water under the bridge.

What still puzzled her was why the Cheapside Hoard had been so important. Yes, the emeralds, rubies, and diamonds were extraordinary in their rarity and value, but they paled in comparison to the profits expected from the sale of raw and cut blue diamonds. The operation here in London was poised to generate hundreds of millions—a staggering sum that made the hoard seem like little more than a distraction. And more on the way, according to Pirate's second, Alfie Morgan. At least she had a first and last name for him. He went by Morgan.

She leaned against a doorway outside a tall, tan colored building in Old Town, Edinburgh. God, she was exhausted.

Her long blond hair, pulled back in a pony tail, had lost its luster months ago. She wore baggy jeans, a long-sleeved turtleneck, and a baggy beat-up coat to hide her tall, slender, sexy body.

She was so close. Just a few more days and all of this would be over. She was sure of it this time. She missed having a proper cup of tea, hated the lukewarm swill they had in this underground hidey-hole. She missed, dare she say it, Georgetown, Grand Cayman. She briefly wondered what the women that she met there were doing now—they had become friends before she betrayed them, but let it go.

Her destination—a four-hundred-year-old abandoned building set back from Edinburgh's historic Royal Mile—was still a few blocks ahead. The Royal Mile, stretching from Edinburgh Castle to the Palace of Holyroodhouse, was approximately 200 feet longer than an English mile, making it a traditional Scots mile—a historic measurement unique to Scotland.

At one end stood Edinburgh Castle, a formidable sentinel perched atop the rugged remnants of an extinct volcano. With roots stretching back over 3,000 years to its origins as a prehistoric fort, it remained one of the oldest fortified sites in Europe—a timeless guardian overlooking the city below. Following the Scots mile to the other end of the road from the castle was the Palace of Holyroodhouse, still used today by royals. It began as an abbey, built on the spot where David I in the twelfth century had a vision of a stag with a glowing cross in his antlers. The abbey was hence dedicated to the Holy Rood, rood for cross. The abbey flourished and was enlarged to include special apartments for use by the kings who increasingly chose to stay there rather than in the exposed and far less comfortable castle.

Anya maneuvered through the busy crowds of tourists, stepped onto a quiet side street, and entered the lone chamber of an empty, forgotten structure that had once been called a close. She lifted her eyes to a narrow column stretching up to the high ceiling. The skylights, coated with a thick layer of soot, allowed only dappled light to pass, creating patterns on the surfaces around her. She trod softly toward the room's heart, her footsteps muffled by the thick dust.

Crouching by a slight recess in the floor, she rapped a covert rhythm against the ground. *So stupid,* she thought. *The existence of this close is unknown to the world, invisible on any known map, yet they still insist on a secret knock . . . whatever.*

Closes, a characteristic feature of Edinburgh's Old Town, were essentially private alleyways nestled between structures that stood so close they nearly touched. These cramped structures teeming with homes and businesses, radiated from the Royal Mile and traced back to the medieval era.

The close Anya had entered lay beneath the bustling Edinburgh City Chambers above. Over time, the original city had become entombed beneath new buildings. The infamous Mary King's Close, a few blocks from here, became the foundation for the new Royal Exchange constructed above it, around 1753. Those who remained in Mary King's Close during construction of the new city above, too poor to move, continued their subterranean existence while life above carried on, until the plague killed the last inhabitants.

This close, likely sealed during the same period, had long been forgotten, perhaps due to its modest size—one room and a small hallway, with two smaller rooms at the end—rendering it insignificant on historical maps.

As the floor latch clicked and the door lifted open, Anya instinctively backed away. Emerging from the shadows was Morgan, a man of medium height and wiry frame, his long, greasy brown hair falling in limp strands below his shoulders, parted in the middle in a style that seemed frozen in the 1970s hippy era. His weathered face, lined with years of hard living, carried a detached expression. Dressed in a faded black sweatshirt and too-tight-for-his-own-good jeans, he completed his peculiar look with scuffed cowboy boots that barely contained his disproportionately large feet. He acknowledged Anya with a slow, disinterested nod. She grabbed the door and climbed down the stone steps into the dank underground chamber, following him.

At some point in the blue diamond smuggling operation, Morgan and his cronies had wired the larger room with electricity. The electric lanterns emitted an orange glow reminiscent of candlelight from centuries past. The walls oozed moisture, giving off a moldy, musty odor. Anya pulled her coat around her as the cold damp air formed condensation on the roof, dripping on her hair.

Voices of the workers below grew louder as Anya and Morgan descended and entered the main room. This was where the raw blue diamonds came in from their connection at the mine in South Africa to be cleaved or cut to smaller sizes. It was easier to move smaller roughs than larger ones, even though the larger roughs brought in considerably more money. Two experts were employed to cut the four or six or larger carat roughs into one, two, and three carats. The cutters sat at a large wood table. Two other workers were employed to gather the cut diamonds and ready them to be delivered to the next operation site. No one looked up when they entered.

"Where's Pirate?" Anya asked, thankful he was not here. She moved to a small table that held an electric kettle and tea bags.

"How the bloody hell should I know?" Morgan said bitterly. "You're his babysitter."

"I don't give a damn about him. Especially after the Cayman debacle." She moved closer to him and said softly, so only he could hear, "He's losing it. You know it and I know it. We don't need that kind of liability."

A subtle expression of agreement crossed his face. He turned back toward the room. "Watch your mouth. He'd kill us both if he heard that."

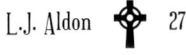

Anya needed to divide and conquer to get the information she required. She moved closer to him, rubbing up against him, holding her bile in check, whispering. "It's you and me, babe. You give me the contact at the S. A. Mine and we're free of him."

He smiled smugly. Looking at her with lust in his eyes, he realized she was right. They didn't need Pirate, but Morgan still didn't completely trust her. He didn't know anything about her background. Where the hell did she come from? How did she know Pirate? Pirate had said something once about another job he'd done with her and some kind of prison connections, but nothing specific. Something still didn't add up for Morgan, despite Anya's loyalty to Pirate over the past few years.

He took a chance. The trouble was, neither of these other goons were trustworthy and he needed help. "I need you to go to the distribution hub tonight, the apartment," he said to her. "Tell them more product is coming tomorrow night. Take these," He handed her a small velvet bag of two carat blue diamonds. "Tell them to get these boxed and shipped now."

Anya's stomach clenched. Showing no emotion, she answered, "Fine. Give me the info now so I can get some food on the way back."

He grabbed her wrist. "No," he hissed. "There and back immediately. Go."

She yanked her wrist out of his painful grip. Contempt flashed in her eyes. She forced a smile as she took the instructions from him. She straightened her back, exuding an air of determination, and moved toward the door with a confident, measured pace that left no doubt she was in control. Her heart raced as she ran up the stone steps, lifted the trapdoor, and ran out of the building and into the sunshine. She looked at the address Morgan had given her. It was up near Newhaven, by the water, north of Old Town. She had little time. He'd know if she veered off her destination but she had to risk it. She sent an encrypted message from her cell phone, ran as fast as she could to the designated drop point, then hailed a taxi to Newhaven.

Chapter 7

What time is it anyway? Pucci checked her watch. Still disoriented from the plane and time change, she realized she had just drunk a beer at 10 a.m. London time, yet the server in the pub from which she just emerged, hadn't even blinked.

She had time to catch the train to Oxford. Actually, it was perfect. She'd get there in a few hours, grab an early dinner and check out her destination after dark, mindful of her promise to attend the funeral tomorrow with Randi. Even though she wouldn't have very much time in Oxford, just to step foot in the city sent a thrill up her spine.

Pucci had always wanted to go to Oxford for two reasons. It contained, in her opinion, the Vatican of libraries. Nestled in the heart of Oxford, the Bodleian Library, one of the oldest libraries in Europe, stood as a venerable testament to centuries of academic pursuit, its ancient walls housing an expansive collection of knowledge, history, and sacred texts.

And second, she was a longtime fan of *Inspector Morse* on Masterpiece Mystery Theatre since its first season in 1987. Filmed in Oxford, she longed to walk where Morse walked.

She caught the train to Oxford. A short hour and a half later, the train pulled into the station. She exited the train and crossed over the tracks in a glassed-in bridge just as an old steam locomotive was pulling out of the station. It looked like the Hogwarts Express from the Harry Potter books and movie. Pucci was a huge fan.

Descending the stairs into the brightly lit long building of the main station bustling with activity, she quickly pulled her purse out of the way of a running man in a navy business suit and briefcase. She walked past a group of college students, laden with book-stuffed backpacks, heading for the coffee kiosk.

Outside, more stairs awaited. Luckily, she had left her large suitcase back in her hotel room. She headed toward the taxis waiting out front.

"Where to, miss?" the middle-aged Pakistani man asked.

Where to is the question? she thought. She needed to get her bearings and formulate a plan.

"How about the Randolph Hotel, please?" It seemed as good a place to start as any.

She'd read that Colin Dexter, the famed author of the Morse series, had written parts of his books in the hotel's small lobby bar. *Maybe they served chips*, she mused. She chose the hotel over the Bodleian as she knew she needed special permission to enter the sacred library, which she didn't have. Plus, she might make a fool of herself bowing and prostrating in reverence at the door to the entrance that held the holy artifacts—the books. Maybe next time.

The cabbie pulled up to the Randolph Hotel, an 1866 Victorian Gothic building that occupied a corner, practically a city block in both directions, in the heart of Oxford. She paid and ascended the worn stone steps beneath the covered entrance that obstructed the towering, pointed arch of the whetstone, upheld by embedded columns on either side.

The entrance, a small hallway to the even smaller reception desk, surprised Pucci. For such a grand hotel, the reception desk was no larger than a reception desk at a small country inn. Maybe that was the point. More room to be grand elsewhere.

Before reaching the desk, to her left, she saw the opening to a smoking lounge bar of days gone by. The wood paneling, low lighting, and leather tufted chairs were strategically placed for intimate conversations. Although cigars were no longer allowed, the scent of old, very expensive ones still lingered like ghosts attached to the walls. Silver-haired, impeccably dressed men lounged on the supple, leather-backed barstools, their movements deliberate and refined as they savored their whisky, the golden liquid catching the warm glow of the chandelier above. Pucci imagined Dexter doing the same with a writing pad and pen next to him. She looked around. Maybe he was here? But, no luck. *Probably off filming the new spin-off series, Lewis,* she thought.

She unbuttoned her heavy winter coat, and removed her hat and gloves, draping them over a chair near the entrance. She stepped into the bar and back in time. She stopped at a wall of black-and-white photographs, featuring the cast from the Inspector Morse series. The casting of John Thaw and Kevin Whately for the BBC series as Morse and Lewis had been flawless. The photos were mainly of Thaw, the actor who played Morse leaning on the signature Jaguar car he drove in the series, along with a photograph of a scene filmed in this bar. She had read every book and watched the complete series at least three times. There they were, hanging on the wall, immortalized as their respective characters.

"Pucci Riddle."

Startled by the sound of her name, she spun around, her eyes narrowing as they landed on the man who just spoke. There stood a man, his polished shoes and tailored suit radiating with the air of self-importance.

"Why, if it isn't Oliver Williams-Tanaka," she said, her voice dripping with mock cordiality as she addressed the man she privately regarded as an insufferable peacock. He was tall, slightly overweight with a cleft chin. He parted his graying hair on the side and combed it over his balding, basketball-shaped head. His brown eyes the color of, well, she wouldn't be that mean, looked at her with surprise, turning into contempt.

Oliver was the most vocal critic of her "Spirits by Pucci" blog. Whenever she wrote about a new and exciting spirit she found, he commented on her lack of taste and refinement. She should stop writing completely and go back into the literary void from which she came. She finally stopped showing his comments on her blog, after figuring out how to curate them. He retaliated by firing back on his own blog, articles he wrote on high-end spirits in prestige journals, and even newspaper opinion columns, always finding a way to call her a hack, using much more "literary" vocabulary. Pompous ass.

They had met once before in a conference in New York with other bloggers, critics, and journalists who wrote about alcohol. He hadn't changed. His recent critique of her Grand Cayman article on rum still stung, and her stomach clenched at the memory. He called Henri, the distiller whom Pucci interviewed, a hack with unrefined taste and suggested he should stop making that swill he called rum. Pucci wrote about how Henri had crafted the nectar of the gods with his unique distilling methods. Besides, she thought Henri was simply wonderful.

"What are you doing here in Oxford, and in this iconic bar?" he said, turning away from his group of men—all drinking single malts, no doubt. His tone insinuated that she had no place here.

"Same as you, I imagine," she said with more confidence than she felt.

"I seriously doubt that. I'm here with some of the leadership of the SWA—that's the Scotch Whisky Association to you. They are consulting with me on a delicate matter that you wouldn't understand regarding the industry." His lip curled as he spoke, perfectly matching his personality.

She turned to the bartender and asked if they had Bruichladdich Black Art, 1989, one of the finest Scotch whiskies ever made, in her opinion. Made by one of the greatest distillers, Jim McEwan, who was deemed "the whisky man of Islay." The band of SWA's leadership turned, eyebrows raised in surprise and appreciation. Clearly, this woman knew something. She even pronounced the distillery name correctly *brook-laddie*.

Secretly, Pucci was hoping they did not have it available, as it would cost her a night's stay, possibly two, at this grand hotel for just a dram—a small pour of whisky, about a shot glass full. She was just trying to impress the git.

The bartender smiled and shook his head and said in a Scottish accent, "Aye, that would be grand if we did." He winked and served Pucci an excellent dram from Bowmore, which was a lot less expensive.

She was determined not to let Oliver's presence ruin her short visit to this wonderful place, but she couldn't help but overhear him talk to his fellows as she waited for her dram. It sounded like he mentioned going to Islay, the southernmost island of the Inner Hebrides, the location for all the best peated, or smokey, scotch whisky distilleries. She truly hoped not—that was her destination after a stop in Edinburgh, and she didn't want to run into Oliver.

She watched him in the mirror behind the bar's bottles of alcohol. She observed a secretive conversation between Oliver, who was now standing a short distance away from the table of the SWA members, and a man in a three-piece suit. Pucci watched as he handed Oliver a small thin package, which Oliver tucked inside his smoking jacket pocket, wearing a conspiratorial look.

After the exchange, they both joined the group at the table. Oliver's gaze lingered on Pucci as she quietly sipped her whisky, the amber liquid catching the dim light of the room. In a low, derisive tone, he murmured something to his companions, causing several of them to glance her way. She turned, their eyes briefly met hers before they turned back with a polite chortle, their laughter soft but undeniably dismissive.

Each sip of whisky did little to calm the simmering anger rising within her. Finally, unable to tolerate the smugness in their collective demeanor, she finished her whisky, paid and approached the table of men while pulling on her coat.

She addressed Oliver. "I've asked you repeatedly to stop targeting me with your pompous attitude and bullying. You, sir, are nothing but a fraud. I'd rather you were dead." She turned and walked out of the bar and onto the sidewalk.

Her heart was racing, sweat beaded up on her brow. She had no idea where that outburst had come from, and why she allowed it to come out of her, especially in front of all those people.

"Totally uncalled for Pucci," she said out loud, looking both ways before she crossed the busy intersection. Another voice in her head said, *Good for you, Pucci*. She liked this voice.

***

Pucci was starving. All she had consumed all day was one bag, and a tiny one at that, of potato chips that morning and a superb scotch. Which probably was partially responsible for the outburst. What she really needed was some food.

She meandered through the cobbled streets of Oxford, enchanted by the sight of ancient spires piercing the sky, each one a sentinel over the city's storied past. Turrets crowned venerable facades of buildings, their once-bright brickwork mellowed to a warm, honeyed hue, now repurposed into charming flats. The dignified facade of the Ashmolean Museum stood as a monument to architectural beauty, its entrance a gateway to the past. The museum, a guardian of history since 1683, was the oldest public museum in the UK, and one of the oldest in the world. She longed to wander the halls, but her stomach growled. The stomach won.

Pucci made her way toward the city center, her steps unhurried as she admired the sculptures scattered along the streets. Busts of unknown figures—believed to be philosophers and researchers, their ivy-leaf headpieces symbolizing wisdom—crowned the towering columns that stood perfectly spaced within a black iron fence guarding the Sheldonian Theatre. Serving as an architectural boundary marker between "town and gown," the statues added an air of scholarly reverence to the site.

A sudden gust of wind whipped her bangs across her face, momentarily breaking her reverie. Spotting an angelic face carved into the stone above a building's arched entrance, its features radiating a quiet divinity, Pucci instinctively reached for her camera, momentarily forgetting her growling stomach.

Just as it started to drizzle, she found an Indian restaurant tucked back off one of the busy streets. She ordered naan, Indian flatbread, and the Palak Paneer, her favorite dish made of spinach, cheese, and spices. While she waited for her food, she opened Valerie's journal again and reread the entry that had brought her to Oxford.

I overheard the three of them talking again. The one they called Pirate raised his voice, saying something like—it's none of your bloody business and if you keep questioning me, I'll kill you both. He told them just to finish the job, the boat will be waiting. I was really scared. What if he would kill me too? Even though I've never seen him, I know his voice. He stormed out. I decided to follow him. There was something sinister in his manner, something that suggested he was up to something more than just stealing the jewels from a drawer in the museum. It was a stupid idea on my part, but I had to find out. Maybe I could use this against him. We went all the way to Oxford. I caught the same train he did. When he got out at Oxford, he took a taxi to a posh neighborhood somewhere off Frenchay Road, I think. I followed in a cab and watched him walk up to an enormous house where the street curved, pretty isolated. But instead of going up to the front door, he went to a side door. I walked down on the other side of the street and saw there was a canal behind the house. I hopped over the fence and walked down the path. I peeked through the hedgerows. Couldn't see where he went, so I squeezed through the bushes and snuck up to the house. I heard voices coming from the basement, strange noises, almost like chanting. I found a small window and peaked in. Jesus still don't believe what I saw. I feel like I made the whole thing up in my head. There were cloaked people chanting in a circle, like they were performing some sort of ritual. Pirate was talking to a man with a different colored robe. Maybe the leader? The man grabbed Pirate by the throat, pressing a knife to it. I heard the leader say they needed something like cipher, or maybe cylinder? I'd never heard of a cipher before. He pushed Pirate down and turned to some animal on an altar, raising the knife. I suppressed a scream and ran for my life. I pray to God they didn't see or hear me.

The job is almost done. I'm going to exchange the last pieces tomorrow and then I'll be free and rich! I just need to keep it together, for mum's sake.

***

Pucci took out a map of Oxford that she bought at the train station and found Frenchay Road. Luckily, it wasn't a long street, and there was only one place where the street curved matching the description from the letter. A canal was behind it. She finished the naan and her tea, paid the bill and flagged down a taxi.

She got out at the corner of Bainton and Frenchay and walked toward the canal. It was very dark out by now, with only a few streetlights illuminating a foot-wide circle around their poles. A chill ran up her spine, as a breeze hit her face. She blinked away tears made by the icy air. She had a plan to go up to the house and act like she was lost looking for someone's residence. *Lousy plan*, she thought.

She felt increasingly intimidated with each step toward the door. The doorbell turned out to be a gong that rang deep in the house. A man in a formal suit answered the door. Pucci assumed he was a servant of some sort.

"Hello, good evening," she said. Her voice sounded high-pitched. Pulling a name from some old English mystery she once read, she continued, "I'm so sorry to bother you, but is this the Carstairs residence? I'm completely lost."

The butler wasn't impressed. "I'm sorry madam, this is not the Carstairs residence and I do not know anyone by that name." He backed up to close the door.

Suddenly, Pucci was accosted by a wave of energy so dark, it hit her in the solar plexus and she almost collapsed. She bent over, tried to breath, reached for the ring in her pocket, and jammed it on without the butler seeing. She felt a flood of positive energy shielding her from whatever it was that had hit her.

Concerned, the butler reached out an arm to steady her.

"Are you all right, madam?"

"Oh, I'm sorry, a sudden stomach cramp. Must have been the food I just ate," she said, slowly standing upright and drawing deep breaths. She had to get out of there fast, but didn't want to lose the moment. "Could you tell me who lives here? I really did think I was in the right place." *Hold it together*. The ring was helping.

"Mr. Smith lives here. I bid you good evening." And with that, he shut the door.

She hurried down the walkway to the street. When she turned to look back at the house that Valerie had once followed Pirate to, an upstairs curtain flicked close. The shadow silhouette of a man moved away. Who was Mr. Smith? What was Pirate up to with these people? She was certain Valerie had heard the word cipher.

So, these people were interested in what Pucci and Olan had discovered in the reliquary pendant found in the Cheapside Hoard. She decided to reach out to Olan, no matter what internal conflict he was struggling with. She needed him.

Exhausted by the dark energy, she hailed a taxi back on Bainton Road and headed to the train station. She got back to Cheapside, to her hovel of a hotel room, showered and collapsed. She dreamt of dark, cloaked people, conjuring dark spirits.

Chapter 8

The hotel was in close proximity to New Scotland Yard. The next morning, she decided against just showing up at the front desk, asking for Chief Inspector Lathen. Pucci didn't want to investigate any further without Olan, remembering how Olan rescued her from the gun pointed at her head in Grand Cayman with Pirate at the other end. She needed his protection.

She called his office. They said he wasn't in and didn't know when he would be back. She tried his cell, no answer. She sighed.

Every time she'd called him since Grand Cayman a little over a year ago, it had been the same story. She didn't understand. They had made such an intimate connection that last night. Yet, he had not spoken to her since. Why?

She decided to call Connor. Detective Connor Davies and Olan had previously partnered on the case in Georgetown. They were dispatched to the Cayman Islands to investigate the blue diamond smuggling case, but were quickly pulled into another investigation when the Cheapside Hoard, stolen from the Museum of London, was linked to Cayman. With intelligence suggesting the hoard had been smuggled to Grand Cayman and subsequently vanished, their orders shifted—dropping the smuggling case to focus entirely on recovering the missing treasure. She was about to dial Connor's number when her cell phone rang, showing a London number.

"Hello?" Pucci answered tentatively.

"Pucci? It's Detective Connor Davies. We met on Grand Cayman. Do you remember me?" Connor's accent was that of a proper English gentleman.

Pucci looked at the phone. *What are the odds?*

"Wow, Connor, so great to hear from you! Believe it or not, I was just going to call you. Have you seen Olan? I mean Chief Inspector Lathen? I'm really worried about him."

"That's actually the reason I'm calling." Fear clenched Pucci's stomach.

"Is he OK, Connor?"

"He's not doing so good, Pucci. He's alive, but a shell of his former self. Ever since we got back from Grand Cayman, his behavior has become increasingly unstable. He's drinking. He's been missing work. He won't get help, doesn't think he needs it and wants people to stop pestering him. I heard from Varv that you were here in London. I thought maybe," he paused, "I know it's a big ask but maybe you could talk with him. As a friend?"

"I would love too, Connor, but he's not answering my calls. Do you know how to reach him?"

"Sadly, yes. He'll be at the Station Pub off Peabody Avenue. I'll text you the address. Pucci?"

"Yes?"

"Be careful. That isn't a safe part of town."

"OK, thank you, Connor. Listen, I have a favor to ask of you as well. Do you remember Valerie Baines, the woman's body that was found in the Thames in connection to the Cheapside Hoard heist? I went to visit her house. I found her diary. Apparently, your men missed it. I have some information regarding Pirate. I might need your help if I don't get anywhere with Olan."

"Pucci, what diary? We searched everywhere for some shred of evidence. We didn't find anything."

"It was in her underwear drawer. Apparently, your men didn't want to get their hands in her knickers—I believe that's what you call them."

"I should very much like to see that diary, Pucci. It could be vital evidence in a cold case."

"I'd like to give it to Olan. I also need to share with him some additional information," Pucci said, thinking about her communication with Valerie's ghost and the dark energies of the house in Oxford. "I'll be in touch with more information. I'll go and try to find Olan now."

"All right, Pucci. Keep that diary safe," Connor hung up.

It was only 9 a.m. What was Olan doing in a pub at this hour? Maybe having breakfast? She doubted it. Oy.

Chapter 9

The neighborhood was ancient, its weary walls bearing the scars of centuries. Cracks spidered through the stonework, and those not hidden beneath layers of graffiti crumbled into heaps of decay. Shadows shifted unnervingly in the dim light, and the lumps scattered along the ground weren't just discarded coats—they concealed old men huddled against the biting chill, their breath visible in the gloom.

A gang of youths emerged from the shadows, their laughter sharp and mocking. In their hands, glints of metal caught the faint sunlight—knives, or something equally threatening. They moved as a pack, their steps echoing against the cobblestones as they fell in behind Pucci. Her pulse quickened. She picked up her pace, her gaze locking on the pub sign ahead.

With trembling hands, Pucci shoved the pub door open and slipped inside, quickly closing it behind her. She leaned against the cool wood, her heart pounding as she waited for her eyes to adjust to the dim interior. Through the haze, she spotted a familiar figure at the bar. Steeling herself, she pushed away from the door and approached cautiously, her steps careful and deliberate.

With each step, the soles made ripping sounds on the old wooden floor, sticky from years of spilt beer, or worse. She came to a stop about a foot behind Olan's hunched back and slumping shoulders. She could see and feel how he tried to bear the weight of the world, but was defeated. He downed his pint and placed the empty glass on the bar.

Their last phone call came flooding back to her. He had told her everything was fine. He said he was fine and told her to stop asking. She said she missed him. He didn't respond. The final words he spoke were "stop calling, we have nothing more to talk about."

"Same again," he called out to the bartender. His head tilted to his right and slightly behind him. "Hello, Pucci. What are you having?"

Pucci approached and reached out to touch his arm. He shrugged away. Her heart ached. She dropped her arm by her side and sat on the barstool next to him. The bartender placed another pint in front of him.

"Hello, Olan," she said. "Just water for me, thanks."

"What are you doing on this side of the pond?" He took a gulp from his glass. His eyes were glassy and watery. His hair was tousled, and not in a sexy way. He saw her looking and raked his fingers through the mess on top of his head. It didn't help.

"I left a message for you. Maybe you didn't get it? I'm doing an article on whisky. I also wanted to see if we could find anything else about Pirate through Valerie." She stopped talking, he wasn't listening.

"How did you find me?"

"Conner said you might be here," she said, nodding thanks to the bartender for the water he set down.

"You mean you didn't ask your ghost buddies where I was?" His slight sneer bit into her. A flicker of pain crossed her face.

"What's going on with you, Olan?"

"Nothing. I told you to stop contacting me," He slammed down his empty glass. He reached into his pocket, threw out a few pounds on the bar, and headed for the door.

"Olan, wait! I need your . . . ." She let the words die as she watched the door close behind his retreating form.

Pucci was about to follow when she looked back at the barstool he'd just vacated and heard a familiar cackle.

"You!" she exclaimed.

When she had first met Olan all those years ago in San Francisco, she had seen this ghost with hollow eyes in an elongated skull and his Satanic tattoos covering his arms and neck. He was haunting Olan. The ghost was powerful enough to knock her down back then. He was even stronger now.

She turned and ran out of the bar. Billowy, dark clouds covered the winter sun, threatening snow, creating an eerie darkness outside. She searched for Olan as the freezing mist seeped into her clothes and into her bones. He was gone.

Chapter 10

Pucci was pressed for time, and had her sights set on catching the northbound train from the iconic Kings Cross Station. She was traveling to Edinburgh to lend her strength to Randi, at her time of saying the ultimate goodbye to a cherished great aunt. This solemn commitment alone drew her from London to Edinburgh. If not for the pull of this heartfelt obligation, she would have stayed in London and continued to investigate the clues she had unearthed. What else had Valerie discovered related to Pirate's actions that ultimately cost her life? Staying in London might also give Pucci a chance to heal her relationship with Olan, and ease some of the persistent pain that tugged at her heartstrings.

She called Connor and told him what happened at the pub regarding Olan. His sadness and frustration emanated over the phone.

"Pucci, please leave the diary at the hotel's front desk before you leave, I'll have one of my lads retrieve it now," Connor said, still slightly unnerved that his men missed it.

"Connor, there is a house described in the diary that Valerie followed Pirate to. I deciphered Valerie's description of the location of the house and went there as well to see what I could learn. It's in Oxford." She felt Connor's agitation. "I know I shouldn't have gone alone, I'm sorry."

"What did you find?"

"Something really evil is in that house, not just the occupants. I didn't get any further than the man servant, who said a Mr. Smith lives there, which of course wasn't true."

"Alright, Pucci. I'm just glad you're safe."

"And, Connor, one more favor. Please have social services, or whatever you call them here, look in on Valerie's mother. She's not doing very well at all since her daughter's death. She needs help."

He promised he would. She thanked him and told him she'd be in touch.

***

She caught the express train to Edinburgh Waverley Station. The express has fewer stops, arriving in Edinburgh in less than half the time, a little over four hours, rather than nine hours for the commuter train that travels a more inland route. Plenty of empty cars remained on the silver and green express, but they were quickly filling up. She lucked out and found a window seat on the east side, facing the direction in which the train was heading. She never could sit backward. This side of the train should afford her a glimpse of the North Sea as they traveled closer to Scotland. Pucci stashed her large suitcase in the luggage rack at the back of the car. Lucking out on that front, too, squeezing it into the last spot.

She settled into the comfortable high back seat, moving her purse out of the way for a passenger that took the seat next to her. The young woman nodded her thanks and settled down with her book.

A recorded male voice announcement bellowed three times, "Mind the gap, caution, doors are closing."

Pucci's stomach lurched with the movement of the train, her excitement mounting as they cleared the station. She had just started to relax when she heard a familiar voice coming toward her. She strained to listen.

"I have a plan, don't concern yourself. I've done my research. I know where it's located," Oliver Williams-Tanaka, hissed under his breath.

"It's not a good idea. We need to follow their directions. You're a fool if you don't." A second voice replied, laced with impatience.

"Never call me a fool." As the two men walked passed her seat, Oliver spotted Pucci. He was startled but quickly recovered his signature sneer. "Well, we both know the train car makes the person. We of course, are in first class."

Before Pucci could come up with a snide retort, the two men walked on. She did not get a good look at his companion—a hood concealed his face.

She seethed with loathing for that man. *Why do I keep running into him?* Her intuition was on high alert. She looked out the window at glorious green pastures, dotted with sheep and old stone barn structures. She vowed to let it go. Oliver was not worth impeding her adventure.

As Pucci first glimpsed the North Sea, her breath caught at the sight. She removed her new small portable digital camera from her purse to have it handy. She imagined the sea to have gale force winds, and enormous waves crashing with churning, portentous dark waters. Maybe a Norse God or two in glorious sailing ships off on the horizon. She let her breath out as the sea came into full view.

On the contrary, it was a magnificent shade of aquamarine, edging toward the gray side. Gentle white caps painted the surface as wispy clouds meandered overhead. And on the horizon, oil platforms. So much for the fantasy of the North Sea. Still, it was majestic in its vastness. She practically pressed her nose to the glass, turning her head left and right to see the entire coast line as it flew past. An old castle ruin came into her view out on a peninsula, about a mile off the coast. She wondered about the history of that ruin, now a scenic picture she had just captured with her camera.

***

It's so interesting how a dash line on a map can come to define a people, Pucci pondered as the train crossed into Scotland. She took out Mr. MacNevin's card, smiling as she remembered his kind eyes and sexy smile. The card was understated—just his name, Mr. Braden MacNevin, and a phone number. Her stomach fluttered at the thought of calling him after settling into the castle over the next few days. She wondered where he lived.

Towns frozen in time with ancient churches and stone houses came and went giving way to more modern buildings on the outskirts of Edinburgh. The train rattled to a screeching stop into Edinburgh Waverly Station. Pucci grabbed her suitcase and got off the train as fast as she could, not wanting to run into Oliver again. *What was with the hyphenated last name anyway? Just added to his pompousness. Was that a word?* She followed the signs to the taxi's, schlepping her large suitcase and carry-ons with her. She needed those upgraded wheels now as she rolled over the cobblestone street to the waiting taxis.

Before Pucci left on her trip, she had consoled her longtime friend Randi Baklen on the passing of her great aunt. Randi had been closer to her aunt than to her own family and felt her great aunt Amalie's passing keenly. Her aunt had no children and adopted Randi as her own. In Amalie's will, she left Randi instructions to bury her in her ancestral mausoleum in Rosebank Cemetery in the Pilrig area, close to the boundary of Leith, a historic port district in the north of Edinburgh. The will contained enigmatic directions to search for Galloway, her maiden name, with the sole message to Randi, "You should know your ancestry."

Upon hearing Pucci would be there in December, Randi had planned her sailing adventure to meet Pucci there. She needed her friend's support and would she mind taking time out of her trip to help bury her aunt? Pucci told her of course.

They had decided, after consulting maps of the area, to meet at a pub north of the cemetery, The Ol' Poison. Maybe not the smartest choice of name. The chosen day was upon Pucci, and she was running late.

The taxi driver jumped out of his car to assist Pucci with her luggage and asked in a very thick Scottish accent, "Where to?" When Pucci relayed the address, he said it would be cheaper to take the bus.

"Thank you, but I'm late for a funeral and do not have time to check my luggage at this point. And carrying this large suitcase into a crowded bus just doesn't seem very smart," she said.

"Oh, aye. A funeral, ye say? I'll nae charge ye the full fee." The cab driver smiled. He was slightly taller than Pucci, with a bald spot on top of his head that made him appear older than his likely middle-aged years. He got into his cab on the right-hand driver's side.

"Thank you, that's very kind of you," Pucci said to the back of his head as they drove away from the train station.

Dusk was just starting to settle on the great city of Edinburgh even though it was only 4 p.m. as they drove north. Behind them, Pucci's gaze lifted as the Edinburgh Castle loomed into view, its ancient stone walls rising like a crown above the city. Her awestruck murmur was enough to make the taxi driver glance in the rearview mirror with amusement.

"Aye, she is a beaut. Is it yer furst time in Edinburahh?" he asked.

"Yes," she turned around. "I have been wanting to come here since I was a teenager. I'm thrilled to be here." She turned her head left and right, her eyes darting to take in everything at once through the cab's wide windows. The city sprawled before her—historic stone buildings, bustling streets, and flashes of green parks—each new sight tugging her gaze like a child unwrapping gifts.

"Well, if that's the case, I'll take ye past Holyroodhouse on our way," he said.

As they drove past the Palace of Holyrood, its tall brick walls and grand gallery teased glimpses of the historic palace within. The thought of being so near a place where monarchs still tread—a living link to centuries of power and intrigue—sent a shiver of excitement through her. Across the street, the stark, modern lines of the Scottish Parliament Building stood in bold contrast, a striking reminder of Scotland's ever-evolving identity.

As the cab followed the curve of the road around the palace, she craned her neck for a final look. Ornate tall black iron gates stood proudly between two moss-streaked brick towers, each crowned with a pair of animals, upright and poised, clutching what appeared to be the Scottish flag.

"Those animals on top of the towers are unicorns," the cab driver said as he looked into his rearview mirror, watching Pucci gape out the back window. "They're our national animal," he said with pride. He turned back around at the roundabout on Queens Drive, back past the palace and up toward Abby Hill. "I'm givin ye a wee tour. I wanted ye tae see some of the grounds of the palace on the other side. I'll get ye tae the cemetery now."

Pucci thanked him again and sat back into the large bench seat. She sighed. *I'm here. I finally made it.*

Chapter 11

Olan

From the shadowy corner near the pub, Olan watched as Pucci burst onto the street, her head whipping back and forth in silent desperation. She was searching for him, and the sight tightened something in his chest. His exhausted, fogged mind struggled to grasp the memory of the last time he'd held her, the warmth of her in his arms now feeling like a lifetime ago.

He walked toward his flat, trying to stay upright, his shoulder scraping the red brick walls of the building. He couldn't remember the last time he was sober.

He stumbled into his ground floor flat and collapsed on a couch riddled with takeaway bags, old plastic sandwich containers, and booze from the convenience store down the street. He also couldn't remember the last time he'd had a decent meal. He didn't care. His guilt was destroying him, and justifiably so. He killed her. The memory of her death, though it had been ten years, was still as fresh as if it had happened yesterday.

"Don't fall asleep, you bloody fool," he said to himself out loud. Falling asleep meant losing control over his consciousness. He had to stay awake. He reached over to the whisky bottle on the coffee table and sucked the last drop out. His eyes drooped, the bottle rolled out of his hand. He lost the battle.

"No, don't shoot! Take me. She has nothing to do with this," he screamed at the man with an elongated skull, holding a gun. The man flicked his dark hair out of his eyes, Satanic tattoos covered his neck and arms. He cackled.

"You're a damn fool, Lathen, if you think I'm going to show any mercy," the man said, looking straight at him while pulling the trigger pointed at Lathen's fiancée. She fell.

The memory of the shot startled him so severely, he woke up. Tears streamed down his face, somewhere between waking consciousness and the dream. He felt like someone was controlling his mind, making him relive this horrible moment over and over. He pounded his fists on his head trying desperately to wake up. It failed.

"NO!" Lathen yelled, running over to Liana and cradling her in his arms. His beautiful Liana. She was already dead. He slowly pulled out his hidden weapon under his shirt, whispered goodbye and how sorry he was, stood, turned, and shot the man dead.

Olan, oblivious to the ghost lingering in his living room—the same ghost that had woven itself into his dreams over the last year—let out another hollow laugh. Its presence, unseen and unfelt, twisted his dreams into nightmares, bending reality and memory alike. The ghost cackled one last time before dissolving into the shadows.

The dream changed. *Olan stood in the basement of some sort of metal workshop. He looked down to see himself putting what looked like a piece of jewelry inside a locket. He heard someone say it will be safe, hidden here, until we can return.*

The dream changed again. *He looked down through a steel helmet cross-hatching to see himself adorned in a white cloak with a red cross on the breastplate. The hilt of the sword in his hand glistened with jewels of sapphire and rubies. He was in a group of three similarly cloaked men.*

One of the men spoke. "We need to break it apart so no one man has access to the whole. Lathen watched as a diamond and gold foiled multifaceted piece was carefully and reverently disassembled. Each knight was handed a piece. "Now go. Only send a message when you have successfully hidden your pieces in the designated places."

The dream changed one more time. *He cradled a woman's face lovingly. He gently wiped the tears that had fallen from her teal eyes. "I won't be long, my love. It's only a day's ride from here," he said, as he leaned down to kiss her one last time.*

Olan started awake. "Pucci!"

Chapter 12

The cab made good time, and dropped Pucci off around 5 p.m. She rolled her suitcase into The Ol' Poison pub. She asked the bartender if she could keep her suitcase somewhere safe for a few hours.

He smiled and said, "Nae problem, your friend over there already warned me ye might need a place for both ye're luggage. I'll have them stored in the office in the back."

Pucci thanked him. In such a short time, she felt an unexpected kinship with the Scots, as though she'd found a place—and people—that welcomed her like family.

Pucci looked around the pub. The brick walls, blackened with long-ago fires, looked old and tired. The brass pulls on the wooden bar matched well-worn wooden stools with brass legs. A small wooden table stood near a crackling fire. A woman with blonde hair, sporting a stylish short cut, glanced up while sipping her beer. A smile creased her freckled face as she put her glass down and stood up.

"Pucci! You made it! My God it's wonderful to see you!" Randi said, hugging Pucci, jacket, bags, and all.

Randi Baklen was a force of nature. She was power itself, kept in check by her compact frame and kind smile. If you didn't notice or weren't aware of that power, you were an idiot; if you negated it, you were a fool. A mechanical engineer by degree, turned shipbuilder, her knowledge of engineering surpassed that of her male counterparts, but she let them take the credit. She supported and mentored the younger generation and had no need for accolades. Her hug would crush you with love if you were privileged enough to get one from her. She rarely showed such intimacy. The sincerity of her loyalty and friendship was unwavering. Her infectious laughter, rising from her belly and framed by squinted, tear-filled eyes, lit up the room. One of Randi's best qualities that Pucci admired was her acceptance of life as it unfolded. Nothing seemed to bother or worry her. She had a deep spiritual understanding that we are who we are, and all of it was OK. No judgment. She was calm waters in a raging world.

"Oh, Randi, it's so fabulous to see you again! And here, in Scotland!" Pucci exclaimed as she removed her coat and sat down. "Do we have time to eat something? I didn't get to eat on the train, so I'm really hungry!"

"Of course, eat. Eat. We don't meet the funeral director for an hour. He's giving us only a few minutes in the mausoleum, they don't use it for burials anymore, and I had to get special permission from the cemetery folks. Auntie Amalie bought her spot there decades ago—you know her, planning ahead," she said as she reached across the table to take Pucci's hand. "Thank you again for doing this with me."

Pucci smiled at Randi and then at the server who had brought over menus.

"I might join you in some food. I've only had a stale sandwich after I docked the boat at Port Edgar Marina," Randi said as she took the menu.

"Would you mind if we order right away? We're in a bit of a hurry," Pucci said to the server as she glanced at the menu. "I'll have the roast beef sandwich and whatever beer Randi ordered."

"I'll have the same, thanks," Randi said, handing back her menu to the server.

The two friends caught up, talking nonstop. Randi told Pucci the story of how her great Aunt Amalie lived in the states most of her life and came back to Edinburgh to live out her final days, knowing she'd be buried here.

They finished and paid. Randi communicated to the bartender their intentions and promised to be back in a few hours.

"Nae worries, Randi. Ye're belongings are safe, and a whisky is on the house when ye return. If ye're burying someone at Rosebank, ye're considered family here," he said, amicably.

Randi retrieved the instructions for the cemetery and a white silk flower out of her luggage. From the pub, they walked down the street to the cemetery. The mausoleum was at the very back of the cemetery, away from the entrance gates. Randi read the instructions on which path to follow once they entered, still chatting animatedly as they walked.

Rosebank Cemetery had opened for business in 1846. Two World War memorials, now weatherworn, were covered in moss and lichen, threatening to cover the list of local men lost in battle. The green grass and leaf-covered path, frosted from the cold, crunched as they walked. The leafless trees looked like skeletons keeping watch over their internments. Here and there, ghosts looked up as they floated around their gravestones to watch the women walk by. One woman still carried a parasol over her shoulder, while another gentleman tipped his hat to them. Pucci focused on her friend, not wanting to make eye contact with any of the ghosts to avoid them approaching her with their stories. *You all really need to go into the light*, she said to herself, looking at some dates on the headstones. Prof. James Harper, 1879, Lady Campbell, 1874. *It's time to cross over for goodness sake!* She didn't look at them, using her will to move the message out. Hopefully, someone would feel it.

"Cemeteries are always a little creepy," Randi spoke, interlocking her arm in Pucci's. "But this one is beautiful in a strange way. Seeing anybody floating around, Pucci?"

"Yes, thanks for asking," she replied dryly. "But it is beautiful, almost elegant in its proper layout and architecture." Randi nodded.

They approached the mausoleum. It was circular, about twenty feet in diameter, with two massive columns inset into the structure, framing the entrance. The bulbous roof blended with ominous clouds, threatening snow. Unaided, the large wooden door opened, creaking and groaning like an old man suffering an agonizing death, as the two approached. Their locked arms tightened.

Mr. Timothy Larchmont, the funeral director, stepped into the doorway. Behind him, Aunt Amalie's casket rested on a gurney in the center of the room, adorned simply with a small bouquet of flowers. The gaping hole of an open crypt, set into the smooth, marbled wall, gaped like a dark wound—her final resting place.

Timothy was tall, bone thin, dressed in a suit and a tie that was the width of dental floss. His voice was deep and somber, and he seemed to choose every word deliberately, from long practice of not offending anyone in mourning. Pucci was reminded of Lurch from the *Munsters* television show.

"Miss Baklen, my name is Mr. Timothy Larchmont, I am handling all the arrangements for your . . . " his low, grave, funereal voice, stopped.

"My great aunt."

"Ah. I apologize. We just now opened the crypt and found that George Galloway's coffin is in the middle of what we call a horizontal companion space. We have not been able to move him over to make room for your aunt. It seems the metallic sides of the coffin are rusted to the spot. I've called for some additional help. We will not be able to put your great aunt into her space until we move him." He said shifting back and forth on his long legs uncomfortably, his sunken eyes not looking at her.

Randi looked into the space that held her ancestors. "Oh, alright. Please do what you need to do."

The open crypt was third in a row of crypts marked with metal plaques engraved with names and dates. In the middle of the opened space sat an antique dark wood coffin with rusted corners. A cookie tin, also rusted and leaking ashes, sat in one corner of the crypt. A faded photograph of a small spaniel dog leaned against the failing tin. Resting alongside the leaking ashes was a rather large urn.

Pucci's stomach lurched, indicating that a ghost just showed up. She turned away from the open crypt. Behind her stood two ghosts. Randi raised a knowing eyebrow at Pucci.

Pucci asked Randi and the ghosts, "Who are these people?"

"George was my great grandfather," Randi said. The male ghost raised his translucent hand in acknowledgement. "And I'm assuming the urn is my great grandmother, Margret." A rather large woman ghost curtly nodded in acknowledgement. Margret had a snooty and annoyed look on her face. They were both dressed in formal attire: Margret in a long dress with a laced high collar and George in a three-piece suit, the vest a slightly darker shade of gray than the rest of his outfit. Leaning against the wall near their feet, the family crypt plaque read George Galloway, 1843 - 1920, shipbuilder; Margret Galloway 1868 - 1929.

"Who's the dog?" Timothy asked unexpectedly. "I really don't know how the dog's ashes got into the crypt, it's strictly forbidden. I won't remove it, but I must insist we put it in a new urn to stop the ashes from leaking."

Randi bit back a laugh, not wanting to offend him.

Two scraggly looking younger men burst into the space, breathing heavily from running, one carrying a crowbar.

"Sorry sir, we dinnae find the crowbar where ye said it should be . . ." the smaller of the two stopped talking when he saw the women. The other young man held a small empty urn.

"Could I ask you ladies to wait outside while I move George's coffin out of the way?" Timothy asked, without looking at either one of them.

"Certainly," Randi said, taking Pucci's arm, trying not to smile.

With a precise motion, the funeral director shed his suit jacket, passing it to the solemn young man holding the urn. He snatched the crowbar from the other's reluctant hands, bracing himself as he began to hack away at the decayed casket, each blow echoing in the still air. The two young men stood silently, transfixed, their expressions caught somewhere between wonder and dread.

"Ye always were glaikit," Margret said to George, disgusted as she watched the operation through the open door, standing next to the two women outside.

"Your greats are here, witnessing this," said Pucci. "I don't think Margret is too happy. What does glaikit mean?"

Now outside of the mausoleum, Randi let herself laugh out loud at the poor funeral director trying to move the rusted coffin. Calming herself with deep breaths, she replied, "It means selfish, thoughtless. Margret is probably accusing George of hogging the space. Which, by the way, Great Grandmother, my Great Grandfather was not glaikit and would never hog anything and you know it. Aunt Amalie told me stories of his generosity and kindness."

Margret harrumphed.

Through the open door of the mausoleum, they could see Timothy crawl into the crypt. Pucci tried desperately to silence Randi's laughter at seeing the funeral director's boney legs and feet sticking out of the crypt. The two young men turned to look outside at Pucci and Randi. One of them swept leaked ashes into the new urn, being extremely careful not to disturb his boss. Margret's lips pursed even harder if that was possible. George cracked a smile and winked at Pucci.

Pucci turned to the ghosts. "Who *is* the dog?"

Randi stopped, caught her breath and wiped away her tears.

Margret softened as she spoke. "Charlie was our Cavalier King Charles Spaniel," she explained before George could. "He adored George and passed away shortly after my husband—I think from heartache. When I died, Amalie arranged to bury him with me, slipping a small bribe to the former funeral director."

"What are they saying, Pucci?" Randi asked.

"I'll tell you back in the pub," she said as Timothy came to the door and beckoned the women back inside.

George's coffin was now on one side of the crypt. The leaky Charlie was in his nice new small black urn, but on the wrong side of the space, far from the coffin. Pucci whispered to Randi that George requested Charlie be next to him. Randi reached in and moved Charlie and his photograph to George's feet.

Timothy and the young men gave Randi a moment alone with Aunt Amalie while Pucci drew back to give her space. Randi was happy that her great aunt was at peace and out of pain.

She faced the casket, "Mar sin leigh an-drasta, goodbye for now," Randi whispered as she teared up. "I'll miss you."

She drew the silk white rose from her jacket, placing it into a small metal ring attached to the wall next to the open crypt, the green stem contrasting against the white marble. She knelt down near the metal plate and ran her finger over George's name, date, and occupation.

"So my great grandfather was a shipbuilder. That must be why Aunt Amalie wanted me to come. It's in my blood, as they say," Randi said, more to herself than to Pucci, wiping her tears. As Randi stood, she saw a small piece of paper protruding out underneath George's coffin. She reached in.

"Pucci, come here. I think there's something under George's coffin," Randi said.

Pucci walked over and leaned around Randi. She watched as Randi slowly removed a folded parchment out from under his coffin, making sure she didn't tear it.

"This must have been stuck under his coffin, but when they dislodged it . . . " Randi said, not completing her thought. "It looks like blueprints of some kind."

Randi reverently unfolded the fragile yellowing paper that crackled in protest. She approached Aunt Amalie's coffin and laid the drawing flat, delicately smoothing its edges.

"It seems to be a sketch of an old ship." Pucci said, admiring the drawing.

"You're right, Pucci. I think it's blueprints, hand-drawn sketches of an old ship. Oh, this is stunning! I've only seen these in museums. I wonder what it's doing here? Maybe my Aunt knew this was here and wanted me to find it," Randi said.

"Is it valuable?"

"No, probably not to anyone except me. Or, maybe a maritime museum." Randi leaned in closer to the bottom right-hand corner of the parchment. "Pucci, look. It looks like one of my ancestors designed it. See the title block?" She pointed to the bottom corner. "There's a faint signature and a date. M. Galloway. And the date looks like 1865. Oh, goodness, Pucci, look at the name of the ship!"

"Cutty Sark . . ." Pucci read out loud, slowly looking up at Randi. They couldn't help but smile at each other.

"Of course we find a rare, hand-drawn sketch of a ship that a famous whisky derived its name from!" Randi exclaimed.

Showing deep respect, she folded the parchment back up and delicately tucked it away in her coat's inside pocket. She brought her hand to her lips, kissed it, and gently laid it on the coffin as a last farewell.

Timothy and company came back in and lifted Amalie's casket into the crypt beside her father and mother. Pucci teared up, bowed her head to the fading ghosts and walked out of the mausoleum behind Randi.

Pucci and Randi walked arm in arm down the cemetery path toward the exit. Suddenly, Pucci felt a familiar evil off to her left. She froze mid step, her breath catching as she spun around. A shadow—a distinctly human shadow—flickered in her peripheral vision, vanishing as quickly as it appeared, leaving her heart pounding in the eerie stillness. *It can't be.* She said to herself. *He couldn't have followed me here.*

Chapter 13

The bartender, Archie, true to his word, poured a wee dram of whisky for everyone in the bar for a toast.

"To our ancestors . . . Slàinte, cheers!" Archie called out, holding up his glass.

"Slàinte!" the bar responded.

Retaking their table by the fire, Pucci turned to Randi, "How are you doing, my friend?"

Randi smiled, "I'm doing really well, Pucci. I am happy my great aunt is at peace." She paused, looking intently at Pucci. "The question is, how are you? What happened as we were walking out of the cemetery? Your energy completely changed."

"Perceptive as always, Randi. And, it's a very long story." Pucci sighed.

"We have all the time in the world," Randi said, sitting back, sipping her second whisky.

"Remember when I went to Grand Cayman last year for my rum article and met the ghost of JD Langer? That crazy adventure?"

Randi nodded. Pucci continued. "I didn't tell you all of it. The last night I was on the island, Olan—Detective Chief Inspector Olan Lathen—and I discovered a piece of jewelry hidden in an old locket. Turns out, this little piece of jewelry is called a jeweled cipher. I studied these a long time ago, so I recognized what it was. The locket was part of the Cheapside Hoard, but the jeweled cipher wasn't documented anywhere as part of the hoard." She paused. Randi nodded again, her eyes intently focused on Pucci.

Pucci looked around to make sure no one was listening. "Olan had a psychometric episode when he touched the cipher. He saw and felt things."

Randi sat up. "Had he ever had one before? The way you described him, he didn't seem like he would believe in all this stuff."

"Never. I had to explain what psychometry was to him. It was fascinating. I think he saw a past-life while he touched the cipher. He saw in his mind's eye, the cipher being hidden inside the locket, then put into a small wooden box, then being buried underneath a floorboard in a basement. His last vision was fire. I've been researching the Cheapside Hoard ever since I got back. The hoard was buried in a jewelers shop, but no one knows why. Then, the great fire of London happened. No one ever came back for the hoard. In all my research, this cipher never appears in any inventory or story about the hoard. No one knew this cipher was inside the locket."

Pucci moved her hand to her neck, moving the turtleneck out of the way slightly and removed a gold chain from around her head. She held her palm out to Randi, who bent her head over it. Pucci opened her palm, and Randi's breath caught at the sight of the exquisite gold and diamond jeweled piece.

"Pucci, my God, are you nuts wearing this sacred piece around your neck?"

"No safer place in my mind."

"OK, good point," Randi said, reaching out to touch it. "May I?"

"Of course. Let me know if you get any psychic visions off it. I got nothing!"

Randi touched the three larger diamonds in the center, looking to be about a carat each, marveling at the other, slightly smaller ones surrounding them. "No, no visions, but wow, it is powerful. That I can feel."

"Olan said as he came out of his psychometry vision, this piece is 'part of a clue to a mythical treasure that dates back centuries.'"

"Oh, come on. It doesn't look that old. Seriously?"

"Seriously. And, one more thing I haven't told you. It's connected somehow to the Knights Templar and Rosslyn Chapel." Pucci put the gold chain around her neck and tucked it back under her layers.

"OK, but you still haven't told me what happened in the cemetery as we were walking out. What did you see?" Randi asked.

"He goes by the name of Pirate. I call him the Shadow Man. He's wanted by Scotland Yard for some big smuggling operation. He almost killed me in Grand Cayman. Olan shot him, but he got away. We think he's still alive somewhere. He has powers much like mine, but they're dark and evil. I thought I felt his energy in the cemetery. I even thought I saw him for a moment. It doesn't make sense. I thought he was just after the treasure hoard, but now. Maybe he's after the cipher."

Pucci shook her head and brushed back the bangs that had fallen in her eyes. With her elbow on the table, her palm felt cool on her forehead as she leaned into it. They were both silent for a moment. Randi felt Pucci collecting herself.

"I don't want to put you in any danger, Randi. I was going to invite you to come stay at the castle with me, but now, I don't think it's a good idea."

"Castle? What castle? Is it haunted? Does it have good food and a good wine cellar?"

"Strathhammond Castle. It's also a spa! And yes, yes, and yes, or so I've heard!"

"You had me at spa!" Randi laughed. "Pucci, I wouldn't miss one of your adventures for the world. What a story! I must see Rosslyn Chapel now, as well. Look what you just did for me and my great aunt. And besides, the new boat I'm supposed to sail back to the states is delayed by at least three weeks. So, you find me with time on my hands, Pucci."

Pucci's smile deepened until her cheeks began to burn. She felt a warmth, the kind of warmth that comes from an abundance of laughter and joy. She leaned over to hug Randi, being very careful not to spill the superb whisky.

Randi got up to go to the Lady's, the polite Scottish name for the bathroom. Pucci's phone rang, and she was delightfully surprised at the name that popped up.

"Varv! How are you, my dear? Where are you?"

"Hi, Pucci! It's so good to hear your voice."

Pucci heard and felt sadness. "Varv, what's wrong?"

"My ex-husband died. It had been coming on for a while, cancer. But, it's still a shock. The kids are struggling. I wish I could help them. I'm still working through the grief. You know, we remained good friends." Varv said through tears. "Pucci, you don't . . . I hate to ask, but do you see him?"

Pucci opened up her energy, taking a moment to center herself. "No Varv, he hasn't come to me, and he isn't here now. Let me know if you want to try and talk to him. We could do it over the phone when I'm not in a pub."

"How about we do it in person, Pucci?" A little energy was coming back into Varv's voice.

"What do you mean?"

"I'm free till after the holidays. I'm driving to London. I've finished my commission in Cardiff after I came back from the funeral, and was wondering if I could come join you in Scotland?"

"Oh, fab, Varv!" Pucci exclaimed. "How about you join Randi and I at Strathammond Castle, just outside of Edinburgh! It's also a spa!"

"That sounds perfect, just what I need. Do you think Randi would mind?" Varv asked.

Pucci looked up as Randi came back to the table. "Randi, Varv wants to join us at the castle, would that be OK?"

"Are you kidding me? Of course, I'd love to see her again! It's been way too long." Randi smiled.

"Did you hear that, Varv? I'll call the castle and get you a reservation! I don't think they're very busy this time of year, so they'll likely have a room. Take the earliest train you can leaving out of Kings Cross, and we'll pick you up at Waverly Train Station on our way out to the castle. Text us your arrival."

"Perfect! And, Pucci? Thank you. I can't wait to see you and Randi and give you both a big hug!" She hung up.

"This will be so much fun!" Randi exclaimed. "Hanging with the gals in a haunted castle-spa, chasing down clues to a mysterious treasure while avoiding getting shot from the Shadow Man! Let's do this thing!"

Chapter 14

Anya

Anya paid the cabbie in cash and got out of the taxi a block from her destination. She walked toward the modern gray cement apartment buildings, which stood in front of a large wall that bordered an expanse of open land. She turned down a small alley and walked toward the end unit. A black iron handrail and six steps led up a white door. Two blacked-out windows faced the entrance.

"Hidden in plain sight," Anya mumbled to herself as she ascended the stairs. Morgan and Pirate called this 'the apartment'—she knew it as the distribution center. She knocked the secret knock again, rolling her eyes. The door cracked open. She saw an eye checking her out. The door opened a crack further to reveal a small Asian man.

"Who are you?" he asked.

"I'm Morgan's second. Open the damn door," Anya said, forcefully.

He stepped aside to let her in. He and two other colleagues, also Asian, were unboxing what looked like cloth ornaments. Anya picked up one in the shape of a thistle, the national flower of Scotland, stuffed so it had a three-dimensional shape like a pincushion. The front had green leaves on either side of a gold embroidered stem, with green and gold crosshatched in the center. The top of the ornament featured a purple velvet rectangle, symbolizing the bloom of a thistle flower. Anya turned it over and read in gold stitching Palace of Holyroodhouse. A gold-covered string was sewn in a small loop above the purple top to hang the ornament.

The man who had opened the door ripped open another box. "Pretty clever, huh? We get these from China, all go to Holyrood except the overfilled ones, we keep. They have special lining. We undo the stitching, put the stones inside with special material so customs machine don't pick them up. Then send them back as rejects to special address. See?" he said pointing to a box labeled "Return - Rejects."

Anya nodded and cracked a good-one smile at the man. He nodded back smugly. She handed a small velvet pouch to the man. "Morgan said these go out tonight."

The man took the pouch, opened it and poured the diamonds into his palm. As he inspected them, Anya stealthily palmed her phone and took a photo of the label on the box. She quickly slipped her phone back into her pocket before the man finished counting.

"OK, we get these out. Lucky, we just got new shipment of tourist trinkets." The man said and turned to speak what sounded like Mandarin to the other two in the room. They nodded and continued their work.

"Morgan wanted me to ask about our guy in South Africa out at the S. A. Mine." Anya lied. "He wants to know how many ten carat rocks he's collected and when is he getting them out? He said you would know." She said it as a statement, hoping her bluff was true.

"Oh, Whiley's got a plan to get three of them out," he said, smiling a toothless smile.

"Nice, but he wants to know how and when."

"The same way he's getting all of them out. He should know that," he said, suddenly suspicious.

"Then why did he ask me to ask you?" she said and turned to go.

"Wait, if Morgan trusts you, fine. I'll tell you. Plus, he'd kill anyone that betrays him. Whiley goes down into the mine when they think they find a vein. Since he's a geologist, he's trusted."

"And is he? A geologist?"

"What do you think? He learned enough to fool people. I made his diploma! Very convincing! The mine was desperate, so no checking his references. Anyway, he inspects what they find prior to anyone else seeing the rough material. He pockets some of the diamonds, not all, that would give it away," he laughed at his own joke. "Everyone is searched when they come out of the mine, so he can't just carry them out. He hides them in the loader down in the mine. When the loader comes up for inspection, he removes them from their hidey-hole when no one is around, then ships them to your little operation in Edinburgh. Had to bypass Grand Cayman since you guys fled."

She cringed at the jibe. "Ingenious," she said, hiding her anger. "I'll be sure to tell Morgan. When's the next shipment?"

"He's got three ten carats, blues. Very rare. He waited a long time for the third one. The loader is about to come up for maintenance, so it shouldn't be long now. Maybe few weeks, maybe days." The man said, flipping an overstuffed ornament into the small pile on a chair in the living room. "Whiley told me rumors going around the mine there's a thief on the inside. So far, they don't suspect Whiley. Tell Morgan he wants out before he's caught. He's done. Too risky."

Anya's stomach clenched with apprehension. She was running out of time. She tried to keep her face stoic. "Whiley quits when Morgan and Pirate say he's done," she growled, hoping to scare this man and Whiley too, next time they talked.

The other workers stopped and stared at the confrontation between Anya and their fellow worker, feeling the anger in both. Anya pointed to the small pouch that she had just handed to the man and said, "Tonight." He nodded.

She walked out of the small apartment and down to the street to hail a cab. While she waited, she quickly sent another encrypted text message with a picture attached. She could only hope they were receiving them.

Chapter 15

The train pulled into Waverly on time. Pucci and Randi waited at the coffee shop for Varv to come through the turnstiles. Pucci spotted her tall, slender Italian friend approaching. Her long brown hair was tied back in a loose ponytail, highlighting the striking blue of her eyes. When they saw each other, Pucci ran toward Varv, arms outstretched, her heart swelling with love. Varv dropped her luggage, and they collided with laughter, hugs, and tears. Their life-threatening adventure together last year in Grand Cayman had bonded the women at a deep level.

"Let's not spill coffee all over Varv." Randi lifted Pucci's coffee cup out of her hand from behind Varv's back. When they broke apart, Randi leaned in and gave Varv a sweet, so-great-to-see-you-again hug.

Pucci and Randi grabbed their luggage. Varv wiped away her tears as they all walked out of the station.

In the cab, they chatted and commented on the beautiful scenery on the way to the castle. They decided to save the big stories of what was happening in their lives until tonight at dinner.

The taxi drove south, through small towns toward Gore Glen Woodland Park in Midlothian. As it rounded the last corner, less than an hour later, the castle came into view. Strathhammond, with its imposing circular tower, turrets, and flag flying high from the uppermost tower was enchantment itself. The walls were burnt orange, made of stones quarried nearby. Arms of peridot and maroon ivy vines wrapped around the belly of the tower in a giant hug.

The three women stepped out, mouths open, looking up at the imposing building. The grand arched entrance was flanked by two enormous pots, each housing a twenty-foot pine tree decorated for Christmas. The taxi driver moved their luggage into a small foyer before Pucci could protest. She then paid and tipped him well, thanking him before he drove away.

"Pucci, this is magnificent!" Varv exclaimed taking in the castle. "How did you find this?"

"I wanted to be near Rosslyn Chapel, but not necessarily stay in the town of Roslin. I found this place, and they were offering a special." The women watched as a barn owl flew from a perch, low across a grass field to a gloved hand of a seasoned falconer as a family with small children watched mesmerized. They were admiring the woodlands across the field when Pucci heard a familiar voice.

"Ms. Riddle? Pucci?"

Her heart skipped. "Mr. MacNevin? Braden?" She turned and saw the man who'd been in her dream—and talked to—on the airplane. Tall and impeccably built, he carried himself with an easy elegance. His short brown hair was neatly styled, and his vest, patterned in green, red, and blue tartan, added a Scottish flair beneath his expertly tailored navy-blue suit jacket. The cut of the jacket accentuated his balanced frame, while his navy trousers draped smoothly over his long legs. Pucci's smile lingered as she caught sight of the faint beard that had grown since their flight. His moonstone eyes, their corners crinkling with his smile, held a warmth that seemed to reach right through her as they walked toward each other.

"What are you doing here?" they both asked.

"You first," Braden said.

"My friends and I are staying here for a couple of days. We're going to see Rosslyn Chapel, and I thought it would be fun to stay in a castle," she answered, as Varv and Randi came closer.

"Will you introduce me to your friends?" Braden asked.

"Certainly. Braden MacNevin, this is Randi Baklen and Varvada Conti." Randi and Varv beamed. "Randi and Varv, this is Mr. Braden MacNevin. We met on the plane from Chicago to London."

Suddenly, a woman dressed in a severe black uniform with a crisp white collar and white apron came running out of the castle toward them.

She curtsied. "My Lord," she said, somewhat out of breath. "I'm sorry tae interrupt, but yer wanted in the main dining room."

Behind Braden's back, Randi mouthed, "My *lord?*" Pucci shrugged.

"Please tell them I'll come directly. And please tell Mr. Anderson my special guests have arrived." She curtsied again and ran off.

"Ladies, I do apologize I cannot welcome you properly. Right now, I am, apparently, needed. Mr. Anderson will take care of you. Pucci, will you and your friends be available for a drink later? Say, 5 p.m. in the library?"

"That would be delightful, thank you," Pucci said. Should she curtsy? *Could* she curtsy? He nodded once, turned and walked swiftly into the castle.

Randi and Varv rounded on Pucci.

"My Lord?" Varv's eyebrows flew up. "You got some 'splaining to do, Lucy!"

"Honestly you two, I had no idea! His card said Mr. Braden MacNevin. No, esquire or Earl or Duke, no title at all!" Pucci exclaimed.

They all laughed. "Only you, Pucci," Randi said, grinning. "Let's get checked in and get settled. You can tell us all about how you met the Earl of Strathhammond!"

***

Mr. Anderson, his gold shiny name tag indicating he was the manager, met them at the front door with a bellhop. He was tall, fair-haired, and impeccably dressed in a gray wool suit and tartan tie of yellows, reds, and browns. It was immediately clear that one of his chief job skills was his gentlemanly manners. Even toward American tourists.

The lobby entrance lay between twin-curved grand staircases, leading down two steps into a dimly lit room, where a plush deep-red carpet softened every step. The women followed their suitcases and Mr. Anderson.

"Welcome ladies! Wonderful tae have you all here. How are you acquainted with the Earl of Strathhammond?" Mr. Anderson asked Pucci.

"Oh, I just met him on the plane from Chicago to London. He mentioned he lived in Scotland, but never hinted he was an earl," Pucci said.

"Och, I'm not surprised. He likes tae keep a low profile as much as he can. But, since the magazine article came out, declaring him one of the most eligible bachelors in Scotland, he's becoming quite a recluse. I'm sure it was refreshing tae meet someone who dinae know who he was!" he chuckled. "He dislikes it when people treat him differently than any other man."

"We'll keep that in mind. We're supposed to meet him in the library for drinks in a few hours. Could you tell us where that is?" Pucci asked.

"Nae worries, I'll give you a tour as soon as we get you sorted with your rooms. Pucci, I have you in one room on the third floor, and your two friends sharing a room on the second floor, if that's satisfactory?" asked Mr. Anderson. The three looked at each other and nodded.

The bellhop delivered their luggage to their rooms, which was a relief considering there were no elevators and narrow stairs. The women decided to meet back at the front doors for a walk in about an hour. Time enough to get settled and changed.

Pucci's bed stood like something from a storybook, adorned with a canopy draped in ethereal white sheer fabric that floated delicately in the soft glow of the room's light. Three polished steps, their edges lined with a hint of golden trim, led up to a bathroom that gleamed with a white marble sink and vanity, and an ornate bathtub at the far end. An antique dresser, its dark wood polished to a warm sheen, stood proudly against one wall, its simple brass handles hinting at centuries of history. A small writing desk rested beneath the picture window, its delicate legs carved with care. Pucci set her purse on the writing table, taking in the scene unfolding before her. The lush green expanse of the grounds, the towering pine standing sentinel, and the full moon just beginning to rise on the horizon stirred something familiar in her being.

Chapter 16

The three friends set out for a leisurely stroll around the grounds. It was just turning dusk. They admired the beautifully manicured lawn that encompassed acres in all directions spanning away from the castle. The woods beyond were a medley of ferns, pines, and towering trees. The ground was saturated with dampness, so they remained mindful of their steps, careful not to slip on the moss beneath their feet. The air smelled of snow. They turned around giving themselves enough time to go back up to the room and change for drinks with the Earl.

Pucci dressed in her nicest gray wool slacks; she hadn't brought anything too dressy. Who knew she'd be in the company of an earl? She thought her cashmere sweater, with green and red beadwork, would be nice and festive. She freshened her eyeliner, touched up her mascara, and ran downstairs to meet the gals in the common area above the lobby.

Pucci was admiring old portraits on the walls when she heard Randi and Varv behind her.

"Varv, you look beautiful," Pucci said reaching over to feel Varv's deep blue fine wool sweater. "So soft!"

"Thank you, Pucci. Randi, I love your silver necklace against your black sweater. Stunning." She looked at Pucci and, feeling her energy, asked, "Pucci, you OK?"

"Intuitive as always, Varv. I'm just nervous about Braden. I have felt such a strong connection to him ever since we met."

"We got you, Pucci," Randi said.

"I'm so happy you gals are here!" Pucci said as they walked into the library.

Braden was already in the library standing next to a tall three-paneled window. A small sitting area with a love seat and two chairs framed the space by the window. A beautifully crafted antique coffee table in front of the couch held a bottle of whisky, a pitcher of water, and eight glasses.

He turned at the sound of the women entering, a roguish grin playing at his lips as he said, "Welcome to my castle."

Braden went straight to Pucci and held out his two hands reaching for hers. She moved toward him and offered her hands. He squeezed them while looking in her eyes and said, "I can't believe you're here!"

"I can't believe this is your castle!" she said, blushing slightly, not knowing if she should let go and remove her hands from his.

He gently released her and said to Randi and Varv, "So wonderful to have all of you here at Strathammond with me."

Varv responded, "Thank you, Braden, it's wonderful to be here." Randi nodded.

He lifted a bottle of whisky. "Would you like a wee dram? This is one of my favorite whiskies and from one of my favorite distilleries on Islay, Bunnahabhain," pronouncing it boonahaben. He removed the top of the bottle, poured a little more than a splash in each of the smaller glasses and handed them all around. "Slàinte, to your health," he said as they all clinked glasses.

Pucci's nostrils filled with a delightful, smoky scent as she 'nosed' the amber liquid. She noticed Braden watching her. She could smell the peat and sweet fruit. Her first sip mellowed the peat and brought out the fruit and vanilla flavors of the eighteen-year single malt. Delicious! Pucci made a mental note to visit this distillery when on Islay.

She looked around the library, admiring the maroon-and-gold carpeting, and leather chairs in intimate arrangements for quiet conversation or settling down for a good read. The bookshelves were filled with antique volumes of all shapes and sizes. Pucci breathed in the atmosphere, her soul content. She loved libraries and a good single malt, let alone sharing this moment with her dear friends and a gorgeous Scotsman.

Varv looked up at the ornate ceiling, its soft yellow hue accentuated by delicate white plasterwork. She had studied the art of decorative plaster ceilings in her interior design courses but seeing it in person was something else entirely. Intricate geometric and floral patterns adorned every corner, flowing seamlessly along the edges, a testament to masterful craftsmanship.

"Beautiful Scottish plasterwork, Braden," she said, still looking up.

"Thank you, Varvada. You obviously know your decorative plasterwork," Braden said, impressed.

"I'm an interior designer. I studied this in school. I was fascinated by how much design-detail went into something that people rarely saw," she said. "So, I always look up."

"I'll have to remember that," Randi said, chuckling. "I look up all the time, but it's to watch the sky for signs of weather!"

"Why is that, Randi?" Braden asked.

"I'm a shipbuilder, Braden. I design and oversee the construction of custom boats and bring them to the owners, all over the world," Randi said, smiling. "So, I'm usually on the lookout for changing weather."

"Pucci, you have fascinating friends!" Braden said.

Pucci had spotted what looked like a first edition of *The Waverley Novels* by the famous Scottish author, Sir Walter Scott. She moved to the bookshelf and took it out, reverently opening it to the first page, then startled at the title of the first book, *The Pirate*.

"Pucci, what's wrong?" Braden asked, watching her face.

"Oh, it's nothing, Braden," she said, quickly recovering. "This library is amazing!" She closed the book and replaced it on the shelf, hoping it wasn't a bad omen.

"Aye, come here, I want to show you something," he said, grinning. "Randi, Varvada, come too."

Near a Christmas tree, decorated with embroidered snowflakes and red ball ornaments, what looked like a wall of books revealed itself to be a facade. Braden reached over and pushed a wooden spacer at the end of the middle shelf. The fake book shelf opened with a clunk. Braden smiled at the women's reactions and opened the door wider.

"A secret passage, Braden?" Varv asked.

"Nae," he said and stood back to let them in. "A bar!" he laughed. The three laughed and marveled as well. "It's under repair, so we can't go inside. But I thought you'd like that," he said, closing the bookshelf.

At the table, Randi and Varv poured themselves a glass of water.

"So, we've heard your castle is haunted, Braden." Varv took a seat on a cushioned leather chair. Pucci sat next to Braden on the love seat.

"Which haunting do you want to hear about first?" His eyes twinkled with mischief.

"More than one?" Randi exclaimed as she sat down.

"Aye. But the famous one is about the Lady of the Stairs. Around the late 1400s, there was a woman who apparently was a mistress of one of my ancestor's lairds. His vengeful wife locked her up in one of the Castle turrets, where she perished from not eating. Some psychics have seen her. She walks the stairways at night."

"That's a lie," a voice hissed in Pucci's ear.

Pucci almost choked on her whisky. She tried not to react any further. She communicated to the unseen ghost with her thoughts. *I'll come find you later.* She hoped the ghost heard.

Randi and Varv felt the shift in Pucci's energy. Not wanting to say anything in front of Braden, they raised their eyebrows in question. With a sharp nod, Pucci acknowledged—a ghost had, indeed, just spoken.

Chapter 17

B raden had a prior dinner engagement. "I hope you enjoy your dinner down in the dungeon!" he smiled. "Nae worries," seeing the looks on the ladies faces. "We converted it into a beautiful dining room." He bowed to the three of them and walked out of the library.

"I wonder who he's dinning with?" Varv mischievously asked. "I'll bet it's the Queen."

"Oh, Varv, quit with the imagination already!" Randi said, laughing.

"Come on gals, let's eat." Pucci said, leading the way to the dungeon.

They descended a narrow cement staircase into an unusual room. The towering walls, at least two stories high, were constructed from bricks of various shapes and sizes, some rectangular, others irregularly cut. Their gray-brown hues blended like the patchwork of an old quilt, and the pale cream mortar between them formed a delicate mosaic pattern that added to the room's ancient and mysterious atmosphere. Swords, shields, and suits of armor decorated the walls and niches. Candlelight created a cozy atmosphere, and the white tablecloths added formality and brightness to the room.

The menu offerings were exquisite. Filled with traditional Scottish dishes, prepared in a French-style cuisine. Pucci wondered at the strange combination of Scottish and French, while ordering the vegetarian option—a squash and cauliflower dish with a Romanesco tart, candied hazelnuts and smoked onions. She paired it with a Medoc from the

Bordeaux region. Randi and Varv chose roast loin of lamb with goat cheese gnocchi and winter vegetables.

The wine came, Pucci sipped the delicious red with flavors of berries and licorice. Perfect.

"These are works of art!" Pucci exclaimed in a whisper, when their food was brought to the table. Her voice barely audible amidst the soft murmurs of the room. Around her, distinguished-looking patrons moved gracefully, their quiet conversations blending seamlessly with the air of refined elegance.

"I don't even want to eat, it's so beautiful," Varv exclaimed.

"Let's take a picture of all of us and our food," Randi said. "Excuse me, waiter. Could you please take a picture of us?"

"Certainly madam," he said. He took a few shots with Randi's camera. "Bon appétit!"

Between bites and moans of delight, they caught each other up on what was happening in their lives.

The story of the cemetery startled Varv. "So you felt the Shadow Man, Pucci? God, I'd hoped we were done with him."

"Varv, I think he's after this," Pucci said, removing the jeweled cipher from around her neck, handing it to Varv. Varv drew in a sharp breath.

"Pucci, this wasn't part of the Cheapside Hoard," Varv said, fingering it delicately.

"You didn't see this piece, Varv. Olan and I discovered it hidden in the reliquary locket that Brent was researching for JD, remember?" Varv nodded. Pucci continued, "He was never able to open it. But Olan and I got it to open when we simultaneously touched the locket—I know, weird. When Olan removed the cipher, he had a vision when he touched it. He saw it being hidden in the locket, then the locket was included with the rest of the hoard that was buried under the floorboards of the jewelers shop in Cheapside. And, as I was telling Randi earlier, he said it was part of a clue to a mythical treasure."

Varv and Randi looked at each other, then back to Pucci.

"One last thing. A ghost is attached to this piece and showed himself in Knights Templar clothing and told me to go to Rosslyn Chapel. He told me 'a key piece can be found there,'" Pucci said, putting the gold chain around her neck, and letting the jeweled piece hang in front of her sweater. "So, Varv, my feeling is the Shadow Man, or Pirate as he likes to call himself, is after this piece. He was never after the Cheapside Hoard. That was just icing on the cake, as it were." The server delivered their deserts.

Varv's stomach was in knots, thinking back to those harrowing experiences they had shared in Grand Cayman. She calmed herself down, enough to nibble on her desert of chocolate and passion fruit crumble. Even though the taste was superb, her nerves wouldn't allow her to finish. She set her fork down. "Pucci, what are we going to do? I mean, is he really back?"

Pucci reached over and squeezed Varv's hand. She felt Varv's fear. "We have to stay one step ahead of him, again, Varv. I know we don't have a specific ghost to help us this time. But, I'm hoping my Knights Templar will come around again when we visit Rosslyn tomorrow."

"Pucci, have you contacted Olan?" Varv asked.

"That's a long story, Varv. I think you know part of it. Connor contacted me in London. Are you two still seeing each other?"

"Yes," Varv smiled, releasing some of her fear. "As much as we can in a long distance relationship. What happened with Olan?"

"He's not in a good place right now. Something is really wrong. It's like his soul got shattered by something. I don't know. He's nothing like his former self. We might have to do this on our own."

"I've got your backs, ladies," Randi chimed in.

They smiled. Pucci said, "Oh, Varv, I'm so sorry. I never asked how you are regarding the death of your ex-husband? Are you OK? How are your kids? Do you want to talk about it?"

"No, that's alright, Pucci. We'll find another time. I'm pretty tired. I might go up to our room and call it an early night." She smiled sadly.

"I'm sorry, Varv," Randi said.

"Thank you, Randi, but I'm fine."

"We'll talk tomorrow," Pucci said as Varv stood.

"Sounds good, and thank you, gals. I'll see you bright and early in the morning," Varv said. "Here's some money for a tip."

Randi and Pucci watched her go. Randi spoke, "She's a tough woman, been through a lot. I'm so thankful to be here with you two, and to get to know Varv better."

"She is amazing," Pucci said.

"Pucci, I've been meaning to ask you. What's next after Rosslyn for you? Do you have any plans?"

"Oh, yes, hah!" Pucci laughed. "I guess I haven't told you. This is also a working vacation. I'm going to the island of Islay to visit three or four distilleries for my blog. It's funny, it's spelled Islay but pronounced 'eyelah.' I've also been asked to write an article for *Wine and Scotch* magazine. The commission is almost paying for this trip! I'm definitely adding Bunnahabhain to the list. I would love it if you and Varv can come with me."

"I'm not a big peaty Scotch fan but would love to come and see the island. How are you getting there?"

"I'm catching the train to Glasgow, then a bus to the ferry. The ferry port is just south of the village of Tarbert. It takes about a day to get to the ferry, but it is a lot cheaper than flying. Plus, you get to see the country. The bus skirts Loch Lomond," Pucci said, taking the last sip of her wine.

"Fabulous, count me in." Randi said, adding her share to the tip. "I'm knackered as well, Pucci. I think I'll turn in, have a soak in our glorious bath, and call it an early night."

"Sounds good, my friend. I'll see you both early tomorrow."

***

Pucci was not tired at all. Images of Braden danced in her head. She'd caught him looking at her during drinks. Was this for real? Did he really like her? She aimlessly wandered the castle, singing *"you take the high road and I'll take the low road . . . for me and my true love will never meet again on the bonny bonny banks of Loch Lomond."*

She thought she was ascending the correct staircase to her room, but something didn't look right. She kept climbing. The air temperature was dropping. "These castles sure are drafty," she said to no one in particular. *But, the air should be getting warmer, hot air rises.* Turning right on a landing, she stepped onto the first step and paused. She could see her breath now. She looked up at the top of the short flight of stairs and saw a magnificent woman, dressed in a blue dress from the late 1400s. The dress, simply adorned, formed a V shaped at her small waist and cascaded out and down to the floor. The sleeves were long and belled out at her wrists. Her locks of white translucent hair flowed down her back. She had her hands on her hips, her lips pursed in annoyance.

The ghost spoke, "I told you it was a lie."

Pucci, recovering from gazing on this amazing apparition, answered. "What is a lie?"

Instead of answering, the ghost asked, "What are you doing in my house?"

"What are *you* still doing *here*?" Pucci asked, slightly affronted by her blunt question. "And what did you mean by telling me Braden's story was a lie?" Pucci tried again, slowly ascending the stairs, getting colder by the minute.

Suddenly, the ghosts' energy changed. Confusion and astonishment were evident on her face. Pucci could see her features more clearly as the ghost came closer, her gown rustling. The Lady reached out her shimmering hand just below Pucci's neck to the jeweled cipher.

"Where did you get that?" she whispered reverently. Pucci, taken aback, backed away slightly, feeling the jewel and the gold chain turning cold, even through her sweater.

"Are you the Lady of the Stairs?" Pucci asked. The ghost nodded, not taking her eyes off the necklace.

She spoke, "I never thought I'd see a piece like this again. I died protecting one just like it. I concealed it on my person, just like you. They tortured me for the information, then killed me. That's when they found it. I don't know what happened to it or who they were. My torturers slandered my reputation by making up the story that I was his mistress, so no one would ask questions. That's why I said the Earl's story was a lie," she said with sadness, not anger this time.

"My Lady, can you remember how the piece came in your possession?"

The ghost tremulously reached out to Pucci. Their energies connected. The Lady of the Stairs smiled and spoke again. "I can feel your energy. You are one of us. A protector of good and a thwarter of evil. I will tell you, but you must swear not to tell anyone and protect that piece with your life. Swear."

"I swear on my life, my Lady," Pucci said.

She nodded and spoke. "What I can remember, when I was alive. My lover, the laird's brother, was part of a secret society, sworn to protect ancient artifacts brought here from the Holy Land by knights ages ago." Pucci's eyes grew wide. "He told me once, in our bedchamber," she said, a sweet smile shown on her face at the memory, "the knights had discovered artifacts in the ruins of King Solomon's Temple in the early 1100s when they were encamped on top of the Temple Mount in Jerusalem. These artifacts are infused with King Solomon's magic and used by Solomon to control evil spirits. They were secretly moved to France later that century for protection. If they fell into the wrong hands, we would experience hell on earth. Whoever controlled the evil would rule the world. In 1307, some knights fled to Scotland before most were persecuted and slaughtered in France. We welcomed the knights in Scotland. They even helped Robert the Bruce defeat the English in 1314. Only the other knights who survived were aware of this history, and passed it down to others who had been initiated."

Pucci had moved up to the same landing as the ghost, astonished at this story. She had forgotten how cold she was. "Please, ma'am, continue."

"I have no knowledge of what the artifacts are. I had heard a rumor, right before my death, that there was a connection to the newly constructed Rosslyn Chapel. William St. Clair, Earl of Rosslyn had connections with the Knights. The Templars have a Parish Church and land very close to here, in Temple," she said, her form was fading slightly. Pucci could feel this conversation was taking enormous energy from the ghost to keep talking.

"Can you tell me anything about this piece? I know it's a jeweled cipher, part of a larger multicomponent jewel. Do you know what happened to your piece? Where other pieces are?"

The lady apparition smiled weakly. "The story handed down was when the pieces are brought together, they hold the key to where the Knights hid one of Solomon's artifacts," her form was fading.

In her last moments, she said, "There is another piece like yours hidden in Rosslyn, connected to the Knights. Find it, before they do." And she was gone.

Pucci slowly descended the stairs, fingering the cipher, mulling over everything the Lady of the Stairs had said to her. She didn't notice Braden coming toward her.

"Pucci! I heard your voice a minute ago. Who were you talking to?" he asked.

Startled, coming out of her reverie, she quickly tucked the cipher under her sweater and said, truthfully, "Just one of your guests."

"They're not really my guests any longer. Do you have time for a nightcap? I can explain."

Pucci had questions. Maybe Braden could help. She agreed and they walked into the library.

Chapter 18

Braden stopped a server on the way into the library, issuing some instructions, and continued walking, allowing Pucci to go before him. She went to the chairs near the fireplace and sat down, still reeling from all the information she had learned and the questions that remained unanswered.

Braden sat in the dark red leather high-back chair on the other side of a quaint, vintage table with ornate legs. The server came toward them and set two drams of whisky down on the table in between them. Pucci looked up, smiled and accepted the liquid he offered, his warm hand touched hers for a moment.

"Thank you, Braden, I'm sorry, I'm a little out of sorts at the moment and maybe a little tired."

They clinked glasses. "Is there anything I can do for you?"

Pucci took a small sip. It was a different whisky than the first one they had shared. "This is delicious! Oh, Braden! This is Bruichladdich Black Art!" she exclaimed.

"I'm impressed, you know your Single Malts."

"Yes, especially the ones from Islay. I'm going there after I leave your castle. It's for my next blog and spirits article. I told you that's what I do for a living on the plane, didn't I?"

He graciously tilted his head in acknowledgement.

Pucci asked, "Now, what did you mean they're not your guests any longer?"

Braden sighed, took another sip and said in a sad voice, "I have sold the grand ol' lass to a large company that has been managing the hotel and spa for the last few years. She's too much for me tae take care of alone. My daughter is in Chicago finishing her degree and will probably make that her home. The deal was just completed this past week." He held up his glass to the library in salute.

Pucci could feel his sadness. She didn't know what to say, or if she should console him. She held up her glass as well, sending her energy out to the heart and soul of the grand ol' lass.

"Do you feel any sort of relief? Loss?" Pucci asked.

"I feel good about it, actually. They will take prodigious care of her for another 800 years, hopefully."

"That's a wonderful perspective."

"My clan's seat is in another town a few miles from here. So, I'll be near, keeping an eye on them. And, I still have private quarters in one wing. That was part of the negotiations. They wanted to turn that into a honeymoon suite. Och, I just couldn't . . . " he said, shaking his head. His bangs fell into his eyes. He raked them back with his other hand.

"Braden," Pucci ventured to change the subject, "do you know anything about the history of your family and any connections to Rosslyn Chapel?"

"Where is that question coming from?"

"Oh, we're going to Rosslyn tomorrow, and since this castle is fairly close, I didn't know if your families had any ties, back in the day," she said, casually.

"Nae, I don't know of anything specific. Except, I've heard that a brother of one of my ancestors helped develop the town of Roslin to house the stonemasons who were employed to build Rosslyn Chapel. There's something written in our family history." He got up and walked over to one bookshelf, running his finger over some titles of the antique books. Apparently finding what he was looking for, removed a book from the shelf and brought it over to the seat by the fire. "Aye, here it is. This is a copy of his diary for the year 1445 on. It looks like his name was Callum

MacNevin. He writes, 'I'm helping to set up a burgh for the stonemasons coming ilk day to aid in the biggin' the kirk and castle.' I think that means, translating from old Scots English, he's helping to build the town for the masons coming in everyday to help build the chapel and extend the castle. He goes on to say, I'll translate into current English for you. 'The best stonemasons, the majority members of the society of Freemasons, all accepted the commissions. Sir William St Clair who is building the chapel, is paying high wages.'

"Well, this is fascinating, I knew none of this about my ancestor. Let's see," he continued flipping pages of the book, "he goes on to write a year later. 'Sir William St Clair was just appointed the title of Patron and Protector of the Freemasons of Scotland by King James II to great joy of the ones that are here. For he is a humble and courteous man, with extensive knowledge of buildings, Astronomy, Alchemy and Esoterica.' Och, I wonder what he means by that?"

"I researched Rosslyn Chapel before I came. In one of the book's references, it is mentioned that Sir William and his co-planner, Sir Gilbert Haye, who is often credited as the architect of Rosslyn, studied the Kabbalah, esoteric Jewish mysticism. Haye was regarded as one of the brightest and most intellectual thinkers of the 15th Century.

"I also read, some of Sir William's personal library was donated to the Bodleian Library by his ancestors. The books included subjects on the Kabbalah, science, astronomy, alchemy among others. Maybe Esoterica is referencing to the Kabbalah?" Pucci suggested.

She was captivated by this firsthand account of history predating the chapel's construction. Her research had revealed that Rosslyn Chapel was sanctioned in 1446, with construction beginning a decade later in 1456—likely allowing time for the town to prepare for the influx of workers needed to build both the chapel and extend the castle, as referenced in the book. She sipped her dram, contemplating the clove and spice cake notes of the golden liquid.

Braden continued, "He goes on about some additional details about the township. Some years go by," he said, turning multiple pages, "here's something. 'I have fallen in love with Lady Davinia. She is beauty and grace herself. I must go away for a while but hope to marry her upon my return.' That is the end of his narrative. I wonder what happened with him and Lady Davinia?"

Pucci teared up. So that was the ghost's name. She knew Lady Davinia would not get to marry her lover. They would kill her first.

She noticed there was no reference to the Knights Templar in the diary. She turned and watched the flames dance, rejoicing over the latest log gifted to them by a stealthy castle worker.

Braden watched Pucci. He saw a tear gleaming in the firelight even though she had turned slightly away.

"I wish I could do something for you, Pucci," Braden said, taking her hand, gently massaging her palm with his thumb.

She felt an electric jolt run through her with his touch. Pucci remembered the dream from the plane. She closed her eyes, feeling his hand. Visions came into her mind's eye. A past-life with Braden. He loved her, but she was in love with his brother, and couldn't return his love. She opened her eyes into his.

"Pucci, I know this is going to sound strange, but I feel . . . I feel. It's like I know you. Deep in my soul there's something that's familiar."

Pucci smiled. She put her hand over his. "We've known each other before, Braden. I don't know if you believe in past-lives, but I just saw we have shared one centuries ago, here, in Scotland."

He pulled his hands away as he sat back. Took a sip from his dram. "Nae, I've never believed in reincarnation. But this feeling for you . . . I'm struggling with it. I want to take you into my arms, kiss you, and never let you go." He stood up, turned his back and walked toward the bookshelves.

She let him go, she didn't want to burst into a past-life recognition story. He just needed to feel it. After a few moments, she walked over to him, gently putting her hand on his shoulder. He turned, pulling her into an embrace as his mouth met hers. The kiss was hard and passionate. Pucci's vision blurred again, seeing this scene play out hundreds of years ago. Her head swooned, from the visions and the kiss. She pulled away.

"Braden, I . . . " Pucci's vision blurred again, she saw his past-life identity overlay his current identity like a holographic projection. His long forest green coat, high collar, and shoulder length dark hair illuminated his moonstone eyes.

"My love." He reached down and kissed her again, with deep feeling and an aching longing that had waited lifetimes.

She fell into the kiss. His soft lips pressed into hers. For a glorious moment, she lost herself in his hot sensuous mouth. She pulled away again. "Braden, ..."

He stopped, his current identity back in place. "Pucci, my God, I . . . I don't know what just came over me," he said as he let her go. "Maybe it was the whisky," he blushed.

Slowing her breath and heart, she said, softly, "You just had a past-life recognition. It happens when both our energies are at a high vibration. Or . . . maybe it was just the whisky." She stepped back, a little embarrassed herself at her response to his energy and body. "I'm going to my room, I'm very tired."

"Pucci, please. I don't know what just happened. I hope I didn't offend you?"

"You didn't offend me, Braden. The kiss was . . . magic. The world dropped away for a breathless moment." She reached up on her tip toes and kissed his cheek.

"Can I see you tomorrow?"

"Of course, Braden. I'd like that very much. Good night." She left the library with his taste on her lips.

Chapter 19

The next morning brimmed with anticipation, especially for Pucci. Visiting Rosslyn Chapel had been a lifelong dream—one sparked in her youth when she first read about its history and the esoteric mysticism surrounding it. Not only did it captured her imagination, she could feel an energetic connection to the mysterious gothic building surrounded by Roslin Glen, in Midlothian, Scotland.

The day dawned cold with snow flurries. But nothing was going to deter Pucci—not the lure of an excellent Scottish breakfast and tea in the newly built dining area, nor a little snow. The breakfast room was solid windows, so the weather was in strong relief compared to the greenhouse effect of the room.

Randi and Varv were already helping themselves. Pucci ordered a pot of tea, then served herself some porridge, toast, and fruit. She sat down at the table, poured herself some tea and said, "Ladies, how did you sleep?"

"Like a log," Randi said. Varv agreed with a mouthful of yogurt and grains.

"Wonderful, I did as well, when I finally got back to my room. Boy, do I have stories to tell you gals!" But before Pucci could continue, Braden approached their table.

"Guid mornin'. I trust you all slept well?" he said, to the three, in Scots English.

"We did, thank you," Varv said, smiling.

"Pucci, how are you today?" he asked, shyly.

"I'm very well, thank you, Braden. We're off to Rosslyn this morning. I'm very excited. Thank you for all that information you found last night. It will add to the exploration," Pucci replied. Varv and Randi exchanged a glance.

"I bid you good day, ladies." He turned to Pucci. "Pucci, I would be honored if you would have dinner with me this evening?"

"Oh, thank you, Braden. But I don't know when we'll be back. I could text you when we return. If it's not too late, maybe we could meet for a drink again?" Pucci said, seeing a slight hurt in his eyes.

"Of course. How selfish of me. Please, we can just see how things progress for you. I'll stay flexible."

"That would be lovely, thank you," Pucci said. Braden turned and walked out of the dining area.

"What was that about?" Varv exclaimed.

"Long story. But to make it very short, Braden and I have had a past-life together. He was in love with me, I was in love with his brother. Oy. We never got together in that life. I think we're playing it out again in this one. I even saw his past-life identity overtake his current identity last night right before we kissed." Pucci reached over and patted Randi on the back as she was choking. "I know, I know, what the heck am I doing with a Scottish romance?"

Varv's eyes twinkled. "What the heck are you not doing? I say go for it! He's an earl for goodness sakes! Maybe this is your time to be together. Unrequited love finally requited. I think that's how you say it. Or finally returned!"

"You're such a romantic, Varv. I love that about you," Pucci said.

"What else happened last night, Pucci?" Randi inquired.

"I saw and spoke to the Lady of the Stairs. Her name is-was Davinia. And, what's really strange, she recognized the jewel cipher around my neck. She told me a story of how she was asked to keep a similar looking one safe. She was killed for it. The Earl's brother gave it to her as he was traveling and didn't want to risk bringing it with him. He was in love with her. She wasn't the Earl's mistress. They slandered her name so no one would care that she was dead."

"Pucci, this is astounding. Did she know what it was? Or why it was so important that people are killing for it?" Randi asked.

"I asked similar questions, Randi, but she didn't know exactly. She did say, however, it's tied to Rosslyn Chapel. I'll tell you all the rest in the car on the drive. But, I don't want anyone to hear, so we'll have to talk quietly in the cab. Oh, I forgot to call one. I'll ask Mr. Anderson to order one."

Just then, a server came up to their table. "Would you like anything else, ladies? Your car is waiting out front," he said.

"What do you mean?" Pucci asked.

"Mr. Anderson asked me to let you know that the car Mr. MacNevin ordered for you is waiting out front, when you're ready." He bowed and walked away.

"I could get use to this," Pucci whispered as they left the table, gathering their coats for the day's outing.

***

The car turned out to be a small limousine. The three tucked themselves into the roomy backseat. Their driver closed the door and pulled away from the castle. Pucci filled in the rest of the information of what Davinia had told her, and what Braden had found in Callum's diary.

"So, somehow, we'll need to look for possible hiding places, related to the Knights Templar within the chapel. I've done extensive research on the chapel, but nothing compares to actually being there."

"Pucci, I'm not very familiar with the Knights Templar. Who were they?" Randi asked.

"The short version is," Pucci replied. "They were a medieval military order founded to protect Christian pilgrims in the Holy Land. But, over time, they became powerful and shrouded in legend—rumored guardians of sacred relics and ancient secrets. The most popular tale ties them to the Holy Grail—not necessarily as a cup, as Indiana Jones would have it, but as I like to think it, a far more profound artifact: knowledge." Randi nodded thoughtfully. "But, other than what Davinia just told me, and our ghost that showed himself when we discovered the cipher, I have no idea how they tie into our mystery."

Varv leaned in. "So Davinia told you that another jeweled cipher might be in Rosslyn, connected to the Knights Templar?"

"Yes. The trouble is, if we do find something, how are we going to explore what's hidden?" Pucci said, a note of urgency in her voice.

"Take a breath, Pucci," Varv said. "We'll open up our intuition and feel out our next move once we're there."

"Since it's snowing, maybe there won't be too many people there today." Randi offered. Pucci nodded.

They drove up to the doors of the visitor's center. Pucci asked how they should get a hold of the car and driver for a ride back to the castle. He gave her a phone number, told her to text him when they were about ready to leave. She thanked him and turned to catch up with her friends walking up to the entrance.

The small visitor's center was an old brick building that created part of the border around the chapel. Men were walking around with what looked like architectural plans in their hands. She walked inside. There was a gift shop with souvenirs, a counter for coffee and snacks, with a few tables scattered in the small area and a cashier to take the admittance fee.

Pucci accepted her change and put it in the small donations box on the counter with a few more pounds. The woman thanked her.

"Can you tell me what's happening outside? I noticed a lot of activity," Pucci asked the kind cashier.

"Oh, aye, we're very excited. We are starting to build the new visitors center. We have more than tripled our visitors coming to Rosslyn since Dan Brown's book, *The Da Vinci Code* and movie came out. It's been such a blessing. We finally have enough money, along with the Rosslyn Trust to save this incredible work of art. That's what I like to call it, anyway," she said smiling. Pucci nodded, feeling gratitude that a book, written by a wonderful author, could save a masterpiece of history.

The women briefly looked around as they walked toward the door leading to the courtyard and out to the chapel. Pucci pushed the doors open and stood transfixed. The snow had stopped, the sun was shining in a glorious lapis sky. For a moment, the three of them stood still. The tiny ice crystals from their breath twinkled in the refracted sun. Varv looped her arm through Pucci's as they approached the north entrance. The buildings' exterior stonework was a kaleidoscope of yellow, pink, maroon, browns along with the green stone-bricks, covered in mold and lichen. There was a light carpet of new snow on the grass. The walkway was clear.

The three looked up at the two gargoyles on either side of the arched entrance. They looked like some sort of wild beast, mouth open, showing sharp teeth. Randi held the large wooden door open for Pucci and Varv. She walked in behind and closed the door. Miraculously, the chapel was empty of tourists. There were two unobtrusive chapel guides on the other side of the interior space. For a glorious moment in time, they had Rosslyn all to themselves. They walked down the north nave toward the Lady Chapel marveling at the extensive stone carvings everywhere you looked. Some have described Rosslyn as "a poem in stone." For Pucci, it was a reliquary building, holding sacred carvings, sculptures, tombs, secrets, and mystical artifacts.

They had agreed on the way over to just enjoy the chapel for a few hours and reconvene to get a plan on additional sleuthing. Pucci looked up at the vaulted ceiling in the Lady Chapel, transfixed. Carved at the base of a stalactite-like structure was an eight-pointed star, symbolizing the Star of Bethlehem from the nativity story in the Gospel of Matthew. Pucci wasn't surprised to see it, as the other name for the chapel is the Collegiate Chapel of St. Matthew. She couldn't help but hold her breath while she kept her eyes fixed on the ceiling. Something looked familiar.

A stone carving in the archway of the vaulted ceiling curved out like a half tube. The formation created a three dimensional carving resembling the jeweled cipher's design. It was so similar, it couldn't be a coincidence. Pucci stepped farther into the Lady Chapel to get a better view of the carving. As she stepped directly under the star, her vision blurred. Current time melted away to a time when the stonemasons were working on the chapel. There was construction noise, chisels, sanding. Stone dust filled her nostrils and teared up her eyes. Observing carefully, she witnessed the completion of symbols engraved into the vaulted ceiling beside the stone cipher carving. Strange markings, all lines with crosshatches and triangles in various designs marked the ceiling. Pucci memorized them as best she could. She wanted to write them down as soon as she could find some paper. She was just starting to see a pattern when someone bumped into her.

Pucci stumbled slightly, completely disoriented. She hear a male voice say in French, "Oh, pardon, madam."

"That's OK," she replied to the retreating back of a man. She shook her head, trying to clear the confusion of where and what century she was in. Varv walked swiftly over, seeing the exchange.

"Pucci, are you OK? What just happened? I saw you looking up and then you just froze," Varv asked, concerned.

"I had a past-life recall, I think, Varv. Everything blurred when I stood under the Star of Bethlehem. Similar to what happened last night with Braden, current time faded into the past, to the time when the chapel was being built. I saw these symbols." Pucci looked up. There were no symbols. "That's weird, there were marks on the ceiling. I just saw them."

Varv looked up. "Pucci, there are no marks." Pucci was still staring. "I have an idea, let's find Randi and go get some tea and a nibble at the café in the visitor's center. Oh, there's Randi now."

Varv explained in a whisper to Randi what happened to Pucci after she walked up. As Randi glanced up, Varv took Pucci's hand and walked her out of the chapel, still in a daze.

They sat down, Varv brought tea and scones over. Pucci drank and ate.

"I need to find a piece of paper," Pucci said.

"Here," Randi replied as she dug a small tablet for notes out of her purse.

"Thank you, Randi. Just give me a minute you guys. Let me get these marks—or symbols—out of my head before I forget them." Pucci proceeded to make strange scratchings on the notepad.

Randi wandered over to the gift shop. She found cute Christmas ornaments of the chapel that would make excellent gifts for her family. She decided to come back to purchase them on the way out. She glanced over to a book that was on display. It was opened to the glossy picture section. The photograph on the page looked to have extremely similar marks that she had just seen Pucci writing. She picked up the book, it was about the stonemasons of Rosslyn. She brought the book over to the table. Pucci was still working.

"Pucci, look at this," Randi said.

"Just a sec, Randi. I need to finish. She closed her eyes for a moment, opened them and wrote down a few more symbols. She seemed satisfied and put down the pen.

Randi put the glossy page down in front of her. "Pucci, these marks look almost identical to yours. They are stonemason marks. It says here, the masons would use these marks to show they completed their work so they could get paid. They're all over Rosslyn."

Varv got up and came around to look at the book and Pucci's markings. "They do look very similar. Maybe that's all they are, Pucci."

"Yes, you're probably right. So weird though. Why would I feel these are significant? And why aren't they showing on the ceiling now?" Pucci wondered.

"Maybe they just got covered over during the restoration back in the 1800s," Randi offered.

"Maybe." Pucci said, munching on her scone.

Chapter 20

Pucci tucked the note away in her Patagonia sweater-vest pocket. They had decided to explore the chapel, inside and out, looking for something relating to the Knights Templar as the ghost of Lady Davinia had mentioned. It wasn't much to go on, but it narrowed down the possibilities of finding the next clue and or another cipher.

"I just bought the official Rosslyn Chapel guidebook," Randi said. "Look what it says here. There is a direct reference to the Knights Templar in this stonework. According to the book, it is a wall pillar of an 'angel holding a seal depicting the lamb of God, and emblem said to be associated with the Knights Templar.' That sounds promising."

They went back into the chapel. There were more people. They found the wall pillar; it was high up in a corner on top of a column about twenty feet up.

"How are we going to get up there?" Pucci wondered in a low voice. The other two shook their heads.

"Split up and let's find the two other references," Randi said.

Pucci wandered back toward the north door, trying to figure out how they could get back in the chapel somehow when no one was around. She was standing in the wide archway of the north entrance. A chapel tour guide was on the other side talking to a woman, his back to Pucci. Pucci was admiring the hollowed out channel that ran the entire length of the arch entryway, in between two skinny wall pillars, when she turned her ear just right. Suddenly, she was hearing the guide as clear as if he was talking directly in her ear, even though his back was still turned away from her.

"Tell Wayne to leave this door unlocked after closing. The new film crew wants to set up some scaffolding to test some lighting tonight," the guide said.

Pucci heard a faint reply, "Which Wayne? There's two working tonight."

Again, as clear as a bell, the guide answered, "Wayne Furrs." The woman nodded and they left the building.

Pucci couldn't believe her luck! She found her friends and told them the story and how she overheard it. "It was the strangest phenomena, his voice sounded directly in my ear," she said.

"It must be an acoustic trick of the channel. I wonder if they did that deliberately or, it just happened by chance? It reminds me of the Whispering Gallery at St. Paul's Cathedral in London. You whisper something into the gallery wall and it can be heard on the other side of the huge dome, about 100 feet away, on the other wall," Randi explained. Pucci and Varv marveled at Randi's knowledge.

"Pucci, we found two more references to the Knights Templar," Varv said.

"So what do you think we should do now?" Randi asked.

"I think we should wait till after closing, mill around the movie crew. We're Americans, the chapel folks might not know we're not part of the crew, the crew might think we're with the chapel. Risky, but it's our best bet."

They agreed. While they were waiting another hour for closing time they walked around outside. They saw the film crew unloading their equipment in the drop-off circular driveway on the other side of the wall in front of the Visitors Entrance.

Varv smiled mischievously, fluffed up her hair and said, "Stay here, gals, I'll be back."

Pucci and Randi watched as Varv strolled over to where the crew were unloading. They saw a few of the men watching her walk and came over to talk with her. The gals watched her work her magic, flipping her hair a few times, and laughing flirtatiously. After a few minutes, Varv turned away from the wall and started walking back toward the chapel. She turned back around and blew a kiss and waved.

Pucci and Randi, shielding their eyes from the late afternoon sun, watched as Varv returned.

"What was that about?" Randi asked.

Pucci replied, grinning madly, "Varv just got us in with the film crew."

Varv giggled. "Right you are, Pucci! I told them we were fledgling independent filmmakers, and can we watch? And of course we'll accompany them to the pub after!"

"Varv, that is brilliant!" Randi exclaimed.

With that new plan in place, they went inside to the café and grabbed sandwiches right before it closed. They didn't know how long the night was going to be.

***

The three came back and watched the film crew set up inside the chapel after the last tourist left. Varv was asking lots of questions, while Pucci and Randi observed with interest. After about an hour, the majority of the lower scaffolding was set up. A few large ladders were also strategically placed by the crew. One man, short in stature, yelled "Break time!" in a booming voice. The crew slowly came down off the heights while the rest walked out of the chapel toward the Visitor's Center café, coolers in tow.

"Now's our chance," Pucci whispered. "Varv, let them know we'll join them at the pub. We're going to stay a few more minutes, then leave." Varv nodded, walked over to the young man she was flirting with and relayed the message. He smiled, winked and walked out with the others.

"Quick, let's move this large ladder over to the Lamb of God wall pillar." Pucci said, walking over to one side of the ladder. The three of them moved it over, close enough so the top was near the stone carving. Pucci quickly ascended. She inspected the carving. Fingering it gently to see if she could feel any sort of hidden compartment. She gently pushed and pulled on the stone lamb. Nothing. There was not much detail in the carving, unlike some of the others she had observed. Probably from the restoration when they covered everything in a solution of silica fluoride of magnesium initially. An additional coating of a white cementitious paint containing shellac was also administered for preservation back in 1954.

She saw what looked like a hand holding a frame in place. She place her hand over the carving and gently squeezed. Nothing. "I don't think anything is here," she called down. She tried a few more places that looked promising. Nothing. She climbed down. "No luck."

"It could be anywhere, Pucci, how in the hell are we going to find it, when no one else has ever done so in the past?" Randi exclaimed.

"We have a ghost on our side. All right, ladies, let's think. Varv, open up your intuition to see if you can feel anything." Pucci said.

"What about Robert I, the King of Scots, or better known as Robert the Bruce?" Randi said. "Didn't you mention the Knights fought with him in 1314?"

"Good point, Randi. And, I read that Sir William St. Clair, the founder of Rosslyn, his ancestors, Sir Henry and his brother, William, fought by Robert's side, as did the Knights Templar."

"If that's the case, maybe it's associated with that sculpture over there," Varv said. "Randi and I found a carving of an angel that is said to be holding the heart of Robert the Bruce. It's in the south nave, on the other side of the chapel. It's not that high up, but I think we should grab that smaller ladder so we can get right next to it."

They walked over, carrying the ladder. The two-foot-high bust of an angel in stone, was at the bottom of the window frame, in the left-hand corner. Its hair, flowing out of a skullcap was down to its collar. An angelic smile shown on its face. Arms reached around, and in both hands, it held what looked like a box with a heart on top of it, all carved from stone. Varv climbed up only about three steps. This carving was much more detailed. Varv, with a critical plasterwork eye, and intuition on high alert, noticed slight discrepancies in the carving.

"Pucci, come here," she said. "I think this might be it."

Pucci climbed up next to Varv on the ladder squishing in on the highest step. Varv pointed out the discrepancies and then descended. They both were looking up at Pucci when Randi heard talking outside.

"Hurry, Pucci, I think they're coming back," Randi exclaimed.

Pucci leaned over, examining the sculpture. She noticed the hands of the angel were in the same position as the pendant keystone carving at the very top of the roof structure in the choir, but reversed. She wasn't sure if it was significant, but the flutter in her stomach suggested otherwise. She had learned to trust her intuition.

Suddenly she remembered her puzzle box at home. She reached out and placed her hands on two sides of the sculpture where the discrepancies were that Varv pointed out. Pressing lightly, she heard a click at the bottom of the heart the angel was holding. A tiny chamber opened. She could just barely get her fingernails inside to reach in and gently pluck out a piece of paper. Her heart was pounding, sweat dripped in her eyes, regardless of the coolness of the chapel. Before descending, she used a pencil-thin flashlight to look inside the tiny opening to see if anything else was there. The chamber was empty. She closed the opening with care and quickly descended the ladder into Varv and Randi's helping hands.

"You were right Varv, look." Pucci showed them the note.

They gathered around and slowly open the fragile paper, hoping the second piece of the cipher would be sequestered inside. Nothing, just writing.

Pucci read out loud. "*I cannot risk the sacred piece being here. They have killed Lady Davinia. I have given it to John for safekeeping elsewhere.*"

They let out a heavy sigh. Now what?

Chapter 21

One member of the crew had stayed behind and was watching the chapel entrance carefully. *What the hell were those women doing in there?* His employer had told him to watch the women and follow them where ever they went. They had not come out of the chapel since the crew had left the building. If he went inside, they might see him and ask questions. So, he waited.

***

The three women swiftly walked over to the south door, Randi checking to see if it was unlocked. It was. They closed the door behind them just as the film crew were returning through the north door. They made their way back over to the Visitors Center, and out the front doors. They continued down the street away from any prying eyes and called for the car.

"Where is the pub we are supposed to meet them at, Varv?" Pucci asked.

"It's just down a little further, toward the town of Roslin," she replied.

"OK, let's wait here for the car. We'll get him to drop you two off. I'll go back to the castle. I told Braden I'd have drinks and/or dinner with him. I'm hoping to get additional information from him, or the diaries in the library. We have to find out who John is. Talk about a needle in a haystack! Also, I want to see if I can make contact with Davinia again. She told me about Callum, her lover. Maybe she remembers if he ever mentioned a John in connection to the cipher or the Knights Templar."

"OK, Pucci. But, I really don't want to stay long. Do you think we should even go?" Varv asked.

"I don't want to force you, but we might need them again."

"Oh, come on Varv. I need a beer and want to hang out in more Scottish pubs," Randi said, grinning. Varv smiled and nodded.

The car picked them up in record time—he must have been waiting close by. As they drove, they explained the plan to the driver before dropping off Varv and Randi at the pub. He said that after dropping Pucci off, he would come right back to pick up the other two.

***

"What did you find out?" the voice asked on the other end of the cell phone.

The man with the film crew had to admit he lost them. He wondered if he'd get paid.

"You what? Did you at least see what they were doing inside the chapel when they were alone?"

"Nae. I didnae see anythin. I didnae dare enter, they woulda seen me," the man replied.

"What good are you? You won't get a pound until you report something useful. If they come back, follow and report."

"Aye. What do ye want with these women, anyway?"

"None of your damn business." The phone went dead.

***

Pucci returned to the castle. Mr. Anderson told her Mr. MacNevin had been called away on business. He handed her a note, bowed, and walked away. Pucci went up to her room to read the note and wash up, surprised at how disappointed she was. She sat on her bed to open the note. He had excellent handwriting. When was the last time someone had written her a note, instead of texting? There's a certain charm to a note written by hand.

"*Ms. Riddle, Pucci, I regret that I will not have the pleasure of your company this evening. Urgent business calls me away. I'm hoping to get back late this evening. I understand you are checking out tomorrow? I wish you would stay, as my guest. But I know you are off to Islay. Perhaps on your way back, we could meet somewhere? If it's not too late when I return this evening, I'll inquire if you are still awake. I would love to see you before you depart. Till we meet again . . . Braden.*"

Pucci sighed, flattered—and, dare she admit it, honored—to receive such a note from an earl. But as she exhaled again, her thoughts drifted to Olan. If she was truly honest with herself, it wasn't Braden who tugged at her heartstrings—it was the inspector from Scotland Yard.

She put the note on the Scottish antique dresser, the top surface slightly uneven because of its age and wear. She then removed the paper of symbols from her vest pocket, unfolded it, and walked to the small writing desk by the window to turn on the desk lamp. She sat on the small wooden chair, which creaked in response. She puzzled at the strange markings of horizontal, vertical, and slanted lines. Some had an x and a diamond shape through the horizontal lines. "Weird," she said out loud.

A plan formed in her mind. She needed to go back to the chapel, put herself into a trance-like state, without being too noticeable, and verify the symbols. She just felt in her gut this was really important.

The knock on her door brought her out of her thoughts. She opened it to Varv and Randi, laughing and leaning on each other.

"You missed a fun time, Pucci," Varv stumbled slightly entering into Pucci's room. "Those guys were so nice and insisted we have more than one beer before we left. Whew! On an empty stomach, and those dark beers. I'm a little tipsy!"

Randi held Varv's arm to steady her. "She's a lightweight, this girl!" Randi said, laughing. "I tell you what, Pucci, these Scots are some of the kindest, most authentic people I have ever met. They treated us with such warmth and generosity." Randi walked Varv over to the bed to sit her down.

Pucci, so happy that her friends had fun, smiled. "I think we'd better have an early dinner!"

***

Randi and Varv went up to their room to change. Pucci met them down in the dungeon dining room. They were seated right away. Pucci told them about the note from Braden and the feelings that it brought up for her about Olan.

"I might never see either one of them again. I don't know why I dwell on what could have been with Olan. If I wanted to change my plans, I could stay here and see where it goes with Braden." She looked away, staring at a suit of armor in the corner of the room.

"I think you should stay true to your heart, Pucci," Varv said, sipping her water.

"Don't change your plans for a man you just met, Pucci. You've got a really exciting adventure planned. Plus, you need to research the Islay distilleries for your article, right?" Randi advised.

"You're both right," Pucci said, smiling at these wonderful companions. "And staying true to my heart means to stay true to my planned adventure. Thank you, both of you." She ran her hands gently up and down their arms, a quiet show of gratitude. "Oy, 'but enough about me, let's talk about you. What do you think of me?'" laughingly quoting Bette Midler from the movie *Beaches*. "But seriously, Varv, tell us how you're dealing with the death of your ex-husband. We never heard about that."

"This has been such a wonderful distraction, so first of all, thank you for this, Pucci. You know, gals, it was so hard, the whole experience. First, being the ex, no one believes you're grieving, let alone have the right to grieve. I was all alone, even ignored by my family, dealing with complicated emotions. There is no pocket in our society for the ex's grief. We were married thirty years! No one comforts you as if you are a widow, even though you are." She was letting bottled emotions out for the first time since the funeral. "I never let anyone know what I was going through." A tear slipped down her cheek, she brushed it aside, preventing it from falling on to the tablecloth. Pucci reached for Varv's hand.

"Oh, Varv. I am so sorry. I wish you had reached out. If not to me, to someone." Pucci whispered, squeezing her hand.

"Thank you," Varv said, and a weak smile reached her lips.

"Varv, you're absolutely right." Randi said. "I've never thought about how we treat ex-wives, or ex-husbands when the ex-spouse dies. It's not like you can really totally cut them out of your life, especially if there are children. You have every right to grieve. People probably thought you were part of the cause of his death."

"That's actually how people were treating me when I was around some folks. Oh, it was awful. The best thing we did was to get a divorce, we were both happier. But no one sees that or remembers it. But, listen you two, I'm fine now. My kids are coping. The older is still very angry at me for getting a divorce. Hopefully one day we'll reconcile." She paused. "Pucci . . . I did want to ask you if you see him around me? I would like to say goodbye."

Pucci opened her energy. Sometimes a ghost would appear if she opened up and asked for them. No one came.

"I'm sorry, Varv. I don't feel him or see him. I can feel, though, he knows you grieved and said goodbye."

"I felt that, too. Sometimes, it's nice to have confirmation," Varv said.

Dinner was another delicious affair of locally sourced trout with citrus and cucumber for the appetizer. Varv got the North Atlantic cod with saffron potatoes, while Pucci and Randi tried the wild mushroom risotto. They were too full to have any of the desserts, even though they were all tempted by the peanut butter and chocolate mousse with caramelized banana topping.

Varv and Randi decided to call it an early night. They wanted to stay at the castle tomorrow for a spa day before checkout.

"Ok, sounds like a good plan. I'm going back to Rosslyn to see if I can get any additional information regarding those symbols. I just know they're important," Pucci said as they left the table.

As they walked up the stairs into the lobby, Varv's cell phone pinged. She looked at her phone. "Oh, wow, I've missed three messages."

"We probably couldn't get a signal in the dungeon, those walls looked five-feet thick!" Randi said.

Varv nodded at she began to read her messages. "Oh my!" she exclaimed as she stopped walking.

"What is it?" Randi asked.

"Ladies, it looks like I'll have to leave you tomorrow. I have been asked for a design consult in Edinburgh tomorrow. They want to meet for dinner. It's an incredible opportunity. They saw my work in Cardiff, and they want to redesign their country house in the Cotswolds area. I think that's near Oxford? Maybe a little west? Sounds like their country home," she said with air quotes, "is over 7,000 square feet. Ah, they put it in square feet for me."

"Wow, fantastic, Varv!" Randi exclaimed.

"Congratulations, Varv!" Pucci said. "I'm disappointed that you won't be able to go to Islay with us. But, I am happy for you."

"Sorry, Pucci. This is a something I shouldn't pass up." Varv said, facing Pucci.

Pucci hugged her. "I totally understand! I am thankful to have you for as long as I did."

Chapter 22

Olan

Olan rolled off the couch onto the floor, hitting his head on the mid-century modern knockoff, white coffee table on the way down and landing on his back. He gave himself a moment to get oriented while the empty whisky bottle underneath him settled in between his shoulder blades. He groaned. His head pounded. His mouth felt like the Atacama Desert, with its annual rainfall of 0.03 inches . . . in the summer.

He got up, headed to the shower, and tried to shake the terrifying dreams he'd been having for two nights since he saw Pucci. He desperately wanted to remember the last one about her before he lost all memory of it, but his brain, throbbing and pickled, wouldn't focus. He showered, swallowed aspirin, and gulped water before leaving for Scotland Yard. He needed to talk to Detective Connor Davies. The dreams had a sense of deep foreboding.

***

Well, at least he's sober, Connor thought as looked up to see Detective Chief Inspector Olan Lathen walking toward his desk.

Olan felt Connor's scrutinizing stare. He draped his coat over his chair and walked to get coffee. He felt Connor's eyes following. *Keep it together. They're just dreams. You're torturing yourself when you have work to do,* he thought, pouring coffee. He walked over to Connor and sat down.

"Chief," Connor said without looking up, picking up the phone on his desk to dial someone . . . anyone.

"Look, Connor," Olan said, putting his finger on the switch to hang it up. "I know I haven't been all together these last few months. Something happened since Grand Cayman. I can't explain it. I . . . I'm sorry," he said, stumbling on the apology. He was bollocks at this.

"Right. It's just . . . I've been trying to help you," Connor said, cradling the handset.

"I know. I couldn't deal with anything. I'm not sleeping, but I need to do my job." He lowered his voice, "I'm worried about Pucci. Do you know what's going on with her? Do you know why she came to see me? I didn't give her a chance to explain. I just walked out on her."

Connor looked at his boss. He saw the taut jaw and the deep worry lines that were more pronounced since a few months ago and felt the silent desperation behind the bloodshot eyes.

He nodded. "Let's go into the conference room. I need to catch you up."

Connor closed the door and laid a diary on the table next to Olan as they both sat down.

"What's this?" Olan asked. He pulled on gloves before touching the pages.

"Valerie Baine's diary. No need to put on gloves, we haven't found any finger prints except Valerie's and Pucci's."

"Pucci's?"

"She found it. She went to Valerie's house to speak with her parents and find out if they knew anything more about who Valerie had been working for during the Cheapside Hoard heist. She was hoping to uncover any clues that might lead us to Pirate—who he is and where we can find him." Connor pointed to the diary. "Found this buried in Valerie's dresser. Look at the last few pages."

Olan gently turned the pages in the diary and began reading. Connor went for another coffee. When he came back, Olan was paging through the diary.

"So, Valerie followed Pirate to a house in Oxford? Have you found anything else of use in the diary?"

"The description of the house in Oxford was detailed enough that apparently Pucci followed the clues in the diary and found the house that Valerie describes," Connor said, watching Olan raise his eyebrows and shake his head, mumbling something about a bloody woman. "I know, she shouldn't have risked it without one of us, but you . . . " he let the insinuation go silent. "Anyway, she knocked on the door to the house in Oxford. She made up some lame excuse about why she was there, claimed to be lost and looking for someone's home. She didn't get anywhere. As she was standing on the door's threshold, she said something evil, really bad energy, accosted her. She said to be very careful when we go."

"Bloody hell. She might have blown the whole thing. They might be suspicious now. When was this, Connor?"

"She went a few days ago, right before she saw you."

Olan was ashamed of himself. He had lost two precious days. He turned away from Connor and let out a sigh. He needed to act, now.

"Grab your coat," he said, standing up and opening the conference room door. "We're going to Oxford. Give the description to Sara, ask her to see if she can find the house and look up who lives there. Find out any history she can dig up. Have her call you as soon as possible. We need to know who and what we're dealing with." He walked to his desk, Connor behind.

"Lathen!" shouted the chief superintendent. "My office, now!"

"Wait for me, Connor. But get Sara working on background," Olan said in a hushed voice. He met the chief superintendent in his office. "Sir."

The chief superintendent shut the door. "Where the bloody hell have you been, Lathen?" He continued before Olan could speak. "I cannot tolerate this behavior. You're not only worthless in this state, but with all your drinking, frankly, you're a liability to the department."

"Sir, I . . . "

"No excuses. You're officially on leave." Softening slightly, the chief superintendent looked at his friend with concern. "Lathen, clean yourself up. I need you back. I can't lose a brilliant detective like you."

Olan stood, gave one nod, and left. He walked past Connor, grabbed his coat and the diary and walked out of Scotland Yard.

"Davies, get in here," the chief superintendent yelled out his office door, again.

Connor stood and walked in. The chief motioned to shut the door.

"What was that about, sir?" Connor inquired.

"Lathen's on leave. I need him to sober up," he said. "I need you to follow up with the Carbuncle smuggling case. Our informants tell us it's coming to a head. What have you heard from your source?"

"I just received an encrypted message last night. It seems that these messages are not coming through immediately. Something about the encryption is holding them up. This was sent a couple days ago," he said, showing the chief superintendent a photo on his phone. "We're following it up with surveillance at the location."

"Good. Go to Edinburgh. Make contact. I don't want anything to go wrong."

"Sir, I wanted to let you know. Lathen and I found additional information on the London Museum case regarding the gang that Valerie Baine was working for. The lead is in Oxford. Sir, I'd like to follow up."

"The cold case from three years ago? The woman who was shot and found in the Thames near Gravesend in 2004? Good God, man, we don't have time for all that. It'll keep till after the smuggling case is over. Focus on that and nothing else. Keep me apprised," he said and motioned Connor out the door.

Connor walked out. He needed to get a hold of Olan and let him know.

"Detective Davies!" Sara called out to Connor from her desk after telling Sergeant Tress to bugger off. *Ugh, he was creepy*, she thought. She looked back at her computer screen. "Sir, I found the address and the occupant. You're going to want to see this."

Sergeant Tress scratched his beard as he slowly walked away from Sara's desk, dismissed but unwilling to let it go. His uniform was rumpled, and the last of his dark brown hair stuck up in disheveled tufts above his ears. He needed to know what she was researching and inform his employer.

Chapter 23

Pucci's mind raced all night, and her sleep was restless. She woke up early the next morning. She needed to think. She did her best thinking while walking. Not wanting to wake the others she snuck out of the castle.

Feeling an inexplicable pull to the north, she turned away from the castle toward the woods. The air felt heavy, charged with something she couldn't quite name. This place, these grounds—there was a strange familiarity about them. In her mind's eye, she pictured a structure—a tower and a courtyard—details vivid yet fragmented, like memories half-remembered.

Drawn forward, Pucci followed the tug of energy along a muddy path strewn with dead and decaying leaves. She recalled the concierge mentioning ruins near the old quarry if they wanted to explore the grounds. The castle's stones, he'd explained, had been taken from that quarry, just upstream from the river that wound its way through these rolling hills. He'd said to keep bearing left along the river's edge, and the ruins would be impossible to miss. Perhaps what she envisioned wasn't imagined after all.

Pucci was feeling the energetic pull to the right. Strange. Trusting her intuition and the energy, she followed the path to the right. She stopped and watched the stream, listening as it flowed over rocks, rushing past her, down to its destiny. The stream whispered an ancient message as it wandered past. With every breath, she could smell the decomposing leaves and the bark of trees rotting in the moisture. The moss was so thick in areas it reminded her of the green pincushion her grandmother used to wear strapped to her wrist like a puffy bracelet. Pucci walked on, slogging through the saturated soil, shoes squelching with every step. She chuckled to herself calling the ground she walked on soil and not dirt. "Dirt is what you get on your face," her soil scientist father used to say.

She approached a divergence in the path and felt the energetic pull getting stronger. The pull was to the left this time. The forest grew denser, its shadows pressing in around her. To her right, separated by a sagging, weathered fence of twisted wire and splintered wood, a small field of brittle, browning grass stretched out. Two hulking, long-haired cows—*hairy coos* as they were called in Scotland—paused mid-chew, their heads lifting slowly as they regarded her with calm, unblinking stares. A murder of crows suddenly erupted from a clearing.

As she came around a bend in the path, she stopped. To the left of the path stood a crumbling ruin—walls worn thin by time, their stones blackened with moisture, the roof long since vanished. Her breath caught. She slowly approached the structure with reverence. This was what she saw in her mind's eye. The crows cried high in the trees. A voice whispered an eerie message of desperation, beckoning her help. The whisper, carried on the breeze, traveled too fast for her to make out the exact words.

Pucci walked toward the pile of collapsed stones. She stepped through a tumbled part of the exterior wall, or curtain wall, into what once was a large room. Her hand brushed against the cold, weathered stone for balance. The world shifted. The ruin stirred, then rose from the ground like a time-lapse movie—walls climbing skyward, windows materializing into place, and heavy doors sealing the space. The interior came alive around her—flickering torchlight, polished wood, and the scent of beeswax and smoke. Laughter and music echoed through the chamber, distant yet vivid, as though the past had never left. People were dancing in the bailey, a fortified enclosure. The smell of cooked meat filled her nostrils, and her mouth watered. A young woman, with the beauty of a delicate flower, materialized. Her laughter carried over the music. Pucci watched as a handsome young man made his way across the room toward her.

"Amaryllis," the young man and Pucci whispered together.

The scene faded back to the present time. Pucci pulled her coat around her as an ethereal breeze kicked up. A millie bug was crawling on her black coat sleeve. She gently cupped it with her hand and put it on the ground. She walked north, toward a wall about seven feet high, around and down a slight incline to her left. A voice, clear now, told Pucci there is an opening behind the wall.

"Please help me," the voice said.

Pucci found the opening and reached her hand up into the gap. She could feel a hand, not of this world, touch her fingers. She opened up her energy to communicate with the apparition.

"What's happening?" Pucci asked. "Why are you here?"

"They killed me and hid my body in this tower," the disembodied voice cried.

Pucci pulled her arm out of the opening. She spoke up into the space. "This is not your tomb, Amaryllis. Break away!"

Pucci heard and saw her scream as men, dressed in medieval attire, violently stabbed her over and over. She then saw as they bricked her dead body into the wall.

"Break away!" Pucci yelled. "Break away!" she yelled again as she put her hands on the wall, willing Amaryllis to hear her and to use her energy to boost her essence out of her imprisoned tomb. Pucci felt an energetic break. It flooded her with overwhelming gratitude. Amaryllis was free.

Pucci looked up to the path. She saw the same angelic being she had seen in the earlier visions. She scrambled through the exterior wall and up the incline. Amaryllis, her long blond hair gently waving in an ancient, otherworldly breath of wind, smiled. Her periwinkle dress, adorned with delicate white embroidered flowers on the bodice, glowed like a full moon on a dark night.

"Thank you," she said, "your energy helped me, I . . ." she stopped and stared at Pucci. She floated toward her. "Lilias? Lilias, is that really you?"

Pucci's vision blurred, her head spun, and she nearly lost waking consciousness. Looking down, saw herself dressed similarly to Amaryllis. Her past-life self approached Amaryllis.

"Aye, t'is me dear one. I've missed you so. I didn't know they killed you. I'm so sorry. I should have protected you," said Pucci's past-life, Lilias.

"You couldn't have known. They would have killed you too. I don't think they got the information they wanted. I remember hearing them saying 'she doesn't have it' as I was dying. Did they kill my older sister, Davinia, as well?" she asked, tearing up.

"Yes, dear one. They got what they were looking for. But we are protectors of the light, my current incarnation will get it back. We will prevail," Lilias said.

Amarylis smiled, "Bless you."

A handsome young man suddenly appeared at her side. The tall, slender red-haired ghost that Pucci saw earlier. He reached for her, gently touching her cheek. "Come with me, my love. I must take you home," he said, softly.

"Alexander," she said, turning toward him. They reached for each other, in the next breath were gone.

Pucci, coming out of her overwhelm, breathed in the cool, forest air. "Another soul released into the light," she said out loud to the millie bug walking by her shoe. "It is done." She bowed her head in deep reverence.

Slowly, she turned and walked back to the castle, observing a leaf, illuminated by the morning sun, softly detaching from its life-giving branch and descending. Shimmering hues of yellows danced in the light before settling silently onto the ground, to begin nurturing the tree from which it had come.

Chapter 24

After saying their goodbyes to Varv, Pucci and Randi watched as the car carried her off to Waverly Station. They waved one last time, their farewell lingering in the cool morning air.

Pucci turned to Randi, "I'm still planning to visit Rosslyn Chapel today. Are you sticking around here for your spa day?"

"Yes, I thought I'd get a massage later."

"That sounds wonderful, Randi." Pucci walked back into the castle. "I really want to get back to Rosslyn as soon as I can to get a better look at those symbols."

Randi turned to her friend with concern in her eyes. "Pucci, why do you think those are so important? There is so much more to Rosslyn than that. Why don't you go back and just enjoy it?"

"I can't explain it, Randi. This is going to sound really out there, especially to you, but seeing these symbols, it was like a cosmic download. Not only a past-life, but also, it was like I could hear and feel the symbols."

Randi dealt in facts and science. But she loved and trusted her friend. She could also feel how important and serious this was to her.

"OK, Pucci. I don't understand, but if it's that important to you, go. Do you want me to come with you?"

"No, you relax and enjoy your massage," Pucci said, looping her arm in Randi's as they walked back toward their rooms. "But, if you have time. Maybe see if you can find any reference to 'John' and the Knights Templar in the library around the time Lady Davinia died. Ask Mr.

Anderson, he seemed quite knowledgeable about all things Strathhammond. Oh, and ask him if we can have a late checkout."

Pucci caught a tour bus from the castle to Rosslyn Chapel. She had her drawing of the symbols, and a notepad and pen with her. This time, she'd be ready.

She got off the bus, walked swiftly ahead of the queue, paid and walked into the chapel. It wasn't crowded, yet. With the other busloads coming, it would soon be impossible to stand in one place. In the Lady Chapel again, she stepped under the Star of Bethlehem. As soon as she was aligned with the star, a low hum began in her head. Her vision blurred. She looked up, and there were the symbols. Pucci, desperately trying to stay in two time dimensions at once, looked down at the original writing from the day before. She compared it to what was coming in and out of focus on the ceiling. She noticed two mistakes. She had swapped the symbols in the middle section and forgot the last symbol in the sequence. Shaking her head slightly, she focused on the paper in her hand and corrected the mistakes.

She failed to notice a man, standing a few feet away, watching her with curiosity and evil intent. He desperately wanted that piece of paper, or at least to see what was on it. The man moved closer, looking at the ceiling as she had. He saw nothing. He stepped even closer, glancing at the paper in her hand. He saw what looked like scribbled lines, but in some sort of order. He dared one more step when suddenly the woman looked right at him. He felt a push of ice-cold air shoving him away from her as he stumbled back. *What the hell was that?* He craned his head back and forth. *Who pushed me? Those were hands on my chest!* He anguished.

Pucci witnessed a peculiar man being pushed by a Knights Templar ghost, the same ghost that had materialized when she had discovered the jeweled cipher in Grand Cayman over a year ago. The stranger ran out the door of the chapel, a look of terror on his face. The ghost was taxed by the energy he had to exert to create the physical push. He was almost translucent, standing next to the Apprentice Pillar. In a low voice, so as not to be overheard, she asked him, "Are you OK? Who was that man, and why did you intercede?"

The ghost, his energy fading rapidly, answered with effort, "Evil is following you, my lady. You must be vigilant!"

"Who is following me? The man they call Pirate?"

"Yes, among others of the same sect. They want the cipher. You must keep it safe," he said and was gone.

"Wait!" Pucci cried out a little too loud. People turned to look. She tucked the paper in her coat pocket and turned to leave. She had gotten what she came for.

***

Pucci took a taxi back to the castle. She had wanted to stay longer but was startled to find she was still being followed. She wanted the safety of the castle and her friend.

She found Randi in the library deeply engrossed in a book. Lady Davinia was looking over her shoulder, shaking her head.

"Hi, Randi. Did you know you have a ghost reading over your shoulder?" Pucci asked, smiling. "Hello, Lady Davinia."

"No wonder I've been so darn cold! I thought it was these old drafty castles," Randi said, wrapping the shawl tighter.

"Could you tell this woman . . . " Davinia cried out in desperation.

"Pucci, this book is . . . " They both started talking at the same time.

Pucci held up her hands for both to stop. "Lady Davinia," she said, addressing what looked like empty space above Randi's head, "what is it you want me to tell Randi?"

"Tell her she's . . . "

"She wants to tell me some . . . ." They both started again.

Pucci held up her hand again. "Just a sec, Randi."

"Tell her she's in the wrong era in the book. Tell her to turn to the last chapter if she wants to find who John is," Davinia said in a huff. "Good thing your friend talks to herself out loud. She mentioned a note with John's name that you found at Rosslyn."

"Randi, what book are you reading?"

"It's fascinating, Pucci. It's the history of Scotland, written in the nineteenth century by a Scottish author. I figured that might be a good place to start. It seems my knowledge of this country's history, which isn't much I might add, came from an English perspective. This is quite different. Listen to this . . . "

But before Randi started reading from the middle of the book, Pucci interrupted. "Randi, Davinia said to turn to the last chapter. She said that's where we might find information about John that was in the note we found."

"How did she know about that?"

"Apparently you talk to yourself, out loud."

"Oh, true . . . " Randi turned to the last chapter as Pucci pulled up to a chair and sat down. No one else was in the library. Randi began.

"The final chapter—looks like it ends with Robert the First, or Robert the Bruce and the famous battle of Bannockburn in 1314. Pucci, wasn't that the battle that the Templars joined to help Robert the Bruce? They defeated the English in that battle, correct?" Randi asked.

Pucci nodded. "Go on."

"There are a lot of details, but, here, it says that Angus Óg—I have no idea how to say that name—anyway, he fought alongside Robert the Bruce. Angus Óg's son is John. John pledged his allegiance to David the Second—who ascended the throne of Scotland in 1341, after Robert—and by doing that, David II gave John Islay, Mull, Jura, and a whole lot of other islands. This happened in 1344."

"Why is this important?" Pucci asked Davinia. Davinia held up a finger.

Randi continued reading. "It says, 'John was a quiet, gentle old man and didn't want any part of the wars that continued to happen between England and Scotland. It is said he moved to Islay and became John of Islay." Randi raised her head to look at Pucci.

"Do you think this is our John? Davinia, is this the John that's referenced in our note?" Pucci asked pulling out the note from her pocket and showed it to the ghost.

"This is what you found at Rosslyn? This looks like Callum's writing. I didn't realize more than one jeweled cipher was under Callum's protection," Davinia said, pausing. "I remember a man named John—not just a trusted friend, but like a father to Callum. Callum once mentioned that John's father had fought alongside the Knights Templar in Bannockburn, and as a result, John had ties to Callum's order. He stayed at Strathhammond several times. One night, John told Callum he was weary of the wars. They spoke of peace. He longed to escape to one of his islands. His young wife was expecting, and he said they planned to settle and name their son John the Second."

"Davinia, do you know what happened to him? It seems too coincidental that it's the same John," Pucci asked.

"No, I do not know. They killed me and took the cipher that had been under my protection. I don't even know what happened to Callum," she said.

Pucci moved closer to the ghost. "My Lady, please, you are our only connection to this time. You have been such a gift so far. But can you think of anything else that might help us—any small thing you might have overheard, or that maybe Callum mentioned—that you can remember? Even something small might be important."

Lady Davinia floated over to the fire, gazing into the flames for a few moments. She held out her translucent hand. Pucci pulled the jeweled piece out from under her layers of clothing and held it out for Davinia. Pucci felt the chain grow cold. Caressing the diamonds, without looking up, Davinia said, "Callum wanted peace as well. We were all so exhausted from the constant fighting. Why couldn't England just leave us alone, he would say. I remember one night he said, 'Maybe I'll go help John on Islay with his new adventure.' He called it 'Aqua Vitae.'" She looked into Pucci's eyes. "Maybe your answer is on Islay." She turned away and floated through the wall back to her staircase, which was her tomb.

***

"Ah, ladies, there you are," Mr. Anderson said at the entrance to the library. "We'll need you to check out now. I apologize, I don't want to rush you, but there are guests waiting. We are booked solid for the holidays coming up."

"Oh, I'm so sorry, Mr. Anderson. We got caught up in your beautiful library. We'll go get our things now. May I ask, could we get a ride into Edinburgh this afternoon? We're going to catch the train to Glasgow this evening," Pucci said.

"Yes, ladies. I will arrange it for you."

"Thank you. By the way, have you seen Braden—I mean, Mr. MacNevin? I'd like to say goodbye," Pucci inquired.

"He's gone for the weekend, Ms. Riddle. I'm sorry."

"Oh, alright. Thanks," she murmured, averting her eyes to conceal her wounded feelings.

Randi replaced the book on the shelf and they returned to their rooms to pack.

***

Braden MacNevin joined Mr. Anderson, their figures shadowed against the fading light as they silently watched the car disappear down the road. Pucci, however, remained unaware of their presence. As she cast one last glance at the castle, the car turned onto the main road toward Edinburgh, the weight of unseen eyes lingering behind her.

"Anything?" Braden asked.

"Aye, I gave them the three books you recommended to me earlier. You were right about what they were looking for. They found a reference to a John whose father fought with Robert the Bruce. I dinnae know how they made the connection, why they were looking for John to begin with."

"I do, continue."

"I overheard Ms. Riddle mentioning a Lady Davinia, almost as if she were in the room. It sounded like they found a note in Rosslyn, referencing John." He paused and looked over at Braden, "Do you really think she's the one?"

Braden raised an eyebrow and nodded. "Aye. I do . . . I'll inform the others."

Chapter 25

Randi's phone pinged as they rounded the corner and merged onto the main road to Edinburgh. She looked at the text and cursed under her breath.

"What's wrong?" Pucci asked.

"Hopefully nothing major. It's the status of the boat we're preparing for the customer. The head mechanic is having issues with one of the engines and might need to replace it. That's an enormous expense. I might need to see to this personally, Pucci. But, hopefully my mechanic can figure it out." Randi said, closing her phone.

"I hope it's all OK, Randi. I'd hate for you to miss the next part of the adventure!"

"Speaking of, where are we in all this?"

"I've been thinking about that, Randi," Pucci paused collecting her thoughts. "I originally came to the UK for the commission with *Wine and Scotch* magazine and to update my blog. But there were two other reasons. One was to see if I could uncover more about Pirate through the ghost of Valerie Baine—which I did. I passed that information along to Detective Davies. Hopefully he's reconnected with Olan, and knocked some sense into him to follow up with the lead from her diary. Pirate is connected, somehow, to this jeweled cipher, which leads to the house in Oxford.

"The second reason was to find more clues about the cipher, beginning at Rosslyn Chapel. What is it? Where does it come from? Why are dark and evil people after it? How many pieces are needed to make the cipher whole again? We haven't got very far on any of those questions. But, we got some good initial information from our two ghosts. We know that the cipher is somehow connected to the Knights Templar and associated with an ancient treasure, or artifacts in their keeping. So far, I have this piece, which was hidden in the locket. Lady Davinia had a second piece that someone killed her for and stole. Now we know a third piece was hidden in Rosslyn and given to a John whose father was granted a bunch of islands by King David II, one of which we're headed toward—Islay."

Randi listened with intensity, but didn't comment.

"We also have those symbols from Rosslyn, which I still believe are significant. Somehow they're tied to this riddle. I've decided to reach out to Varv and email her a picture of the symbols. Maybe she could go to the National Library of Scotland in Edinburgh to research them."

That sounded like a long shot to Randi, but she held her tongue.

"I can feel what you're thinking, Randi," Pucci said, smiling. "I know it's a long shot. But, we're being watched and followed, so I know we're somehow on the right track."

"Alright, Pucci. I'll trust your intuition, but it seems like we need more to go on than your gut," Randi said, grinning.

Waverly Station loomed closer as the taxi sped forward. Pucci had arranged to stay in Islay starting Monday at a bed-and-breakfast she had booked before leaving the States. She also had meetings scheduled with several head distillers on Monday and Tuesday for her article. Knowing that reaching the island by public transport would take at least a day and a half, they had no time to visit Varv before catching the next train to Glasgow.

As they stepped out of the car, Pucci asked Randi, "By the way, how did you know where to look in the library to find that reference to John? Did you feel a tug, maybe from Davinia?"

"No paranormal help needed, Pucci. I did as you suggested and asked Mr. Anderson. He pulled out three books and said I should probably start with this one, which was the one on Scotland's history, and it turned out to be just what we needed," Randi said, rolling her suitcase toward the entrance.

"Curious," Pucci said under her breath. "Very curious."

Chapter 26

Olan

DCI Lathen slammed the front doors open as he walked out of Scotland Yard. He stormed down the street, heading for the nearest pub. He saw one of his haunts, crossed the street and stepped inside. He stood, letting his eyes adjust as the closing door slowly diminished all outside light.

He looked around the pub. A solitary drunk slurring his words asked for a refill at the bar. Two men in a booth near the back didn't bother to look up as they nursed their drinks.

Olan stood still, feeling the tremor in his hands from withdrawal. He took in the sweet scent of the alcohol being dispensed into the mug of beer for the drunk. Feeling his willpower fail, Olan desperately wanted to go to the bar and join the man. The tremors would stop and his demons would drown for one more day. If he walked over to the bar, it would be over. If he turned and walked out, he'd have a fighting chance of recovery. He could continue to run from his nightmares into the bottom of a bottle or face them.

He recognized the hold his past had over him, the way he clung to the ten-year-old story he had woven about it—the death of the woman he loved, Liana. There was a choice before him: to let go of that narrative, to accept that he wasn't to blame, and to extend himself the forgiveness he had withheld for so long. But deep down, he wondered—was self-forgiveness even possible? He took a step toward the bar. From the inside pocket of his overcoat, Valerie's diary bumped his leg. He felt Pucci. Olan reversed directions and threw open the door to the blinding sunlight reflecting off the recently fallen snow of London. God, he loved this city and breathed her in. He spotted a coffee shop a few doors away and made his way toward it—and toward recovery.

Coffee in hand, Olan found a table near a window and texted Connor that he was going to Oxford. On leave or on the job, he still had his badge and gun. The chief superintendent, at least, hadn't taken those.

He looked at Valerie's description of how she followed Pirate as he reread her diary. *If Pucci could figure this out, I'm sure a detective chief inspector can—even if I am on leave.* He took a deep breath of the coffee aroma and took his first sip. The coffee burnt his lips slightly as he drank through the small opening in the plastic lid. It also soothed the tremors slightly. He breathed again, studying every detail.

He drove to Oxford, making good time. Following the clues from the diary, map in hand, he drove slowly along the street of the house Valerie described. He saw it. A Tudor home, adorned in ivy, featuring two towers and a large wooden door with a pitched roof over the entry.

The neighborhood was dead quiet. Olan rolled down his window to listen. He heard a solitary bird's wings as it took flight from a giant oak tree to another across the street. He heard his phone ping. Connor's text with the research that Sara found. She could ferret out information like no one else. The text said to check his secure email. She must have found a lot. He'd read it later.

The frigid mist hit him in his face as he got out of the car. He looked up to see a second-story curtain flick shut. Was someone watching?

Olan had a plan. He rang the doorbell and heard the gong reverberate deep inside. His Scotland Yard ID was at the ready.

A tall formally dressed gentleman answered the door.

"Yes, may I help you?"

Olan quickly assessed the man as a servant. "I need to speak to the owner of the house, please."

"May I ask what this is about and who you are?"

He quickly showed his ID. "This is a police matter."

"Certainly, sir . . . " But before the man could finish his sentence, Lathen walked past him and into the house. "Please wait in the drawing room, to your left," the man said, in an irritated tone. "I will get the master."

Olan walked into a room that was smaller than a formal dining room, but larger than a study. Deep green velvet curtains were pulled back off the floor-to-ceiling windows to let in the winter light. The walls were covered in art, copies of the great masters, DaVinci, Renoir, Rembrandt, even a Monet.

He felt something shift in the energy of the room and the house. He could feel powerful negative energy kept in check. He didn't like this place. It was a facade.

"A police matter?" said an impeccably dressed man with a pencil-thin mustache and even thinner eyebrows, one arched in question as he stood in the doorway. His three-piece black suit covered a slim, slight frame. The gold fob chain glinted as the man reached into his vest pocket, retrieving a gold watch. He checked the time, the chain looping neatly through a buttonhole. "Who are you, sir, and what can I help you with?" He closed the watch with a click and pocketed it.

"Chief Inspector Lathen, sir. May I ask who you are?"

"Clouding, Sir William Clouding. I am the owner of this house," he sat, indicating Olan should do the same.

Olan remained standing. "We have reason to believe a man connected to a murder and a museum heist visited this house."

"Indeed?" Clouding said, his mouth twitched in one corner. "Pray, tell me, Chief Inspector, when was this, and who?"

"Three years ago. We don't know his real name. He goes by Pirate."

Clouding had the audacity to laugh, "Three years ago? Oh, come now. And you're just now coming to inquire about this? Why so late? And what kind of a name is—Pirate, did you say? You're putting me on."

"I am not, sir. We have recently recovered a diary from a woman murdered in connection with the museum heist. It seems that she followed the ringleader of the heist to this address one evening, three years ago. The next week, we fished her body out of the Thames." Olan watched the man closely. He felt a shift in the man's cocky energy. Fear, perhaps?

Clouding's poker face was back in place as he said, "Well, that's dreadful sir, but your diary must be mistaken. I have no idea what, or whom, you're talking about. I cannot help you." He rose and walked to the door.

Olan followed but was not deterred. "Is there someone else in the house I can talk to that would have been here during that time?"

"No, Chief Inspector. Now, I'll kindly ask you to leave my house and quit wasting my time."

Olan took a step toward him, looking directly into Clouding's eyes, "This is a murder inquiry, sir. I'd like your cooperation."

"Apparently, Chief Inspector, you have no idea who I am. I would suggest you ask the head of Scotland Yard," he said as he turned toward the butler. "James, show this man out."

Olan watched Clouding's back as he walked down the hall. He had no choice but to leave. Olan descended the entry stairs, hearing the door slam behind him.

* * *

Clouding turned and walked back into the drawing room. He slowly took a breath, turning his gold signet ring back around. The blue diamond winked in the firelight. He walked over to the landline phone and dialed. "Get here now, you were followed."

He hung up and walked into his study, accessing a hidden door behind his mahogany antique desk. Opening it, he hurried down a flight of stairs. The underground chambers were dimly lit with candles. Shadows darted on the cold stone walls. Five men waited for him, standing in a circle. Clouding told his second, "Go get the cipher."

One of the five shifted nervously, struggling to maintain his composure as fear surged and bile churned in his stomach.

The man was gone less than a minute and reentered the circle, fear in his eyes and terror in his voice.

"It's gone."

Clouding's anger surged. Ten years—a relentless decade of research, past-life recall, and travel across the world—all for that cipher. After it was stolen and smuggled out of Scotland by his decedents of a dark sect, somehow the Templars had recovered it years later. He finally traced it to Istanbul, hidden within the ancient House of the Virgin Mary in Ephesus, where Mary was said to have spent her final years. The cipher lay concealed within a statue of Mary Magdalene, hidden in plain sight for centuries. His research had led him there, knowing that Mary held deep significance to the Knights Templar, her relics believed to have been taken to Constantinople—modern-day Istanbul—before its fall. And now, after everything . . . stolen.

Billows of negative energy rose up and the other men murmured.

"Gentleman," at the sound of his voice, the other members fell silent. "We have been betrayed."

Chapter 27

Anya

Anya walked into the underground hideout. No one was around. The stonecutters were gone, along with all the equipment off the old wood table. Her stomach sank and fear rose in her throat as she ran down the small hallway to Morgan's room. She breathed a sigh of relief. All of his personal belongings were still there. *They must have just packed up this part of the operation. Damn it. I knew they were close.* She slowly walked down the ancient walled hallway of the forgotten close. She heard voices and stopped. She hid behind a corner wall.

"What the hell do you mean, 'you've been summoned'? Summoned by who?" It was Morgan's voice. "I'm sick of this Pirate, it's over. I've ordered this operation shut down. I'm just waiting for Whiley to send word of the three blues and I'm out."

Silence. Anya dared a peek around the wall. She saw Pirate in a standoff with Morgan. Both men, chests puffed out, almost touching, staring at each other, neither daring to blink first. Fear gripped her again, feeling like she was going to throw up or scream. She'd have to come up with an excuse as to why she was down this hallway. She listened.

Pirate spoke, his voice rough and ragged, still raw from the bullet wound. "You're lucky I agree with your decision, Morgan. Otherwise, I'd have killed you right now. I've decided to shut everything down. Tell Whiley to get out but not until we get the diamonds. Tell the apartment and their contacts in China it's over. The coppers are getting too close. Our informant at Scotland Yard overheard a conversation about our operation. He didn't hear much, but enough to know they're close." Anya grabbed the wall in shock. An informant at The Yard? She concentrated all her attention back to the conversation. She watched Morgan relax his stance slightly and nod.

Morgan asked, "You never told me who summoned you and why."

"It's none of your damn business." Pirate suddenly grabbed Morgan by the collar, and with the other hand held a knife to his throat. Blood trickled down Morgan's neck. "Never ask me again," he growled as he shoved Morgan back so hard, he hit the wall and collapsed.

"You're a fool, Pirate," Morgan coughed out the words, covering the wound.

"Get up and get the hell out of here. I need to go to Oxford. I'll get in touch with you at the apartment. Stay there until Whiley completes his mission, otherwise nobody gets paid."

After taking a few steps back to make it seem like she was just coming around the corner, Anya made a noise and called out, "Pirate?" Looking as calm as she could, she asked, "Where the hell have you been?" She walked toward the two men. Her shaking hands were deep in her coat pockets. With no emotion, looking at Morgan, she said, "You're bleeding."

"I know I'm bleeding, you bloody women. What the hell were you doing down there?" Morgan was incensed, his hand still covering his seeping wound.

"What do you think? I was looking for you," she spat back, hoping her bravado would keep them at bay, masking her lies and fear.

Morgan seemed to accept her excuse. Pirate, however, was studying her every move. He spoke, "It's over, Anya. Whiley is moving the last of the three out in the next couple days. I told Morgan to go to the apartment, which I'm sure you overheard."

Anya, sweat beading on her forehead, her heart pounding in her chest, stayed silent. The overhead light flickered and buzzed.

The strained silence was broken with a trill of a landline phone. Pirate reached for it. "Ya," he said, then listened, turning his back. "It'll be done tonight. The operation is over so who the hell cares if Lathen thinks he's close. It's over," he paused. "I'm not going to discuss the other. The Riddle woman isn't a concern right now. I'll get the piece back in a day or so."

Anya's senses were on high alert with the mention of Lathen. God, she wished she knew who was on the other end of the line. She had never heard that phone ring before. And what the hell is Pucci doing in all of this? She turned, reaching for water to boil tea, keeping her breathing and her hands in check. She thought back to Georgetown, Grand Cayman, and her betrayal there of Varv and Pucci—who at one point, she had considered friends.

Pirate grunted a few times and hung up. She shook herself out of the memory. Anya gestured if he wanted tea. He nodded. She didn't bother asking Morgan.

When she handed Pirate a steaming mug, she said, "I didn't know that phone even worked. Who has this number?"

Pirate rounded on her, grabbed her wrist, his face so close he spit tea in her face. "As I warned Morgan, it's none of your damn business. Pack up and get out of here. Go with Morgan. I'll send word about payment when I get the three stones, and not before." He slammed his mug down on the counter so hard it bounced, rolled, and clattered into the sink. He walked out of the hidden close for the last time.

Chapter 28

By the time they boarded the train to Glasgow, darkness had already fallen. Randi stayed focused on her phone, continuing a text exchange with her mechanic. They were troubleshooting what should have been a simple oil leak, but on a yacht's inboard motor, even minor issues could turn into complex engineering problems—problems Randi hoped to resolve without having to be there in person.

Pucci looked out the window, watching the lights go by, dozing. Her closed eyes revealed images of sinister shadows and red templar crosses, illuminated by the passing flashing lights.

She woke as the train pulled into the Glasgow train station. She looked at Randi, felt her energy and sighed, "You have to go back to the boat, don't you?"

"You scare me sometimes, Pucci," Randi said with a small smile. "Yes, we can't figure this out remotely. I need to see it and get my hands on the hardware. If we can't figure it out and fix it ourselves, it will be an extreme expense I cannot afford, and neither can my client."

"Let's get our bags and find the next train back to Edinburgh. I won't leave you until you're safely back on a return train."

"Thank you for understanding. I hate to miss the next part of this journey! Maybe I should start documenting your adventures, Pucci. I could be your Watson," she said as they grabbed their bags and left the train.

Pucci waved to the departing train, despondent. It was so fun and energizing having her friend with her. *Well*, she thought, *it was a treat, not planned, and now you're where you thought you'd be all along. Alone, on an adventure to my favorite distilleries.*

Her spirits picked up as she walked toward her hotel to stay for the night and catch the early morning bus to the city of Tarbert. She was back to her original plan of taking the bus, excited to see some of this country's enchanting landscape.

After a quick bite in the hotel bar and tucked up in her hotel room, she was too tired to go out and was soon fast asleep.

***

It was still dark and extremely cold the next morning as she boarded the bus to Tarbert via Campbeltown. Luckily it wasn't very crowded and she grabbed a seat behind the driver with no one next to her. The bus was like sitting in a mobile freezer. Apparently, the heater was on, but not doing a good job of warming anything except the driver. Pucci wrapped her heavy coat tighter and put her gloves back on.

She watched as the city of Glasgow turned into more rural country. The snow had not fallen in this part of the country yet, so the green pastures and hills carpeted the landscape as far as the eye could see. After making a few stops in small towns, the bus skirted Loch Lomond, and she caught her first glimpse of the famous deep lake through the bus window opposite her. The bus had warmed up a bit. She rose and removed her heavy coat and gloves. She left them on the seat and asked a man in a neon rain jacket sitting across the aisle if she could lean over him to take some photos.

"Oh, aye," he said as he leaned back out of her way. "American?" Pucci nodded, taking her camera out of her purse.

"You'll be wantin tae keep that camera out. Inveraray is coming up soon as we wind around Loch Fyne and you'll want a shot of the castle."

"Thank you, that would be lovely. I'm off to Islay."

"Oh, aye, you'll be takin the ferry out of Kennacraig?"

"Yes, I'm so excited," Pucci said. "Thank you for letting me take some pictures."

"Oh, aye, nae worries," he said and promptly fell asleep.

Pucci moved back over to her seat, taking in as much scenery as she could. The loch's serene surface reflected the surrounding greenery and the distant hills, creating a mesmerizing panorama. The dense forests along the shore seemed almost to embrace the loch, adding a sense of seclusion and peace. The bus weaved closer to the water's edge. Pucci was thankful the bus driver's hands were thoroughly thawed by now. With her camera, she captured the imposing peaks of the Trossach National Park perfectly reflected in the still water of the loch along with the puffy stark white clouds against the true blue of the sky.

The bus climbed the winding roads, offering ever-changing vistas of rugged mountains and deep glens of the Arrochar Alps. The Rest and Be Thankful pass was announced by the bus driver. Pucci thought he was kidding until the kind man in the neon rain jacket pointed out the dramatic views over Glen Croe, prompting gasps and hurried clicks from Pucci. A delicate veil of snow dusted the otherwise stark peaks. Below, the highland grasses cradled pockets of deeper snow, their golden blades bending beneath winter's harsh, unyielding hand.

Descending from the pass, the bus meandered toward the town of Tarbert, passing through lush valleys and alongside sparkling streams. Her fellow passenger once again called Pucci over as the bus rounded Loch Fyne, and pointed out the imposing Inveraray Castle, its dark gray turrets and towers in sharp relief against the crystal-clear sky behind, and the frost-covered manicured lawn of the extensive grounds in front.

The bus finally rolled into the charming village of Tarbert. Pucci felt a sense of having traveled through a living postcard, each view more captivating than the last. She thanked the kind man as she departed the bus. He was going on to the last stop on this route, Campbeltown. That area had good whisky as well. Maybe next trip.

She rolled her luggage down the street toward her hotel. She was slightly early for check-in. Across from the hotel was a quaint-looking shop of lotions and potions. She squeezed her luggage through the front door, aided by a tall man with kind eyes. A young woman stepped out from a small back room through a dividing curtain, carrying bottles for a display. "Welcome!" she said, smiling at Pucci.

"Thank you, do you mind if I have my luggage in here?" Pucci asked, hoping it was not too much trouble as the shop wasn't very big.

"Not at all, love," she answered. "I'm going to nip to the back, please let me know if I can help. My name is Maisie if you need anything."

Pucci loved everything in the shop. From organic skin care products to specialty designed aromatherapy candles that captured the wonderful smells of Scotland in a candle. She wanted to buy everything. But, knowing she couldn't pack much else in her already crammed suitcase, she bought some sample items.

"I've been looking for some new skin care and your products are just perfect!"

"I'm so glad you like them. I make them myself with the finest ingredients, sourced here in Scotland," Maisie said, ringing up the samples.

"I'm sorry I can't buy more, my suitcase is totally full! But I promise to order more when I get back to the States," she said, putting the shop's business card in her wallet.

Pucci rolled her suitcase across the street to her hotel. No official office or check-in, just a note inside the small entry way with her name on an envelope. Her room was on the third floor, no elevator. Oy vey. By the time she'd schlepped all her suitcases upstairs, she was sweating and her muscles were aching. She grabbed the complimentary bottled water and sat at the tiny desk next to the window overlooking the harbor.

Tarbert, nestled on the shores of Loch Fyne, was a picturesque fishing village that seemed almost untouched by time. Its charming harbor, dotted with colorful fishing boats, bustled gently with the rhythm of the tides, and quaint stone houses with slate roofs lined the narrow, winding streets.

Sipping water and looking out her room window, Pucci noticed how high the tide was. Two swans swam gently past an old wooden boat moored in the harbor. She wondered how the ancient boat stayed afloat.

She walked to a nearby restaurant. The scent of the sea mingled with the aroma of freshly caught seafood. The ancient Tarbert Castle looked down on the town, its ruins silent sentinels whispering tales of bygone eras. The sign by the harbor welcomed her to The Kintyre Way. She wondered what that meant. Maybe it had something to do with the Kintyre peninsula on which Tarbert was located.

As she walked back to her hotel after a delicious meal of fish and chips, she passed the Tarbert Loch Fyne Yacht Club, filled with very small boats, none of which she would call yachts. Maybe they moored the larger boats further out in the Loch. She took a picture for Randi, thought she'd get a kick out of it. She continued to her hotel to call it an early night since the ferry was leaving early the next morning.

Chapter 29

Pucci brewed herself a comforting cup of Scottish Breakfast tea, letting the rich aroma fill her room as the kettle whistled softly. She held the mug against her chest, feeling the warmth and the scent of the steam as she looked out the window. The tide was extremely low. The old wooden boat was now sitting on solid ground, with the water a good five feet away.

She hired a car to take her to Kennacraig Ferry Terminal on the small peninsula of Eilean Ceann Na Creige. She asked her driver about the name of the peninsula. He told her it was Gaelic for Head of the Rock.

"Where you're going, you'll see a lot more Gaelic," the driver said, knowing Pucci was headed to Islay, pronouncing Gaelic "gahlick," with a soft "a." "A lot of folks speak only Gaelic. We like tae keep the language alive."

Pucci paid and thanked him as she left the car. She entered a small terminal building, converted her reservation to a paper ticket, and walked back outside to wait to board in the warming sun of another beautiful day in Scotland. She knew she had been blessed with the weather so far—everyone had told her she was crazy going to Scotland in winter as it was colder than . . . each person utilizing their own adjectives.

She saw giant trucks outfitted with enormous stainless steel cylinders. She wondered what fuel was in those cylinders. She doubted they were filled with milk, like she'd seen in California. She read a sign on one of the cylinders. "Bowmore 10Y."

"Oh my goodness, these aren't filled with fuel or milk, they're filled with whisky! I have to get a photo of this! This is definitely going in my article," she said out loud, stepping back to get the entire rig in the picture.

She watched as the ferry's massive hull yawned open, swallowing the rumbling semitrucks one by one like pieces of licorice as they disappeared into its cavernous interior. These were not the kind of ferries that ran across the San Diego Bay from the mainland to Coronado Island, holding about fifty tourists. This massive, four-story ship carried empty tankers bound for Islay, where they would be filled with whisky before making their return journey to destinations unknown. Alongside them, cars, vans, trucks, and passengers made their way into the belly of the ferry, each with a journey of their own on the way to the island.

Pucci walked up the pedestrian ramp, thankful once again for her upgraded luggage wheels—the ramp surface was made of rough metal spikes to give pedestrians a good grip. A beefy, tall man in a vest with a small red lion in a yellow circle insignia, indicating he was a CalMac employee from the ferry, grabbed Pucci's luggage like it was a grocery bag and carried it the rest of the way up the two story ramp. She wanted to thank him, but he just walked past her, smiled and nodded. Very busy man.

The ferry's interior gleamed with polished mirrors and bars adorned with gleaming brass counters, reflecting the warm glow of the lights. There were places to sit everywhere—by the windows, in the center, up front at the cafeteria tables, and on the open upper level. It felt more like a modern cruise ship than a ferry.

Pucci stashed her luggage and went up top. Deep in the bowels of this enormous floating building, the rumbling of the engines vibrated all the way up to the metal chairs on the deck—and her bum. White water boiled as the shore and the pier fell away. She wanted to wave to someone but only watched as workers walked away from the departing vessel.

She faced where the ferry was headed, wind whipping her hair. The temperature dropped due to the wind chill, but she didn't care. It was exhilarating!

She had dreamed of this moment for so long. She breathed in the crisp salty sea air, her eyes watering from the sting of the wind and the feeling of reverence for the moment. She asked another brave soul who had just walked up the stairs if they would take a picture of her, and to please get more of the scenery than of her.

The Sound of Jura sliced the two land masses in half, creating a breathtaking view of two sides of densely forested peninsulas, giving way to rocky, brown peaks, as the ferry continued its journey toward Islay.

Islay, the southernmost of the Hebridean islands, was located on the west coast of Scotland. It happened to be at the same latitude as Glasgow. The island was the eighth largest in Britain. Home to about 3000 residents and eight whisky distilleries.

They pulled into Port Ellen on the southeastern side of the island. She debarked and caught a taxi to her destination, a bed-and-breakfast right down the street from the Bruichladdich and the Mhurachaidh distilleries.

She rolled her luggage up to the large two-story house and entered through the white picket gate connecting the small moss-covered stone wall that surrounded the property. Behind her, a narrow country road hugged the shoreline, separating Pucci from the dark, glassy waters of Loch Indaal. On the far side of the loch, the lights of Bowmore distillery and town shimmered in the early evening, their golden reflections dancing on the water. To her left, Bruichladdich stood watch on the near shore, its pale walls catching the last traces of daylight—two legendary distilleries facing each other across the vast, tidal sea lake like ancient stewards of Islay's whisky heritage.

She walked into the entryway of the bed-and-breakfast. There was a small guest book to sign in to her right, stairs in front of her, *oy, more stairs*, and a dining area to her left. The proprietor came from a side door with a welcoming smile on her face. Her light brown hair, softened by the faintest traces of silver, complemented her warm brown eyes, which sparkled with hospitality. She radiated charm and poise.

"Ms. Riddle?" she asked in a Scottish accent as she came closer.

"Hello! Yes, you can call me Pucci," Pucci answered, holding out her hand. They shook. The exchange was heartfelt.

"How was your journey? It takes a bit to get to our island, if you don't fly in."

"It was wonderful! That ferry is amazing! More like a luxury cruise liner," Pucci marveled.

"Oh, aye," she said, her eyes looking at Pucci's luggage. "Your room is at the top of the stairs, but I'll help with your bags."

"We might need to do this one together, it's pretty heavy. I've packed for a month, even though I'm only here for a few days. Do you need me to sign in, or give you a credit card?"

"We'll settle up before you leave. My name is Catriona, you can call me Cat." At that moment a fluffy yellow Labrador came around the corner to check out the new guest. He nosed Pucci, tail wagging furiously, begging for some pets. Pucci bent down and scratched his head. "That's Angus. As you can see, he loves attention. If you'd like to follow me," she said and picked up Pucci's large suitcase, climbing the stairs. "You are the only one here this time of year, so you'll have the bathroom to yourself."

"Really? I thought you'd be booked up! That's a beautiful name, Catriona," Pucci said, feeling guilty for letting Cat take her heavy suitcase.

"Thank you, here you are," Cat said as she opened the door on the upper floor to a fairly large room with a couch, double bed, and a window that overlooked Loch Indaal. It was a sweet space, with its own radiant heater and an old wooden dresser.

"The bathroom is to the left. Breakfast is served from seven till about nine. Please let me know if you need anything," Cat said, handing Pucci the keys before heading down the stairs.

Over the next half hour, Pucci settled in and was soon eager to explore some of the island before everything closed. Putting her heavy coat back on, she picked up her purse and strolled a block to the Mhurachaidh distillery.

Chapter 30

The tasting room at Mhurachaidh was smaller than Pucci imagined, about the size of a large living room. It had a tasting bar in the back and branded merchandise, from T-shirts to jackets to whisky, taking up the rest of the space.

To her utter horror, she saw and heard her nemesis leaning up against the bar, holding court—Oliver Williams-Tanaka. She was tempted to turn around and leave but felt frozen to the spot. How could he possibly be here? It came back to her that she had overheard him on the train, mentioning Islay. But, to be here at the same time, in the same distillery? Her stomach turned as he caught sight of her.

"Well, look who just can't keep away from me, Pucci Riddle," he called out, turning to some of the people that were gathered around him. They all looked at her. Heat rose in her face, turning the otherwise pale Pucci red.

She took off her coat, and slowly walked up to the tall, lanky, pathetic excuse for a man.

"Well, if it isn't Oliver, the bully of the internet," she said, hoping no one saw her blush. "Spouting your usual drivel to these poor unsuspecting souls?"

"How utterly droll you are, Ms. Riddle. Why don't you take your pitiable prose somewhere else. I don't think this distinguished distillery needs any help from your uneducated readers," he spouted, making sure his makeshift audience heard as he returned to them.

The woman behind the counter rolled her eyes at Oliver's comment. She came around from behind the counter to

Pucci with a hand extended, and said, "Pucci Riddle? The author of Spirits by Pucci?"

"Yes," Pucci answered, a little flustered.

"Oh, I love yer blog! Did ye come here to write about us? Aye, that would be grand!" the short, older woman exclaimed. She wore an oversize branded T-shirt, white with the blue letters of the distillery's logo.

Pucci read her name tag, "Thank you, Anne. I'm so flattered you know about my blog!"

"I loved your article on the rum distillery in Grand Cayman. Such a wonder that they age their signature rum in casks under water, in the sea! Just brilliant. That was fascinating," she said as she walked back behind the counter.

Pucci beamed. She dearly hoped Oliver was listening, but it looked like he was still expounding his nonsense to folks.

"What can I get you, love. We're about to close, but I'll get ye a dram. How about our new whisky, just came out," she turned to get a small sampling glass. She handed the dram to Pucci, in a low voice, asked, "What was that all about?" tilting her head toward Oliver.

"He doesn't appreciate my articles, or my blog. We write about similar alcohols, and we have very different tastes. He thinks he's so much more refined. I just wish he would fall off the face of the earth," she said, a little too loud, as some patron's heads turned.

Out of the corner of her eye, she thought she saw Oliver's traveling companion from the train, still dressed in a gray hoodie. She couldn't be sure as he rounded a corner and out the front door.

Pucci sipped her dram, admiring the peat that didn't overpower the notes of sweet maltiness of the whisky. She didn't have time to do much more at this distillery, and vowed she'd come back and get a proper tour.

"Thank you, Anne, that was delicious! Could you tell me, so I don't make a fool of myself, how do you properly pronounce your distillery name?" Pucci asked as she set her glass down on the bar.

"Oh, aye, Mu-ra-chee, emphasis on the 'ra.' It was named after the last whisky smuggler of Islay, Baldy Mhurachaidh. There's a legend of a cave somewhere around the McArthur's Head by Proaig, that can only be seen by boat if you know where to look. Whisky was made illicitly and smuggled out by Baldy. Alas, Baldy was betrayed by a friend and he had to flee, leaving all the equipment behind. We named the distillery in his honor. It's fun to hear all different folks try to pronounce the name. However you do it, we don't mind, just as long as ye like our whisky, we're happy."

Pucci said goodbye to Anne and walked out the door. She spied a small convenience store, realized she needed to get something to eat before breakfast tomorrow, and headed that way.

After buying a cold tuna sandwich and some crisps, she walked along the back of the distillery toward her hotel. Beyond the wall, across a wide open space, she spotted Oliver and the man in the hoodie slipping into a large building. She stopped and stared, but they were soon out of sight. She wondered if she was just imagining them sneaking around or might have read the body language wrong. They didn't emerge after a few minutes, so Pucci went about her business, munching on some of the crisps she bought, walking back to the B and B.

After finishing her snack, unpacking and organizing her clothes and toiletries, Pucci crawled into bed, determined to get up early to explore. She was just dozing when that familiar sensation twisted in her stomach—the telltale sign that a ghost had just shown up. Pucci kept her eyes shut for a moment, steadying herself. It wasn't a surprise; old buildings held echoes of the past, and this one was no exception. But still, she braced herself before cracking open one eyelid—then jumped out of her skin.

"Oliver Williams-Tanaka, Jesu . . . what the hell? What are you doing here? How did you find me? . . . Why are you dead?" she yelled, hyperventilating.

She calmed her breathing and grabbed a sweatshirt and sweatpants and her sacred ring. She dressed and slipped the ring on before she made herself look at Oliver again. The ring helped calm her energy. His translucent self wasn't looking at her. His head was turning back and forth, and his eyes were darting all around with an extremely confused look on his ghostly face.

Pucci could see and feel his confusion. "Oliver . . . Oliver," she said gently, trying to get his attention. Finally, he looked right at her. "Oliver, what happened?"

"Ms. Riddle? What are you doing here? How did I get here? What is going on?"

"Oliver, do you know you're dead?"

"Dead? . . . Dead!! What are you talking about, you crazy women?"

"Oliver, I've seen this before. When someone dies a violent and sudden death, some souls don't understand that they're out of their body. It's almost like ripping something out of a package," she paused. "Do you know what happened to you?"

"What do you mean, what happened? Dead? NO!"

Pucci took a step back. These were the hardest cases when dealing with the newly deceased. If he won't even accept that he's dead, he won't be able to move on. Acceptance has to be the first step in transitioning toward the light.

Oliver was mumbling something Pucci couldn't make out. She was just about to ask him what the last thing he remembered when he exclaimed, "I need to retrieve it!" and disappeared.

She sat on her bed, contemplating what to do. She had just seen Oliver at the distillery—alive! What had happened to him in those few hours? She needed to find out. He had been acting so strange. The incident in the Randolph Hotel bar accepting a mysterious package; the snippet of conversation in the train with the man in the hoodie regarding some plan. She dressed in her warmest clothes and slipped out the front door not wanting to wake her hostess.

Pucci returned to the spot where she last saw Oliver and the hoodie man, outside of Mhurachaidh distillery. With a swift hop over the small stone wall, she hunched down and stealthily made her way across the exposed driveway and loading dock to the building. Everything was in darkness. Luckily there were no lights on, and her movement didn't trigger any motion-detection lights.

She made it to the corner of the tall white and blue building, leaning against the icy wall, panting and sweating slightly due to all the layers she was wearing. She caught her breath and peeked around the corner. No movement, only silence. At the end of the building, a door, slightly ajar, led into another building. She pressed herself against the rough wall, feeling her way with her hands as she had forgotten her gloves. The wall was so rough, skin scraped off the fingertips of her right hand. She inhaled sharply. "Ow, damn it, that's painful," she murmured, trembling as she cradled it in her other hand, blood seeping from the wound. Her hands burned from the bitter cold.

With enough illumination from the moon, she abandoned the wall and made a dash toward the door. One side of the large double door, slightly ajar, opened silently at first, then let out a loud creak. Pucci stopped. She squeezed in the rest of the way, not wanting to make any additional sound.

She smelled the oak before she saw the barrels. *This must be one of the aging rooms for the whisky.* Barrels were stacked two, three, and in some places, four high, each cradling the sacred liquid, resting until its time had come. Some waiting more than ten years for their grand debut. The high, arched ceiling skylights let in the moonlight, casting eerie shadows over the perfectly stacked casts.

The wooden barrels, each unique in character, were bound by sturdy metal hoops encircling their bellies and sealing their ends. As she walked further inside, she noticed no two were exactly alike—some bore the deep, weathered patina of age, while others gleamed with newer wood, still rich with the scent of oak. Their surfaces ranged from pale honey to deep chestnut, with some branded or stamped with distillery marks, while others remained unmarked, their secrets locked within.

The end covers varied—some were single, solid slabs of wood, while others were pieced together from multiple planks. Pucci knew that these casks had once nurtured wine, bourbon, or sherry, their past lives infusing their essence into the whisky now maturing inside. A few, pure and untouched virgin oak, held the promise of untainted influence, ready to shape the whisky with nothing but the wood's own essence.

She breathed in deeply, the scent of aged oak mingling with the briny sea air, a heady mix of salt, earth, and time. Beneath it all, she caught the unmistakable whisper of the "angels' share"—that ethereal wisp of whisky lost to evaporation, perfuming the air with a warm, honeyed richness, a silent tribute to the spirits lingering in the rafters.

She heard a noise at the far end of the row and quickly ducked behind a cluster of upright barrels. She listened with all her might, ears straining for sound. None came. Tiptoeing down to the end of the row, she saw a gruesome and sad sight. Oliver's body, crumpled on the ground, blood pooling under his head. Oliver's ghost was there as well, bending over his own body, trying desperately to reach into his own coat pocket, his hand passing through the coat each time.

Pucci looked around before approaching, hoping the murderer had fled. She slowed her breathing.

"Oliver," loudly whispering to the ghost. He didn't look at her, just continued his desperate act of trying to reach into his coat pocket.

She approached his lifeless body and instinctively checked for a pulse by placing two fingers on his neck, despite her certainty of his death. She knew that sometimes, souls can travel out of their bodies with the body still alive. Pucci had seen this in coma patients. She had helped families communicate with their trapped loved ones and aided coma patients in getting messages to their families. Unfortunately for Oliver, this was not the case.

She didn't like the man for causing her pain and anger, but still couldn't help feel compassion for Oliver Williams-Tanaka. No one deserves to be murdered.

She turned to the ghost. "Oliver, stop! What are you doing? What are you trying to get from your coat?" No answer. She tried again. "Oliver, do you know who did this to you?"

"What is happening? Why does my hand just pass through my coat?"

"Oliver, you're dead. That's your body. Who did this?" Pucci said, then stopped. She heard footsteps walking in her direction. Not knowing what else to do, she ran to the corner of the building, hiding behind some barrels.

"I coulda sworn I heard talking," a man's voice called out.

Another man answered from a few rows away, "Aye, something isn't right."

"Holy shite! Geo, get over here. There's a body!"

"What? You're daft. Bloody hell, you're not," the other man said when he saw the body. He leaned down and checked Oliver's wrist for a pulse. "He's dead. Let's get out of here and call the police."

Pucci begged her heart to stop pounding so loud as she watched the two men swiftly walk away. She gathered her wits about her and walked back over to Oliver's body. She reached into his pocket and found a small flat jewelry box. She grabbed it and fled out the exit into the freezing night air. After getting her bearings, she identified a building, knew where she was, and ran as fast as possible, leaping over the wall and returning to the B and B and her room.

Pucci peeled off all her top clothing layers and sat on the bed. She fanned herself with a magazine off the desk. Her breathing finally slowing to a semi-normal pace. She took the jewelry box out from her coat pocket. It was flat, about three inches long, black velvet on the outside. Taking a deep breath, she slowly opened it. Nothing. She felt around the soft material inside. Nothing. *What was Oliver after? There must have been something really important in this case*, Pucci thought.

Exhaustion overwhelmed her curiosity, putting the case on the dresser. She got ready for bed and fell asleep immediately.

Chapter 31

Pucci woke late, nearly missing the designated breakfast time. Catriona, ever kind, invited her to the warmth and cozy kitchen instead of the cold dining room, where atmosphere made for a far more inviting start to the day.

"What can I make for you? Porridge? Eggs?" Cat asked.

"Tea and toast would be lovely, thank you. Catriona, may I ask you a question?"

"Please, call me Cat."

"Cat, it sounded like there was a disturbance in the distillery near here last night. Did you hear anything?" Pucci casually inquired.

"Aye, I've already heard from my neighbor what happened. They found a tourist murdered in one of the smaller warehouses that store whisky barrels in the distillery near here. Can you imagine? Murdered! In our wee village!" Cat exclaimed.

"Do they know what happened? Who it was?"

"I dinnae catch the name of the man, but apparently, he's a famous journalist. Writes for prestige magazines. He was here to write about our whiskies," Cat said, boiling more water. "I believe you're in a similar profession, Pucci. Maybe you can help the police. I hear they don't have a lot of information about him."

"Oh, no, Cat. I'm just here to sample your whisky and learn about your island. I like to keep to myself. But, please keep me posted if you hear anything else," Pucci said, trying to sound nonchalant, getting up from the table. "I'm off to the other side of the island to visit Laphroaig and Lagavulin distilleries. A taxi is going to pick me up in a few."

"Don't miss the Kildalton Cross. One of the best preserved, and famous Celtic crosses in all of Scotland," Cat said, smiling proudly.

Pucci was about to go up to her room to get ready for the day when she stopped and stared at the photograph on the front page of the newspaper lying on the edge of the kitchen table. The headlines screamed out, "Heinous Ritualistic Murder in Oxford." The photograph showed a blurry distant picture of a crime scene. Below it, there was a photograph of the murdered man, Mr. Owen Nell of Oxford. Pucci slowly picked up the paper and carefully studied the man's face. *My God, this is the man Oliver met with at the hotel bar in Oxford. The man Oliver accepted a small package from.* As she read over the account of a ritualistic murder, negative energy accosted her, hitting it in her solar plexus. Another paragraph caught her eye.

"One witness claims to have seen a shadow running from the scene in the early hours of the morning. 'It was so strange,' the witness said. 'I just couldn't get this figure in focus, even with the moonlight, he was just a shadow.' No other witnesses were reported." The article ended saying the investigation was ongoing and Scotland Yard had been called in.

Cat was looking at her strange. "You OK, love?"

"What? I'm sorry, uh, yes, I'm fine, Cat. Thank you for breakfast." She put the paper down walked up to her room. *It can't be. The Shadow Man is somehow connected to Oliver?* Pucci thought. Fear welled up in her. *What is going on?*

When she got back to her room, she heard her computer ping. Taking advantage of a spare moment before the taxi arrived, she opened her email. It was from Varv.

Hi Pucci, hope all is well and you made it to Islay safe. How's the whiskey, or is it spelled whisky in Scotland? Wish I was there sipping that glorious liquid with you.

All is great here in Edinburgh. I met with my clients and they're wonderful. The schedule is still up in the air, so I can't join you yet. Soon, I hope.

I had a little time to look into the symbols you sent. I went to the Scottish National Library, wow, what a beautiful building! I didn't find anything there, as now I realize, I wasn't looking in the proper areas.

You'll laugh. I figured out what the symbols mean, not the library however, but in my favorite place to go . . . yes, you guessed it, an esoteric bookstore. I was looking at the tarot decks, bought some wonderful decks I've never seen in the States! Anyway, I was looking at a Green Man deck, the ancient wisdom of the trees. I turned to the page with the symbols and the corresponding letters, and lo and behold, there were your symbols! It's called the Ogam Alphabet, or better known as the Ogham Alphabet. Ogam was a language used as part of the teachings of the Druids and found on carved standing stones throughout Britain, Scotland, and Ireland from the 4th century on. The inventor of the language was the namesake, Ogam. Some believe Ogam to be a god of literature, light, and learning, associated with divination, and the transmission of secret knowledge! That's the pagan, spiritual, myth version at least. It was fascinating to learn, and when we have time, I'll tell you more. But, meanwhile, here is a picture of the symbols and the corresponding letters.

I hope this helps, I'm super excited to hear what your message translates into in English! - All my love, Varv

Pucci read and reread Varv's email. Could this be correct? She retrieved the paper with the symbols from Rosslyn Chapel and compared it to the attached picture Varv sent. They matched! Excited, she started to translate the mysterious symbols into the corresponding English letters. She got the first word completed when she heard the taxi honking below her window out in the street. She stared at the word. *Diombaireachd*. What? Maybe she translated it wrong, or maybe Varv sent her the wrong picture?

She didn't have time to contemplate it any further, the taxi honked again. She grabbed her coat and her favorite notebook and ran out the door.

Chapter 32

The young woman taxi driver held the door open for Pucci as she got in. She was dressed in a puffy navy-blue ski jacket, black turtleneck, and jeans. Her light brown hair cascaded down her jacket. She flipped it back out of her face as she got into her taxi.

"Hello. Thank you for picking me up. My name is Pucci," Pucci said as they began their drive toward the other side of the island.

"Hiya, my name is Tam. Welcome to Islay. How long have ye been on the island?" she asked, peering in the rear-view mirror as she spoke to Pucci. The rising sun illuminated her lively green eyes.

"I arrived yesterday on the ferry at Port Ellen. But it was already sunset, so I didn't really get to see any of the island. What a beautiful place!" Pucci exclaimed, gazing over Loch Indaal on her right, watching seals frolicking in the water.

"I personally think where we're going is the prettiest part of the island. Although, all of us have our own opinions! I understand you want to go to the distilleries? Did you want to include Ardbeg as well?"

"I'd love to see all your distilleries. So many distilleries, not enough time. I should make a T-shirt of that! I've chosen the first two on the Three Distilleries path and then I'd like to go to Kildalton to see the cross. I don't think I'll have time for Ardbeg. Would you have time to do all this with me? Or should I call another taxi after the distilleries?"

"I'd love tae stay with ye. It's a slow day, not a lot of tourists this time of year, so it works out well," Tam said, grinning.

"Oh that's wonderful, thank you, Tam. And, if you have any fun interesting facts along the way, please don't hesitate to fill me in," Pucci said, craning her neck, looking all around the town of Bridgend as they passed through.

"I'll tell you what," Tam said taking a slight left at the edge of town, "I'll take the high, straight road to get us there faster and if we have time when we're coming back, I'll take the long way around through Bowmore."

"Sounds perfect," Pucci said sitting back and enjoying the wide open hills on one side and what looked like a bog out toward the Loch.

"See where those small diggers are?" Tam spoke a few minutes later, pointing to her right at equipment that looked like farm back-and-front hoe tractors. "That's where they're digging up the peat for the distilleries. Used to be the folks that lived here could dig their own for heating their houses, but environmental groups came in and tried to stop anyone from digging up the 3000- to 8000-year-old decayed soil. There was an outcry from the distilleries who needed the peat to create our famous peaty whiskies, so they received special permission. That's what you're seeing."

Pucci could see sections of soil being removed from the brown grassy topsoil by small front diggers. Tam explained each distillery had a different color digger. The stacked peat looked like dark bricks, stacked about seven feet high, waiting to be taken to its designated distiller. They reminded Pucci of large piles of dung.

They drove past the vast fields, heading toward Port Ellen. Pucci got to see the outskirts of the town and the port in the daylight. A giant ferry was coming into port as they drove past.

Tam pulled into Laphroiag just as the sun burst out from the cloud cover. The white buildings lit up like wedding dresses in a display window. Pucci had read that the distilleries were painted white to improve visibility, allowing boats to spot the docks more easily when whisky was transported directly from the distilleries. Additionally, the white lime wash served a practical purpose—it helped deter pests due to its strong scent.

The sun's reflection danced on the mirror-like surface of Loch Laphroaig, with fluffy clouds adding to the enchanting scene. Pucci sat at an empty picnic table as Tam walked inside. She felt embraced by a deep and profound calmness, absolute tranquility, filling her lungs with the salty peaty crisp air. She fingered the cipher around her neck. She desperately hoped to get some answers regarding John and his Aqua Vitae. The distillers might have knowledge about the ancient history of the island's first distillers.

Pucci got up from her serene moment and walked into the tasting room/visitors center, glittering with the crown jewels of Laphroaig. The date etched on the building before she entered, claimed the distillery had been established in 1815—about 300 years too early for her timeline. She approached Tam who was enjoying a "driver's dram." Even designated drivers should be able to enjoy a small sip or two.

Pucci sampled a few offerings as she walked around the center, reading the information on the walls. One fun fact she giggled at:

"During prohibition, Laphroaig could still be bought in America—Ian (the founder) persuaded authorities it was for medicinal purposes—lucky for the American consumers."

Good one, Pucci thought. It actually does cure what ails ya!

Pucci came around a corner and saw a display about the first woman distiller and distillery owner in the twentieth century, Bessie Williamson. A photograph showed a smiling, shrewd-looking woman rocking a pair of cat-eye glasses. A familiar sensation in her stomach signaled to Pucci that a ghost just showed up. She looked behind her, "Hello Bessie, I love the glasses," pointing to the picture.

"Hello, and thank you," Bessie replied, staring at Pucci with a quizzical look. "Ye can see me?" Pucci nodded. "How?"

"It's a gift. Or a curse, depending on the day."

"And today?"

"A gift. What a gift to be able to meet the first women distiller! Not a lot of living folks can say that," Pucci said, smiling, a little starstruck. She had a thought. "Bessie, if you don't mind me asking, could you tell me any ancient history of distilling on Islay?"

Bessie thought for a moment, "Aye, the oldest distillery is Bowmore. They were the first. But there was talk of a man who came over to Islay around the late 1400s or early 1500s, two hundred years before Bowmore. I don't recall anything more. We were so busy with our operation here, I really didn't have time or a life outside this distillery. To this day, we're the world's number one Islay malt whisky," she said, swelling with pride.

Pucci was curious about how ghosts maintain human feelings even in the afterlife. Maybe that's partly what keeps them earthbound.

"Thank you, Bessie. That's actually about the time frame I'm looking for. Um, Bessie, may I ask, why are you still here? Don't you want to cross over into the light?"

"Oh, aye, but not until they get their new whisky distillation process correct. I've been tryin to tell them that the second distillation, they're making the cuts too fast, but no one is listening!" Bessie floated toward a building where, Pucci assumed, the copper stills and the spirit sample safes were located.

Pucci pondered the information that Bessie had given her. She wished she could have talked with her more, but she saw Tam waiting for her by the taxi.

"Hiya. How'd ya get on?" Tam asked.

"Good, thanks. What a beautiful setting for these distilleries. I guess all of them are located near the water for ease of shipping purposes?" Pucci inquired.

"The old distilleries, yes. Some new ones are popping up more inland," Tam said, not elaborating as she pulled the taxi out of the drive, turning right toward Lagavulin.

They had a wonderful time tasting and talking at Lagavulin. Pucci inquired again about any ancient history regarding distilleries. No one had any additional information to share.

The drive out to Kildalton was filled with woodlands on one side, the sparkling loch on the other and glimpses of the snowcapped Beinn an Òir, the highest peak of the Paps of Jura on the island of Jura. The ruin of Dunyvaig Castle silhouetted at the water's edge, with the distillery of Lagavulin in its sights.

Tam pulled into the parking lot in front of the ruined church and walled in graveyard that held the Kildalton Cross. Getting out of the car, she said, "I've never seen this place empty. Usually it's filled with tourists. Ye caught it on a rare day."

Pucci stood to take it all in. The three-foot-high moss-covered rock wall surrounded a ruin of a roofless medieval church, its gravestones of parishioners nestled in the sacred land. There stood the Kildalton Cross, off to the north side of the church, towering over the standing gravestones like a sentinel. She reverently walked into the graveyard, toward the cross. Pucci could see this early Christian cross had carvings of Celtic designs on one side and, according to the sign, biblical scenes on the other. Unfortunately, the carvings were extremely worn from weather and age. Archaeologists had dated it to the second half of the eighth century, before Vikings and Norse settlements besieged Islay. This cross had outlived it all.

She read the sign welcoming folks to the Kildalton High Cross attached to the inside of the stone wall surrounding the perimeter. "Crois Chill Daltain" was written underneath "Kildalton Cross."

"That's Gaelic," Tam said. "Most signs here are in English and Gaelic."

"Oh, thanks, Tam. That makes sense." Pucci said, still reading the rest of the information. "Inspired Carvings" translated to Gaelic as "Obair Snaighidh Deachdaichte." Something stirred in the back of her mind. Something she'd recently seen looked like these letters. Long words with multiple consonants together that made no sense. "Oh my God!" Pucci said out loud. Tam turned back to look at her as she had moved toward the car.

"You OK?" Tam asked, slightly startled at the outburst from this American who seemed to know her whisky.

Pucci didn't respond, too engrossed in the discovery—the word wasn't translated into English, but Gaelic!

"Of course, that makes sense," she murmured. "Let's see . . . Rosslyn wasn't finished until the late 1400s. I bet Gaelic was the prevailing language among the stonemasons. Holy cow, I wonder if their symbols were derived from the Ogham language."

She looked up to see Tam leaning against the car.

"No hurry, Pucci. Take your time. I'm just going tae grab some lunch in the car," Tam called out as she took her lunch box out of the trunk.

Pucci's stomach growled. She hadn't even thought of food given all this excitement and attention out on this glorious land. She decided not to rush back to the room to finish translating. That could wait a little longer. She walked around the graveyard, thankful no ghosts appeared. Climbing up a small hill behind the walled-in structure to take a panoramic photo, she could now clearly see the snowcapped peaks of the mountains over on Jura. The sun illuminated the snow, glistening like tiny diamonds contrasted against the baby blue sky. In the foreground, white sheep dotted the greenest grass Pucci had ever seen, like cotton balls dotting an emerald quilt. The cross stood in silent vigil over it all, awe-inspiring in its solemn presence.

Chapter 33
Olan

Olan turned his head away from the camera at the scene of the gruesome murder. Sara had called her chief, knowing he was on leave, but also knowing he'd want to know about this murder. Still in Oxford, he had drove to the scene on the outskirts of town.

They had identified the body as Mr. Owen Nell of Oxford. Sara's research, which he finally managed to read, identified this man as part of Clouding's inner circle and told a story of Clouding's power manipulation in all aspects of government, law enforcement, money laundering, and smuggling. Blue diamonds, to be exact. Sara had identified five men in Clouding's inner circle. Owen Nell, it read, was mainly involved with money laundering. His background was as an accountant. He had been arrested for embezzlement early in his career. After that, nothing. Clouding must have recruited him.

The rest of the research revealed one thing—Clouding remained untouchable. Evidence vanished without a trace, informants either fell silent or disappeared entirely.

It seemed the smuggling operation was the primary source of funding for his enterprise, covering everything from historical artifacts to precious gems—including the rare blue diamonds. *Unbelievable*, he thought, *my search for the blue diamond smugglers that started in London, Edinburgh, and Grand Cayman has brought me here, to Oxford.*

He pulled his hat down low and turned his collar up against the biting wind. As he trudged away from the crime scene, his steps were slow, heavy with sorrow. Things were falling into place, but major pieces were still missing. He needed to talk to Connor.

Why such a brutal and ritualistic murder? The candles and ancient lettering around the body, the organs removed. Poor bastard. Probably to send a message to anyone else thinking about betraying this lot, he thought. *What did this poor sod do to deserve this brutality? His death would have been slow and excruciating,* given Olan's assessment of the crime scene.

Olan got into his car and dialed Connor.

"Chief."

"Connor, I need your help, again," Olan began.

"Chief, before you say anything, the Carbuncle blue diamond smuggling case is coming to a head. I told the super I needed you to complete this, he reluctantly agreed. You're officially off leave. We need to go to Edinburgh, sir."

"Good. I'll fly out from here. There's usually a nonstop leaving from Oxford twice a day," Olan said, starting the car.

"Excellent, I'm on the flight out of London, gets in around eleven p.m. What did you need from me?"

"I need you to ask Sara for additional information on Clouding and a Mr. Owen Nell. He was just murdered here in Oxford. Sara says he's in Clouding's circle. Ask her to concentrate on any esoteric affiliations. Nell's murder was ritualistic—candles, ancient lettering, and other specific details—I need to understand why, or was it just for show?"

"Right, will do. See you soon then," Connor rang off.

***

Connor spotted Olan sitting at a table in the Edinburgh airport, finishing a sandwich. They exchanged a nod and Olan paid his bill.

"Chief. Car's waiting out front," Connor said and headed toward the exit.

Olan followed, and together they walked out to the waiting unmarked police car. In the front seat were two high-ranking detectives from the Edinburgh office. The passenger door swung open and out stepped a wiry man with a crew cut of red hair and a watchful gaze.

"Hello, I'm Detective Ried, that's Detective Stewart. Welcome to Edinburgh," he said as Olan and Connor got into the car.

"This is Detective Chief Inspector Olan Lathen of Scotland Yard, I think both of you know me, Detective Inspector Connor Davies. The chief inspector has been on this investigation for over three years. He's in charge and will brief your men." The two men up front nodded. "Our undercover detective has provided intel on the main headquarter's hideout. We thought the diamonds were coming out of the famous Cullinan Mine in South Africa, but our investigations—confirmed by our informant—revealed they have someone inside the S. A. Mine. We know their man there. We also know where and how the diamonds are shipped from the mine to the distribution center here in Edinburgh. Our informant sent us a photo of a mailing label, so we know where the diamonds are being shipped to in China, police are standing by. The team in China have been watching the warehouse for the past week and have gathered additional leads on the scale of the operation in their region. They're awaiting our word on when to move, cautious not to jump the gun and alert the smuggling organization—on either side." He continued, speaking to one man up front. "Detective Ried, you'll be in charge of coordinating with China. Detective Stewart, you'll be in charge of the raid on the distribution center. Chief, where do you want me?" Connor asked.

Olan considered for a moment. Connor was good with the lower ranks and the local police. He made them feel part of the operation and included them in celebrated successes. But he wanted Connor with him.

"Davies and I will go to the smugglers' headquarters," said Olan. The three men nodded. "We understand that the primary operation has been shut down in this location, but the two heads of the smuggling operation might still be there. Their names are Alfie Morgan and the lead, a man who goes by the name of Pirate. He's wanted in another matter altogether that somehow ties into all of this."

"The business with the Cheapside Hoard, Chief Inspector?" Detective Ried asked.

Olan was impressed. "Aye, we retrieved the hoard, but he got away from me in Grand Cayman. Not this time." Ried gave out a low whistle.

In the Edinburgh police station, Olan, Connor, and the two Edinburgh officers briefed the special team on the operation ahead. Olan spoke his final words as he passed around a photograph. "Remember, this undercover operative is one of ours. This detective has put her life at monumental risk. Do everything you can to protect, and keep her safe," he emphasized this last statement by looking into everyone's eyes. "Right, let's go."

Chapter 34

As Tam had suggested, she and Pucci took the winding road to Bowmore back. Pucci decided to stay in Bowmore to look around, so she thanked Tam for a great morning, said goodbye, and planned to take the bus back. At a grocery store, she grabbed a sandwich, an apple, and a cola. She found a picnic bench outside of Bowmore distillery and sat next to the water.

After lunch, she checked Bowmore's hours for tastings. They were under construction and closed for a month. She wouldn't be able to tour that famous distillery. *Shoot*, she thought. *Well, that leaves time to try others that weren't originally on the list.*

Pucci caught the bus back to her B and B.

***

Sitting on the bed, Pucci compared her sheet of symbol drawings with Varv's email. She double-checked the first word. It was translated correctly. She continued with the other symbols. They spelled out "nathacomasach**.**" With a possible space between the two words: "Diomhaireachd nathacomasach."

Pucci heard Cat's car drive up alongside of the house, around to the back. She took her message down to Cat to see if she could help. Maybe she knew Gaelic, or at least knew someone who did.

"Hi, Cat!" Pucci said walking into the kitchen where Cat was putting groceries away.

"Hiya. How'd ya get on?" Cat said.

"Oh, Kildalton Cross and that side of the island are magnificent! I had a wonderful time."

"I see you had beautiful weather!" Cat smiled.

Pucci changed the subject. "Cat, do you know Gaelic?"

"Which Gaelic? Scot's, Irish, or Old, middle, or modern?" Cat asked, her eyes twinkled. "Not a lot of folks understand the complexity of the ancient language."

With a mix of curiosity and awe, Pucci looked at her. "I had no idea, Cat. How do you know all this?"

"I studied it in college, along with my nursing degree. I knew I was going to be interacting with all sorts of folks on this island, so I wanted to get to know the language better. We speak Scot's Gaelic, obviously, but because we're so close to Ireland, we also combine some dialects."

"I have a message that I've translated from Ogam, or Ogham, I believe."

"Oh aye!" Cat jumped in. "Ogham is believed to be the original ancient Gaelic writing system. It transitioned into Old Gaelic around the sixth century, I think, if I'm remembering my history. This transition happened mainly with the influence of Christianity. I read it changed rapidly when the Latin educated priests were replacing the Druids priests. Over the centuries, it became what is known as Irish Gaelic and Scot's Gaelic."

"I saw these symbols in my travels," Pucci said, not wanting to give any specifics away to a relative stranger. "I believe the symbols were written around the end of the 1400s. When I translated it, using the Ogham alphabet, this is what I got." She showed Cat the words.

Cat studied the message for a few minutes, after making some tea for the two of them. "Well, I do recognize 'comasach.' That translates into the word 'possible.' So, if that's a separate word, the phrase would be 'Diomhaireachd na tha comasach.' I would translate this into 'The mystery of what is possible.'"

Pucci was amazed and excited. At least she had something closer to what she could decipher, but had absolutely no idea what it meant. "Thank you so much, Cat. You are amazing! But what do you mean, 'I would'? Would someone else translate it differently?"

"Depending on the dialect you learned, someone else might translate it slightly differently. I'll tell you what, go to the Port Charlotte Hotel. There's a bar there where the locals hang out. There's an old gentleman, usually there on Wednesdays. His name is Alasdair. You can't miss him. He might be able to help you with a different translation," she said, turning to feed Angus who had just bounded in from the backyard. "Who's hungry?" A flurry of excited barks from Angus filled the kitchen.

Pucci smiled at the conversation that had started with the dog. She waited till Angus was eating before saying, "Cat, one more thing. May I borrow your phone? My cell isn't dialing a local number correctly. I have an appointment with the distiller at Mhurachaidh Distillery today at five, but I'd like to still make it out to the Kilchoman Distillery. I need to rent another taxi," Pucci said, taking the phone from Cat.

"Oh, why don't I take you? It sounds like it's a short turn around for you, so I'll drive. I've been wanting to go out there and see the new tasting room since they've just finished it. I don't get out on that side of the island much," Cat said, taking back her phone.

They got in the car along with Angus and drove north to catch the road leading west to the distillery, as there was no direct route over the uninhabited hills on this side of the island.

The tasting room and gift shop of this distillery were the largest ones yet, with a restaurant in the back. A friendly woman with kind eyes and short brown hair greeted Pucci at the tasting bar.

"Hiya. Is this your first time here?" she asked.

"Yes! I'm very excited to be here, I've heard lots of great things about your distillery. I understand you are one of the only distilleries on Islay that grow the barley and malt, distill, mature, and bottle all on Islay," Pucci said, taking out her notebook. "The majority of the other distillers send their whisky off the island to be bottled, I believe."

The woman answered proudly, "Aye, the whisky is called 100% Islay. We like to say, 'Single Farm Single Malt Scotch Whisky, produced here at Kilchoman from barley to bottle.' Here's a sample."

"I am writing an article for *Wine and Scotch* magazine and I write a blog as well. Do you mind if I ask you some questions?" Pucci asked. "My name is Pucci Riddle."

"Nice tae meet you, Pucci. I'd love to answer any questions ye have. My name is Freya," she answered, pointing to her name tag. "And whatever I can't answer, I'm sure someone here can."

Freya expressed herself with impressive intelligence and passion. She told Pucci she had been working at the distillery since it opened, but she had been involved in the whisky industry as long as she could remember, just like her parents, and her grandparents before her, here on Islay.

Freya shared a fascinating story about one of their whiskies called Comraich, the Gaelic word for refuge, sanctuary, or asylum. Near the ruined Kilchoman Church, half a mile west of the distillery, stood ancient stones marking a sanctuary—some dating back to the 800s. In medieval times, such sanctuary stones were common, designating areas known as "Comraich," where individuals could seek protection from harassment or arrest.

"This whisky is distributed only to certain bars around the world. The idea is for people to find solace and sanctuary by entering and seeking asylum from their everyday lives, share a dram with each other, sipping this marvelous creation," Freya said.

Pucci nosed the whisky, smelling notes of a slight hint of butterscotch and something like an apple tart. Taking a sip, she let the flavors of deep-roasted peat and creamy vanilla expand in her mouth. As it went down, it was like a balaclava inside her, warming every crevice. Closing her eyes, she pictured a scene of people from different parts of the world, joining together to experience a moment of peace. In the background, a fire crackled while they found comfort and companionship, all with the help of a golden liquid.

She took the sample and walked over to the window as Freya moved to help another customer. She looked out at the fields of barley. Her thoughts turned to her feeling for this amazing island. On Islay, the boundary between its people and the land dissolved into a seamless unity. The rugged terrain and the Ilich, the people of Islay, shared a symbiotic relationship, their lives interwoven in a rich, intricate tapestry. Out of this synergistic energy flowed forth a glorious liquid called whisky, a testament to the deep connection and harmonious bond between the island and its inhabitants.

When Pucci returned to the tasting bar, Freya spoke. "Here's another fun fact, Pucci, your readers might not know. I'm sure you've heard of the Angel's Share—the evaporation of the whisky, about one percent that is 'lost to the angels' during the distilling, maturation, bottling, etc. But, do they know about the Devil's Cut? After aging, when the liquid is removed out of the barrel for bottling, some liquid stays trapped deep inside the wood. That's the Devil's Cut," she shared, grinning. "How did you like our Comraich?"

Even though words were her craft, Pucci found herself speechless. Finally, she managed, "This must be a spirit fit for the gods."

Freya smiled, "The first monk distiller called it 'aqua vitae.' Friar Cor was a monk at Lindores Abbey in Fife. Aqua vitae means 'water of life' in Latin. We like to call it Uisge beatha, pronounced Oosh kih beh-ha, the Gaelic translation, meaning whisky."

Pucci's heart skipped a beat when she heard the Latin words. Davinia had used the exact words Callum once spoke when describing his vision of creating something with John on Islay. As calmly as she could, asked, "Do you happen to have more information about the Latin reference, specifically pertaining to Islay?"

Freya answered, "Sadly no, but one of our distillers knows a historian who specializes in Islay's distilling history. I'll see if he's available. Maybe he could come down here tae meet you."

Twenty minutes later, Freya returned and let Pucci know the distiller had called his friend, and he would be available in about a half hour. Pucci thanked Freya and let her know she'd be in the restaurant.

As Pucci walked up, she found Cat admiring the photographs on the wall. Agreeing that lunch sounded good, they headed into the restaurant. Cat ordered their famous homemade Cullen Skink—smoked haddock chowder with fresh bread—while Pucci opted for a panini sandwich.

They were just about finished when Pucci saw Freya directing a gentleman to their table. He was smartly dressed in a tartan wool suit of deep green. He would have been a tall man in his youth, but now he was hunched over with age. He stood only as high as his back would let him.

He pulled out a chair saying, "Good day to you. I hear you're interested in the history of distilling here on the island." His bushy gray eyebrows lifted in curiosity.

Pucci replied, "Yes, very much so! I'm a journalist, doing a magazine article about the distilleries here on Islay."

"Oh aye." He looked over at Cat. "It's grand tae see you, Catriona. How are you?" He asked, putting his hand on top of hers.

They squeezed hands. "It's good tae see you again too, Mac. I'm doing well, thank you. Pucci, this is Mac."

Pucci wasn't particularly shocked that this elderly man, Mac, was acquainted with Cat, since almost everyone on the island knew each other.

He turned back to Pucci and asked, "How far back do ye want to go?"

"The 1400s. There was a gentleman by the name of John who was the son of Angus Óg. Angus gave John the island of Islay, along with other islands. I believe John came over in the early 1400s? I understand he had a friend by the name of Callum who came over years later, probably to visit John's son, John the Second. It gets a little confusing with all these Johns! I heard—read—they may have started distilling here."

Mac raised one eyebrow and studied Pucci for moment before slowly replying, "Aye. Not a lot of people know that story as it's not documented anywhere. I've only pieced it together from my deep knowledge of Scottish history. I am very much impressed, my dear. Yes—John's son and Callum you say? Interesting. They built a small farm and cottage fairly close to here. I can show you on a map. It's difficult tae find as the ruins are so old—there's not much left. One of John's other sons learned how to distill from a monk, Friar Cor, who was making what we now recognize as whisky at Lindores Abbey on the mainland, and brought the knowledge back to Islay. Although, my guess is their father, John the First, distilled some concoction himself and passed it on to his sons."

"Freya was just telling us about Friar Cor," Pucci said, smiling at Freya as she set down a dram for Mac.

"Slàinte." He took a sip before continuing. "These men of Islay were actually the first to grow, malt, distill, and bottle it for small distribution around the island. Kind of like what Kilchoman is doing today. We believe they even sold some bottles on the mainland in Campbelton. They named the distillery, Stone . . . no, Standing Stone distillery. I think it may have been named after the Cultoon Standing Stone Circle found in this part of the island. I have not had that substantiated by anyone. It's just my little pet theory," he said, winking to both Pucci and Cat.

Pucci was madly taking notes as he was talking. The server cleared the plates, and Pucci brought out the tourist map of Islay. She asked Mac to circle where he believed the ruined barn and cottage were.

Mac took out his readers, studied the map, and put his finger on the location of the Cultoon Stone Circle. With his finger, he followed the road back down closer to Kilchoman distillery and then moved his finger slightly northeast and circled the spot.

"There's actually a small road right here," pointing to the map, "that's not on this map. Drive down that road a ways and you should see the top of the ruined barn. When you see that on the right hand side, park. You'll have to walk to the ruins." Pucci wrote down his instructions.

"Really Mac?" asked Cat. "I did not know that anything was out there."

Mac smiled. "This history is not very well known. A few of us old, retired historians, not many of us left now, know about it. It's not written anywhere, it's been handed down in stories."

Both Pucci and Cat said, "You need to write a book!"
They all laughed.
Mac chuckled and said, "Aye, I might just do that."
"Thank you, Mac. This has been extremely helpful and fascinating," Pucci said, paying the bill.

"Nae bother, I always enjoy a wee dram with old and new friends."

***

Pucci bought driver dram samples as she could not take any of the large bottles in their beautifully crafted boxes back home with her. No room in the suitcase! She desperately hoped that San Diego had all these available except, of course, the whisky that is only sold at the distillery.

As they were driving back, Cat asked, "Should we see if we could at least find this place? Do you have time before your interview?"

Pucci looked at her watch and weighed the importance of finding the old ruins with being slightly late for a distiller. She opted to take Cat's offer. They drove to where Mac had drawn a little notch, approximately where the road should be on the map. It was there, on their left. Cat steered onto a rutted, rain-slicked dirt road, the car lurching with every bump. Pucci clutched the door handles, their bodies jostled about like a ride in a rickety rollercoaster. They drove about a half a mile, craning their necks to the right to see if they could glimpse the ruins over the top of the high grass growing near the road. Cat finally saw it out her side of the car, through a gap in the grass.

Pucci marked the spot more precisely on her map and documented how long it took after they turned off of the main highway to glimpse the ruins, deciding to come back early in the morning.

Cat turned around with great difficulty on the narrow road, executing repeated K-turns. Mud caked up underneath her car and on the tires. She seemed not to care and smiled.

"I love learning new things about my island."

***

Pucci thanked Cat for a wonderful outing. She rescheduled the appointment with the distiller. She needed time to think.

Pucci set the small bottles she'd purchased on the dresser. She'd pack them later. She sat on her bed and wondered. What was the significance of the old distillery? Why did Davinia tell Pucci that she would find answers there? Could that ruined site actually be John's distillery, the John from the note they found in Rosslyn Chapel? *'I cannot risk the sacred piece being here. They have killed Lady Davinia. I have given it to John for safekeeping elsewhere.'* Did this John bring it—whatever was hidden in Rosslyn—here? Could it be another piece of the cipher? If so, what did he do with it? And what was this 'sacred piece'?

"Oh, this is so frustrating!" she exclaimed, punching her fists down at her sides. "Damn, I really wish I could talk to Randi or Varv about this. OK, Pucci, instead of focusing on what we don't know, focus on what we *do know*. Maybe that will help to figure out next steps." She grabbed her notebook and sat in the window seat, watching the light fade and the loch's surface change from blue to black. She wrote:

- Oliver murdered: connected to the murdered man from Oxford, seen in bar in the Randolph Hotel giving something to Oliver.
- Pirate possibly seen fleeing the crime scene in Oxford.
- Jeweled cipher: Davinia recognized mine. She was murdered for a similar one, which was stolen from her.
- Davinia's story of King Solomon's Temple: how the knights discovered artifacts in the ruins when they were encamped on Temple Mount in Jerusalem. Artifacts infused with King Solomon's magic, used to control evil spirits.
- Rosslyn symbols on ceiling: Ogham to Gaelic, translated to 'mystery of what is possible.'

- Note found in Rosslyn Chapel: connected to the Knights Templar, referencing a 'sacred piece.' Davinia said there was another piece like mine hidden in the chapel. The note must refer to that.
- When the ciphers are brought together, do they hold the key to where the Knights hid one of King Solomon's artifacts?
- Found a distillery that could be Davinia's John: what's the significance? Did he have a cipher piece? Did he bring it to Islay?
- Jewelry box found in Oliver's coat . . .

Pucci was caressing the jeweled cipher around her neck as she wrote. When she wrote the last line, the cipher began to buzz in between her fingers. Her intuition on high alert, she went to the dresser to retrieve the jewelry box that she removed from Oliver's coat. Gently removing the piece from around her neck, she lowered it into the open box. The indentations left from whatever was once in there fit almost exactly. *My God, Oliver must have had another piece of the cipher*, Pucci thought, *that must be what the man in the Randolph Hotel gave him. I've got to talk to Oliver.* "Oliver," she said out loud, hoping he would hear her and appear. "Oliver," a little louder this time. She waited. Nothing. *I need to go back to where he died*, she thought. A lot of ghosts will dwell in the area where they died, sometimes confused about where to go, waiting for someone to help them.

After placing the cipher back around her neck, snapping the jewelry box shut, she put on her coat, bundling up, and snuck down the stairs, hoping Cat wouldn't hear her.

She walked back to the distillery and the barrel storeroom where she had found Oliver's body. The distillery was deserted, the back door still open. She stood by the bloodstain on the floor. She called out to Oliver. No answer. She walked down a row of whisky barrels, looking for Oliver, when she heard someone cry out.

"Look out, Pucci!"

It sounded like Oliver! With a jolt of panic, she turned just in time to evade a large wooden plank, its rough edges inches from her face. The hooded man gripping the other end. Her scream echoed through the warehouse.

"Over here, men, quick!" a man called out from the entrance.

The hooded figure dropped the plank with a thud and ran in the opposite direction. Pucci, her heart racing, adrenaline pumping through her, suddenly felt faint, stars popping into her vision. She slowly sunk to the floor. The next thing she saw were several feet and felt hands pulling her up. They kept their hands around her arms as she swayed slightly.

"Ms. Riddle?" a police officer said.

Pucci looked up, "Yes."

"Yer under arrest for the murder of Oliver Williams-Tanaka."

Chapter 35

Olan

Olan and Connor arrived at the building that concealed the entrance to the close—the hidden passage the smugglers used as their headquarters. They stepped out of their unmarked car. Officers of the Armed Response Units strategically placed themselves around the area to block multiple exit points from the building. They waited for Olan's command.

The two approached the building that held the hidden door to the close. They were about to enter quietly when they heard a voice shout.

"I wouldn't do that if I were you, Lathen!"

Olan spun around, his stomach plummeting. Halfway down an alley to the right of the building, Morgan stood with unsettling calm, his gun pressed against Anya's skull.

"Dinnae move, or I'll put a bullet in yer undercover snitch," he said, sneering as he cocked the gun. They were standing next to a van near the back. Olan could see Anya's hands were tied. Fear and desperation were in her eyes.

Olan held up his hands showing he was unarmed. Connor stayed dead still, watching his chief.

Olan moved slightly toward Morgan, "Don't do anything stupid, Morgan. You're surrounded, you can't get away from here. Drop your weapon, and you'll be charged with smuggling—not the murder of a Scotland Yard detective."

"She's my ticket out of here. You think I don't have a plan? You're an idiot, Lathen. Step back and tell your lads not to follow or she's dead. Whiley warned me you'd be coming. Seems your lads in South Africa at the S. A. Mine jumped the gun. Whiley got word to me," Morgan said calmly. He knew damn well the police wouldn't do anything to endanger Anya—she was one of their own.

"Let her go, Morgan."

"I don't think so," he said, shoving Anya into the back of the van. He ran up to the driver's seat and jumped in. He started it up and careened backward down the alley. Tire smoke and screeching noises filled the air. Olan ran down the alley toward the van as Morgan backed into a nearby street, throwing the van into drive, and sped away. Olan heard a gunshot. He didn't know if it was at the van, or in the van. *God, no. It can't be Anya*, he thought.

***

Connor ran back to the unmarked car, jumped in, and sped toward Olan. As he pulled up to the curb, Olan leaped into the passenger seat, yelling, "Go! Go!"

They sped down the alley and turned right where Morgan had turned, following him. There were so many tributaries off the alley, they couldn't be sure they chose the right route. The van was not in sight.

"Where the hell did it go, Davies?" Olan asked in desperation.

Connor didn't answer. He turned down another street, frantically looking.

Olan got on the phone to the head of the Armed Forces Unit. "Did you see where they went?"

"No sir," was the answer.

"Did any of your men fire?" Olan heard a muffled question before the man came back on the phone.

"No, sir."

His grip tightened on the phone. Dread coiled in his gut.

***

Olan and Connor drove around for another hour, searching. The sun began to rise over Edinburgh. Connor looked up out of the windshield to watch a police helicopter fly over.

"They got the air unit mobilized, sir," Connor said. "We'll find them."

Heading back to the station, Olan was silent. He couldn't lose Anya. Not after all she'd sacrificed for years on this assignment. Olan had learned about her undercover status on Grand Cayman. He couldn't tell anyone, not even Pucci.

Before Connor was assigned to Grand Cayman, he had heard whispers in the London office that an undercover officer was already in place. He was later instructed to completely ignore her if he ever came across her on the island. What he hadn't expected was to recognize Anya at a jewelry store in Georgetown. They had worked together on a previous case right before she went undercover, but when their paths crossed again—both deep in their respective covers— they had to pretend not to know each other.

Connor considered her a friend and an excellent detective, but he kept his orders. He didn't even tell Olan about her presence in Grand Cayman—not until their recent meeting at Edinburgh Airport, when they finally admitted they had both been sitting on the same intel.

The station was buzzing with frantic activity. A monitor had been set up to watch the helicopter camera. Calls were coming in constantly from all the units looking for the van. No sightings so far. And no sign of Pirate.

As Olan and Connor searched for the van, officers searched the headquarters. It had yielded nothing—their operation was completely shut down. Olan and Connor went to the hideout later in the afternoon to see for themselves. Olan found drops of blood on the floor. He told the crime scene team to get a sample and walked out.

Olan was briefed on the bad news at the end of the day. A whole day wasted. Connor brought news of the bust at the S. A. Mine. Whiley wasn't talking. He claimed he didn't know anything about a smuggling operation. Connor could only report that were no new findings on the rumored large raw blue diamonds. Must have been a rumor.

Olan went into a vacant office and shut the door. He needed to think, to figure out his next move. It was late and he needed food. He hadn't eaten since the airport, over 24 hours ago. There wasn't really anything else he could do here. Connor and the rest of the force were doing everything they could to find Anya.

A uniformed officer knocked once and opened the door. Annoyed, Lathen looked up.

"Phone call for you, Chief Inspector, line one," he said and shut the door.

Olan was surprised. Who would call on the landline? He picked up the phone, pressed line one.

"This is Detective Chief Inspector Lathen."

"Chief Inspector? Finally. I was told ye'd be there when I called Scotland Yard, lookin for ye," said the Scottish accented voice on the other end.

"Who is this?"

"Och, sorry. This is Detective MacKay of Oban. I've been sent over to Islay tae investigate a murder, sir."

Olan sat up. "Aye."

"We've arrested a woman for the murder. She claims an acquaintance with you, Chief Inspector. Her name is Pucci Riddle."

Chapter 36

Pucci spent the night in the police station on a cot in a small windowless room with a door locked from the outside. No phone call was allowed. She didn't know who she would call anyway. She didn't know if Olan would even talk to her.

In the morning, a police woman moved Pucci into a cramped room, likely meant for interrogations, it had no windows and four stark white walls. A metal door loomed behind her. A table stood in the center, surrounded by five wooden chairs—one at her side, three across from her. A couple more lined the wall. The setup struck her as oddly multipurpose. Did they also use this as a lunchroom?

The scene was all too familiar. Back at the Georgetown Police station, she'd been grilled about the death of JD Langer—the ghost who had asked Pucci for help. That was a mistaken arrest as well. Why did she keep finding herself in these positions? *I guess when you deal with death, you're bound to be caught up in murder*, she thought.

Thankfully Sirius, her spirit dog was by her side. His wolf-like coat of black fur, the white-speckles on his nose, the soft patch on his chest, and that ever-curly tail—it was all a comforting, familiar sight that eased her heart. He appeared to her in spirit, just as he had been when he was her beloved pet in this life. He had also appeared in Georgetown, protecting her from bad guys at that police station, ready to bite their butts. The Scottish police seemed to be kinder than those in Grand Cayman. Still, Sirius brought comfort.

Back in Georgetown, Olan had intervened on her behalf. He had vouched for her work with Scotland Yard to the lead detective. Thanks to him, she was released immediately. Would he come again? She doubted it. There was nothing to worry about—the police had nothing on her. She didn't even know why they arrested her.

The door opened. "Miss Riddle, I'm Detective MacKay from Oban. Islay doesn't have many resources for murder cases, so I flew over tae help out." He took a chair across from her. He was in his late forties, his thinning strawberry blonde hair sticking out at all angles. His brown wool suit was well made, but not tailored to his medium frame, and was a size too big. His maroon knitted tie was surely from the seventies. Pucci liked him immediately. She smiled. He responded with a slight grin, then dropped it. "This is a serious matter, Miss Riddle." Sirius growled, but only Pucci could hear.

"Why have you arrested me, detective? And did anyone bother to look for the person that tried to hit me with a large board?"

"A few reasons. A witness saw a women fleeing the scene on the day of the murder matching yer description, running in the direction of the bed and breakfast where ye're staying. Plus, the large wooden plank looked like it had been lying there on the floor for quite a while, not just dropped by someone you say, tried to kill you."

"Unbelievable, detective. I almost died, and you're claiming I'm lying."

"We found a fingerprint on the neck of the deceased. And, when my lads entered that fingerprint into the system, guess who came up? Seems you have a record for getting arrested." He leaned back in the chair.

Pucci searched her memory of why her prints could have been on Oliver. She *had* checked his pulse on his neck to see if he was still alive. Damn.

MacKay watched her carefully. His instincts told him she was no murderer, but the evidence pointed otherwise.

"Why was your fingerprint—in blood, I might add—found on the victim?"

Pucci's stomach clenched. Her mind raced. She looked down on her healed fingers under the table. Sirius sniffed her hands, giving a comforting lick. *Oh no*, she thought, her heart sinking. *I scrapped my fingers on the wall outside the distillery. I must have checked for a pulse while they were still bleeding. How the hell am I going to get out of this?*

She decided on stall tactics. "Detective, did someone call Detective Chief Inspector Lathen of Scotland Yard? He can vouch for me."

"You're not answering my questions, Miss Riddle."

Pucci started to panic. How was she going to explain this? MacKay didn't look like he would believe her story about Oliver's ghost coming to her.

MacKay continued. "And, I understand that ye and the victim," he opened his folder on the desk, "Oliver Williams-Tanaka, had words at one of the distilleries. What are the odds, Miss Riddle," he leaned forward, staring into her eyes, "that two people that don't like each other, are on this wee island at the same time, havin' a barney in one of our distilleries, and now one ends up dead?"

"I'll ask you again, detective, did you call the chief inspector?" desperation started to creep into Pucci's voice.

"Yes, I called the chief inspector," he thought he'd bluff. "He said he'd never heard of you."

The door opened. "That's actually not quite true, MacKay," Olan said, walking in the small room.

Pucci's heart leapt. Sirius started barking and circling Olan's legs.

"I said I *wished* I'd never heard of her," he said to Pucci, a sarcastic grin on his face. He raised one eyebrow.

Pucci couldn't help herself, she leaped up out of her chair and hugged him tight. It was so unexpected, Olan didn't have time to move his arms around her.

She broke free, still standing a breath away, "Thank God you're here."

"We've got to stop meeting like this, lass."

Chapter 37

"Guid mornin, Chief Inspector," MacKay standing, taken aback at Olan's sudden entrance that caught him in a bluff.

"Guid mornin to you, MacKay. This woman isn't a murderer, but I am anxious to hear her explanation of all your evidence against her," Olan said, guiding Pucci back to her chair. He moved another chair toward the table, and sat on the end, kitty-corner to Pucci and MacKay. As he removed his signature trench coat, Pucci noticed he had zipped in the wool lining. More insulation needed here than in the Caribbean islands.

The two men scrutinized her. Pucci composed herself. Sirius looked up at her and nodded his approval curling up at her feet.

"Now that I have someone here that actually might believe me, I'll tell you the truth, and what I know," Pucci said.

Suddenly, the door burst open again. Cat was breathing heavily, an officer behind her, looking very annoyed. "I can vouch for this woman, she's done nothing wrong!" Cat loudly exclaimed. "She's a good person; she'd never hurt anyone."

"Rest assured, mum, we just need to get the facts. If you have any information regarding this incident, please let this officer know. He can take your statement," MacKay was formal and polite. He nodded to Officer Parr to remove Cat.

Pucci's heart swelled with appreciation, knowing she had another advocate on the island. Even though they hadn't known each other long, she felt a kinship to Cat. Pucci smiled and mouthed, "Thank you" as Cat backed out of the room.

"OK, let's try again," MacKay said, closing the door.

Pucci took a breath, gathering her thoughts. She needed to figure out how to tell these guys how she found Oliver's body, without revealing that his ghost had told her.

"Let me start at the beginning, Detective MacKay. I came to Scotland to write an article for an American magazine, *Wine and Scotch*, that specializes in information about top-shelf and unique alcohol. I am a journalist and a blogger, sir. I have always wanted to come to Islay, as this is the famous island for peated scotch whiskies, as you're well aware. By the way, I love the whisky from the town you're from, MacKay. Anyway, I flew into London, and for unrelated reasons, I visited Oxford." She glanced at Olan. He raised an eyebrow.

She continued. "That's where I first encountered Oliver Williams-Tanaka on this trip. He and I are in similar fields, but he is more established, well respected, and an expert in all things alcohol. I believe he found me as a threat, an upstart, and over the years, he took every opportunity to discredit me online, on my blog, in comments, and in his own articles. We ran into each other a few times at conferences. He always took the time to call me out as a hack. So you see, detective, there was no love lost between us. When I walked into the bar at the Randolph Hotel in Oxford, I was shocked to see him. We had words there as well. Yes, I even said I wished he were dead." Olan shook his head. MacKay looked up from his notes, both eyebrows raised.

"Before either of you say anything, please, let me continue. Olan—sorry, Chief Inspector—when I was there, I observed an exchange. Oliver accepted a package from a man who, I just saw in the newspaper headlines, was recently brutally murdered."

Olan sat up. The hair on his arms did as well. "What do you mean, Pucci?"

"At the B and B where I'm staying here on Islay, the innkeeper, Catriona—the woman who just burst in here—had a newspaper. The headlines caught my eye. Then I saw the headshot of the man who was murdered, and I recognized him from the hotel bar. He gave something to Oliver. I'm now thinking that whatever that was, it got both of them murdered."

"Pucci, this is incredible. What you're saying means that this murder ties into what we were investigating in Oxford," Olan said with intensity.

"What are you two talking about?" MacKay asked.

"It's a very long and complicated story, MacKay. And, no need to focus on it, yet. Pucci, continue on with what happened here," Olan directed.

"I left Oxford for Edinburgh and lo and behold, Oliver was on the same train. He was now accompanied by a younger man in a hoodie and jeans. I never could see his face. I overheard Oliver say something about sticking to the plan and going to Islay. I didn't hear anything else before he saw me and moved away. I hoped that they weren't going to Islay, as that was my destination as well after a stop in Edinburgh.

"So, when I walked into Mhurachaidh Distillery, and saw Oliver was there, my stomach turned cold. He bullied me, again, in front of people in the tasting room. That's why we had words, or a barney, as you say. After I left the distillery, I went to a shop and bought a little food. When I was walking back, I saw Oliver and the man in the hoodie creeping around the distillery. I didn't think anything more of it, and returned to Cat's." She paused. "Detective MacKay, I'm a person with very strong intuition. It often turns out to be right. The chief inspector can vouch for me. Later that night, I got an intuitive 'hit,' as I like to call them, a feeling that something was wrong, that something had happened to Oliver."

Olan nodded, "She's helped Scotland Yard quite a few times, using her psychic abilities."

Pucci was surprised that Olan had actually used the 'psychic' word in front of MacKay. MacKay leaned back in his chair. Pucci could feel skepticism come up in him, but he looked at Olan with respect.

She continued. "I crept into the distillery around one or two in the morning, I didn't get the exact time. I scraped my fingers on the rough wall outside the storage warehouse. They were bleeding. When I got inside and found Oliver's body, I knew he was already dead, but I checked for a pulse, that's why my bloody fingerprint was on his body."

"Why were you back in the warehouse when we arrested you, Miss Riddle?" MacKay asked.

This was going to be even harder to explain. She chose not to mention the jewelry box she had taken from Oliver's coat—at least not yet. She'd tell Olan when they were alone.

She sighed, playing the concerned citizen. "I just felt like I needed to help somehow and decided to go back to where I found his body and look for clues."

"Instead of calling the police, and letting them know what you found?" MacKay sounded annoyed.

Olan held up his hand for MacKay to back off. Pucci was grateful.

"I know it was stupid, but something told me to go there. I didn't find anything and was just about to leave when I heard . . . " she thought back now to what she did hear. Was it Oliver that gave her a warning? Why would he try to save her?

"Heard what, Miss Riddle?"

"I heard a noise behind me and saw a giant beam coming down on my head. If I hadn't screamed and moved, I would have been dead, detective." Pucci's voice was fierce.

"Pucci, what happened? Did you see who it was that tried to kill you?" Olan asked, reaching over, gently placing his hand on her hand.

She felt a warmth spreading through her. "I believe it was the man in the hoodie, but I only saw a figure that was hooded, nothing else."

Olan nodded. "MacKay, given all this information, I believe you need to start scouring the island for a man in a hoodie that came onto the island recently, traveling with Williams-Tanaka. He shouldn't be that hard to find. It's not a large island. You can release Ms. Riddle to my custody if you still have questions, but she's no longer a suspect. Agreed?"

MacKay hesitated. Sirius stood up, ready to bite his butt.

"Agreed."

Chapter 38

Pirate

Oxford, two days earlier

Pirate did what he needed to do to make the scene look like a ritualistic murder. He followed Clouding's instructions perfectly, arranging the victim's hands, the ancient symbols, the organ removal. He walked away before the man died.

Pirate drove about a mile, got out of his car on the side of the road and vomited. *This was it*, he thought. *I'm done. After the payment of the diamonds, I'll disappear. Evil will come for me, not them. They keep their hands clean.* The shadows had already started to close in. He had heard the whispers creeping though the silence. His gaze darted wildly. Fear gripped him. Every monstrous act, every murder—what awaited him on the other side?

When Nell was begging for his life, he'd told Pirate how he'd taken the cipher from the hidden compartment in Clouding's sacred room and given it to Williams-Tanaka. Nell had found out that, through years of extensive research, Clouding had discovered a connection to a historic distillery on Islay—even older than Bowmore. Nell had heard about Williams-Tanaka's expertise regarding the history of distilleries and hired him to help find the other cipher. Nell entrusted the sect's cipher to Williams-Tanaka, hoping it would create an energetic connection to the other piece to help locate the second one.

Nell said he wanted the cipher and the treasure for himself. He was sick of being low man in the sect. He would show them. Nell had overheard Clouding talking one night about the cipher's history. There were three pieces and when joined, the ciphers were thought to form some sort of key that would open a hidden compartment in Rosslyn Chapel that held an ancient artifact of King Solomon's. Legends claimed this artifact could somehow control evil spirits. Nell admitted he had enlisted Manier from the sect to follow Williams-Tanaka and find the second cipher. When they found it, kill Williams-Tanaka to keep him from talking. Manier was expected to bring back the two ciphers to Nell, in exchange for a considerable sum of money.

Talking to himself, Pirate wiped his mouth on his sleeve. "So, these ciphers form some sort of key to open a compartment that holds an artifact capable of manipulating or controlling evil. Now I know why Clouding and this sect want it so badly. Clouding said something about ultimate power. I know the Riddle woman has a piece. Now, since Nell—idiot—stole their piece, where is it? It must still be on Islay. I need to contact Manier."

Assigning Eric Manier from the original gang from the hoard heist to Williams-Tanaka without Clouding—or even Nell—realizing it had been a calculated risk, but one that paid off, he thought as he sat in the driver's seat. *Nell believed it was his idea all along, which worked to my advantage. Manier had proven his worth when he helped steal the Cheapside Hoard a year ago, but he failed to retrieve the most critical piece—the cipher. That fell into the hands of the Riddle woman. He saw she had found it back on Grand Cayman at the restaurant. An unforeseen complication.* He caught his reflection in the rearview mirror. "But now, I have the chance to retrieve both ciphers."

Pirate drove into Oxford, and parked behind Clouding's house, making sure no one saw him. He felt the energy before he descended the stairs. Waves of negative, dark, cobweb-like energy billowed up from the ritual room below. The main, larger gathering room was empty. He heard the distant murmur of chanting and walked toward the cave below the basement. This room was used only for esoteric work to move into the other side of the veil, in-between worlds. *This is how they had communicated to him when he was in Grand Cayman. This was how they had watched him for all those months.*

He crept down the stairs, hands on both sides of the moist stone walls, careful not to slip on the mold-covered worn stone steps. The air was dank and cold, and got colder as he descended. At the bottom of the stairs was a dimly lit corridor, and at its end, a large wooden door framed in black metal.

The chanting grew louder and faster, a rhythmic pulse of low, guttural voices weaving through the air as he walked towards the door. The words, ancient and indecipherable, carried the cadence of Latin or perhaps old Gaelic, each syllable rolling into the next like a hypnotic incantation. The negative energy pounded fiercely in his head. A wave of malignant energy hit him so powerfully that he felt it physically, in his stomach, he keeled over.

Suddenly, the chanting stopped. He stood up, leaning against the frigid wall for support, and crept forward and slowly opened the door. At the threshold to the cave, he saw the remnants of a dark energy ritual. Four men, cloaked in robes, stood in some sort of trance around the center altar, dripping with blood from their wrists.

Each of the four men, shrouded in red robes had bled into metal bowls. A sacred blade lay next to their bowls. In his black robe, Clouding stood in the north end of the alter. In his right hand, he held a sacred Highland dirk, a long knife historically used in Scotland for skinning and cutting through animal bone. It was also used as a close-combat weapon. This one, however, was used for evil. With a raw blue diamond embedded at the end of its handle, it radiated such energy that it emitted a visible glow. In his other hand,

Clouding held a book of great antiquity and read an incantation in Latin. He brought the knife to his forehead as the others dipped their finger in their own blood and brought their hand to their foreheads, mimicking Clouding.

Pirate could feel they were not in this world. He took his place in the back of the room, the only witness to this dark ritual, concentrating on holding the negative energy at bay.

Waiting. He kept what he had learned from Nell to himself, guarding the knowledge carefully. Finding the three pieces of the cipher would be his task alone.

As the men emerged from their trance, two of them collapsed, drained from exhaustion and blood loss. Pirate stepped over them and faced Clouding.

"What did you 'see'?" Pirate asked without any preamble. He could tell Clouding was weak as well. *Good, his powers are diminished, he won't be able to read what I have learned from Nell*, he thought.

"We saw another piece of the cipher on Islay. Manier is there. He must have been working for Nell, damn him. He has our piece with him and looking for another piece of the triad on Islay." Clouding hissed.

"I'll handle Manier. I'll get him back over here and get the cipher from him."

"Yes, and dispose of him as you did Nell. No one betrays us."

"Right," was all Pirate said.

"We also saw the Riddle woman. What the hell is she doing on Islay? You didn't tell me she had the cipher that you were supposed to retrieve from the hoard." As Clouding's strength returned, his anger grew.

"I lost her in Glasgow. I didn't know she was on Islay."

"Find her, find Manier and retrieve the stolen cipher and the one the Riddle woman has. Find the last piece on Islay. They are rightfully mine!" Barely containing his fury, Clouding stormed out of the chamber.

Chapter 39

Morgan and Anya

Morgan navigated the twisting side streets of Edinburgh, keeping to the shadows. The city offered plenty of places to disappear—for now. He gripped the wheel tighter, his mind working through the next move.

Having earlier been shot by Morgan, Anya was slumped in the back of the van, her breathing ragged. Blood seeped from the wound in her upper thigh, pooling beneath her. She was fading fast.

His jaw tightened. He needed to get rid of her—soon. Dead or alive, she was no longer of any value to him. The only thing that mattered now was getting the three blue diamonds from Whiley and vanishing. He didn't need the dead weight—or all of Scotland Yard hunting him down.

After a few hours, he drove the van to a hidden car he'd stashed on the outskirts of town. He threw an unconscious Anya in the back seat of the old maroon Morris Minor, circa 1970s. The police wouldn't be looking for this car. He smiled, proud of his preplanned escape.

He drove into the country, toward Glasgow, heading for his family cottage in the middle of nowhere near a tiny village near Broxburn. His parents had left him the cottage, hoping maybe he would come home to it before they died. He didn't make it and didn't give a damn. But now, it would function as a hideout. He'd lie low a few days and plan his next move.

***

Anya groaned in the back seat. She didn't want to admit to herself she was weak and getting weaker by the minute from loss of blood. Her constant self-talk about how stupid she had been back in the hideout wasn't helping either. Why didn't she see it coming? She had felt Morgan's energy shift when he got off that damn phone. Pucci had taught her to trust her intuition. She hadn't and had been caught off guard. In moments, he had the gun pointed to her head, demanding her phone. He flipped through the photos and saw the ones she had taken of the package being mailed to China, and the cryptic messages she had sent to Scotland Yard. Even though he couldn't decipher them, he knew she had betrayed him.

Her hands still tied; she tried to stem the blood flow by wrapping part of her ripped shirt around the wound. The bullet had hit a major artery and gone clean through. If it had hit the femoral, she'd be dead by now. She sat up, trying to see where they were going. Her vision blurred, dark spots filled her view, and she lost consciousness.

Morgan pulled into the driveway of the abandoned cottage. He got out of the car, pulled the passed-out Anya out of the car into the garage at the back of the property that had no room for a car, but enough room for a body. He left her there to die.

Chapter 40

Pucci walked out of the police station and into the crisp, icy air. The sunlight was bright and hinted deceptively at warmth, but the chill was unmistakable. Cat had left the police station and returned to her B and B. Olan walked behind Pucci. He stopped, wanting to wrap his coat around her and pull her into his warmth, to feel her body against his.

Pucci felt his presence behind her. The electric heat of their closeness sent a shiver through her. She leaned her body into his. They stood, savoring the moment of unspoken passion pulsing through them.

"I need tea," Pucci broke the silence, bumping off Olan's chest. She followed him to his rented car. They drove down the street toward the Bowmore Distillery and spotted a sign for tea, upstairs in a bookstore near the distillery. The car ride only took a few minutes, as it was right down the street from the station. No time for her to ask how he was doing.

The bookstore had jewelry, clothing, and fun knick-knacks besides books. Pucci realized she hadn't had time to do any touristy things, like buy a baseball hat that said Islay. She picked up a baby blue hat, tilting it slightly before settling it on her head.

"I'll buy that for you," Olan murmured, his gaze lingering just a moment too long. A slow smile curved his lips. "It brings out your eyes."

They went upstairs, ordered two cream teas and sat at a small table by the window. The sun was streaming in, taking off the last of the chill of the morning.

Pucci studied Olan's face. It still showed signs of deep worry, but the wear from alcohol, the glassy, watery eyes and pasty skin were fading. He felt her eyes on him. "I haven't had a drink for a while now, Pucci. Six days. I stopped since you found me at the bar," he said, dropping his head shamefully.

"I can feel that, Olan. I'm happy for you," she smiled. "And, once again, like Georgetown, thank you for saving me back there."

"Aye. Now, Ms. Riddle, catch me up. What are you doing here, and what really happened with the murdered man?"

"Oy, where to begin," she paused as the tea, scones, clotted cream and jam, were delivered to the table. She added a dab of milk to her tea and took a sip. She buttered her scone, added a smear of clotted cream and took a large bite, and another sip of tea, savoring the flavor of the two tastes together in her mouth. "You just can't duplicate this taste in the US. Must be the water. OK, Olan, where to begin? I will assume Detective Davies gave you Valerie's diary. Did you follow up with the Oxford house?"

Olan shook his head in frustration. "I found the house just as you did. Which, I might add, was incredibly stupid of you, Pucci. You put yourself and this investigation in danger." He paused, taking a breath. "I met the owner, a Mr. Clouding. I've since learned that we have an extensive file on him and his mates. We have never been able to trace anything illegal back to him. He has powerful men in high places on his payroll. We get close, but no charges ever seem to stick, extortion, money laundering, etc. Owen Nell, the murdered man, was in Clouding's inner circle. He died a horrible death by having his organs exposed while the tide came up and eventually drowned him. What we have been able to dig up is Clouding and company have esoteric ties to a sect. Dark magic. My gut says Clouding is the ringleader. I know Pirate works for him, which Valerie found out as well when she followed Pirate to the Oxford house. I also believe Pirate murdered Nell, based on a witness of a 'shadowed man' leaving the scene."

Pucci ignored the scolding. She knew he was right, but water under the bridge. She nodded at his assessment of Pirate.

"Yes, I read that, too. So, Mr. Smith's real name is Clouding. The dark sect makes sense given the negative energy that accosted me at that house." She saw Olan's pained expression. "I know, I know. OK, moving on. I already mentioned the incident with Oliver being handed that package at the Randolph Hotel. From Oxford, I went to Rosslyn Chapel. You remember I told you about the Knights Templar ghost attached to the jeweled cipher we found in the reliquary locket in Grand Cayman? That ghost told us to go to Rosslyn Chapel, as the answers are there." She pulled out the jeweled cipher from underneath her sweater. She saw Olan pull a face. "No safer place to hide it, in my opinion." He shook his head again, but she thought she caught the hint of a smile. She told him about the note they found in Rosslyn Chapel. The clues in the library in Strathhammond, leaving out Braden MacNevin, the earl. She told Olan about the ghost of Lady Davinia in the castle and how her lover had ties to an old distillery on Islay.

"Davinia also told us a story of King Solomon's Temple and his artifacts that were under the protection of the Knights Templar. Davinia's lover was a descendant of the Knights. So, almost firsthand knowledge, so to speak."

Finally, Pucci told him she thought she'd found the old distillery—the ruins she and Cat saw through the grass—that might hold a clue to another cipher.

"When I saw Oliver's ghost, he was trying to retrieve something from his coat, but of course, he couldn't. So I went over to his body and searched the pocket of his coat. I found a small black jewelry box. It was empty. This cipher," she pointed to her necklace, "fits almost perfectly in the indentation in the box. I think Nell stole it from the Oxford house."

"So given everything you just told me, Nell stole a cipher piece from Clouding, then gave it to Williams-Tanaka, who brought it here to Islay. And you found the box but no cipher. Why bring the cipher here?"

"The only thing I can think of is the Oxford sect might have learned about the cipher's movements—or perhaps they knew about another piece that had also ended up on Islay. If they performed divination on their cipher before it was stolen, they could have psychically traced its connection to the others." Olan's puzzled look prompted Pucci to clarify.

"Divination works by establishing an energetic link between similar objects, almost like a mystical resonance. That could explain how they knew to search the Cheapside Hoard," she said, thoughtful, the idea still unfolding in her mind.

She continued. "My theory? The sect—or maybe just Clouding, and Nell found out—connected the cipher to an ancient distillery on an island, but no further. Through divination, they likely saw fragmented images, lingering echoes of its location. With this knowledge of an ancient distillery, Nell enlisted Oliver Williams-Tanaka, the foremost authority on whisky history, which brought Oliver to Islay. My guess is that Nell suspected if Oliver had its counterpart, the connection might amplify, making the missing piece easier to locate. That's why he lent it to him."

"You're way out of my realm, Pucci. But I trust your intuition."

She smiled, accepting the compliment and continued. "I've been trying to contact Oliver, but he's still confused and doesn't realize he's dead, so he won't be of any help," Pucci replied, draining the teapot. "Olan, I have an idea. I think we should go out to the ruins of the old distillery together. Maybe we can find another clue, or maybe even the missing cipher, the one that was once was hidden in Rosslyn Chapel."

Olan took a deep breath, his expression darkened as he leaned in, "Pucci, I have something to tell you before we go any further." Pucci's stomach churned. Something was terribly wrong. She could feel it.

"We have wrapped up the blue diamond smuggling case, in which we suspect Clouding was involved, but again, there is no direct connection or evidence to convict him or his sect. We lost Pirate. Again." The words came out tight, edged with frustration. "We've had a deep undercover detective on this for over three years." A heavy pause. "Pucci . . . it's Anya."

Pucci inhaled and sat back in her chair. Scenes of Grand Cayman came flooding back. There had been a deep knowing inside her—Anya couldn't truly be on Pirate's side. Her intuition had been right. Anya was undercover. My God.

"Pucci, during the raid of the headquarters in Edinburgh, the second in command to Pirate—his name is Morgan—found out Anya was one of us. He kidnapped her and got away. I heard a shot. I believe he shot her . . . Pucci, please," he paused, hating to ask the next question. "Do you see her? Is she dead?" Olan's voice wavered, trying to keep his emotions in check.

Pucci stared at him with such intensity that he sat back. She then took a cleansing breath and extended her energy out to the other side, calling for Anya. Nothing. It was a tremendous relief. It probably meant she was not dead. Probably.

"I don't see or hear her, Olan. My psychic sense feels she's not dead, but in danger. She's weak, she can't escape. I can see her lying in some cluttered room—can't get a sense of where she is, though. I'll have to go into a meditative state to see if I can astral travel to where she is to get additional information. We need to do this tonight. I can feel she's running out of time."

Olan released a wavering sigh, tinged with both doubt and relief. Anya was still alive—hopefully. He called Connor and told him what Pucci saw. Olan added that he hoped he'd have even more information later tonight.

Pucci texted Varv. *We need to talk, I don't want to text this. Call when you can.*

Chapter 41

Pucci and Olan drove to Cat's bed and breakfast to check Olan into a room. Cat was happy to have him and showed him to a room on the same floor, next to Pucci. *Oy*, Pucci thought. *Now we have to share plumbing.*

Olan put his kit bag in his room, while Pucci put on another layer of clothing, and grabbed warmer gloves before heading down. The weather was still holding—blue skies stretched overhead—but large, snow-laden clouds were building on the other side of the loch, rolling in toward Bowmore.

They got in the car and drove to the ruins of the distillery where Mac had sent Pucci and Cat the day before. Parking on the road, they walked through the tall green and yellow grass, the wet ground swallowing each step. Off in a near field, sheep and a few hairy coos were grazing. One looked up as they passed.

Olan stopped a few feet from the rubble that had once been a cottage. Nothing really left there besides partial outlines of rooms, and proceeded to walk toward the barn with Pucci, its stone walls still standing. The wooden roof was long gone. They stepped through what might have once been the entrance. Pucci could see a faint holographic ghost-image of the old barn doors that once hung in the large opening between the walls.

Olan stepped over a low stone structure. Perhaps an interior wall? He bent down and rummaged under some small white stones. Pucci walked another twenty feet deeper into the ruins. On the back wall, she spotted some sort of drawing and words, barely visible. With her gloved hand she gently wiped dirt and lichen off the words. She could make out 'Standing' something 'one Dis' something. *So, Mac was right. This was the Standing Stone Distillery.*

Beneath the words was a sketch—almost like a logo. Pucci examined it closely. The image depicted a boulder with a distinct curved ridge along its top, giving it the uncanny resemblance of a molar tooth. In the background was a hill and a setting sun—or rising sun—depending on how you look at it. She ran her fingers over the drawing. She took out her phone and photographed the whole wall and then zoomed in on the drawing. Her intuition was telling her this was significant. Maybe the jeweled cipher is behind this, sequestered in the wall? Or, maybe nearby. Olan approached.

"Find anything?" she asked.

"No, you?"

"Look closely at this wall. Do you see the words and the drawing?"

"Aye . . . but just barely. I don't think I would have noticed if you hadn't pointed them out. What do you think it is?"

"Maybe some sort of logo for the Standing Stone Distillery."

"I think you're right," Olan marveled, running his fingers over the drawing as Pucci had done. As soon as he touched the wall sketch, his fingers began to tingle. "Pucci, why are my fingers tingling?"

"I think we found it, Olan. We found John and Callum's distillery. We should look to see if we can find a hiding place for another piece of the cipher. I'm going to guess that it's going to be similar in size to the one around my neck," Pucci said, rubbing her fingers over more of the walled area, searching for hiding places.

They searched for another hour or so but found nothing of significance. The sun was low in the horizon, they decided to call it a day. They still had work to do tonight.

***

In the distance, a hooded figure crouched in the tall grass, watching through binoculars. His car was concealed behind a deserted stone cottage. It didn't seem like they had found a cipher piece—but it looked like they had discovered the distillery he and Oliver had been searching for. That fool Oliver had been looking on the wrong side of the island, near Bowmore. It was obvious now—he had been useless, despite Nell's insistence that his expertise in whisky history would lead them straight to it. Nell and Oliver, both idiots. He needed to report this progress to Pirate. Pirate was right. This Riddle woman had powers. How did she find the distillery before he did?

They were returning to their car. Crouching low, Manier ran to his car to follow.

Chapter 42

Pucci and Olan drove in companionable silence, both contemplating their next move. Pucci spotted a small sign on a fence indicating a point of historical interest from the Islay Heritage. She saw standing stones in the distance as they drove past, the small sign illegible from the car.

"Olan, please turn around. I'd like to go back to the sign on the fence. This might be the site of the Cultoon Stone Circle. Cat told me about it, and I've read about the circle. It's believed to have had ceremonial or astronomical significance, similar to the Stonehenge. Cultoon dates back to the Neolithic age, I think."

Olan turned around and parked. Pucci got out of the car and read the small sign on the fence post. "It *is* the Cultoon site. This says it dates to the Bronze Age, c. 2000BC. It also says to follow the fence line. Come on, let's go have a quick look. I love the energy of standing stones."

Olan grunted, "You've got ten minutes and then we're finding a pub." He pulled his coat tighter as the wind picked up, masking the low growl of his stomach.

The grasses were high and green in this part of the island as well. Pucci could smell the peat soil, not to be dug up near this sacred site. They ascended a small incline up to the circle. No one else was around. Now and then, a car drove by on the road below.

Pucci walked up to a gray and white stone adorned with moss and lichen. It stood about five feet high, and about three feet wide, with curved sides. She stopped and put her hands on the stone. She felt and heard a soft hum coming from it. There were only three stones still standing. The rest had fallen over. This was no Stonehenge, but it was built at approximately the same time as Stonehenge's inner circle.

She walked unsteadily toward the center of the circle, over uneven moist ground. At the outer edge of the circle, Olan squatted down to inspect one of the fallen stones.

She stood in the center, waiting for something to happen. An energetic surge? A vision of how it use to look? The heavens to open up? Nothing . . .

Pucci, a little disappointed, still marveled at the sight of these stones, lying and standing for centuries. She spun slowly around, recording a video on her phone, wishing she had her digital camera with her. The sun was on the horizon, next to a small hill to its left, peeking through some clouds, illuminating the sky and clouds with bright orange and yellow hues. One of the three standing stones, the largest, slightly blocked the hill behind it. This stone, about eight or nine feet high, looked almost like one of her molars . . .

"Oh my God! Olan!" Pucci yelled over the high winds. "Olan, come here, quick!"

He looked up and ran over, stumbling in the dense grass.

"What, Pucci?" he asked slightly out of breath.

She stared off into the sunset. He followed her gaze. He didn't understand and she wasn't explaining. Suddenly, she started fiddling with her phone. "Och, Pucci, quit with your phone already and tell me what you're looking at."

Pucci found the photograph on her phone and raised it up so Olan could see. He inhaled sharply. "Bloody hell." The logo of the old distillery, the drawing on the wall, was the exact replica of the scene they were both looking at. The stone, the hill and the sun. "What do you think this means, Pucci?"

At that moment, Pucci felt a soft vibration coming from the cipher around her neck. When she moved her attention to it, it felt as if it was tugging on the chain. She pulled off the necklace and held the chain between her first finger and her thumb. There was a definite tug toward the ground. She held it out from her body and took a few steps away from the center. The chain sharply tugged down at an angle, like a fish tugging on a line, pointing back to the center of the circle. Could there be another clue—or another piece of the cipher—here? They looked at each other in wonder.

"Olan, can you lift this stone?" she asked, putting the cipher back around her neck. She pointed down to a small, moss-covered fallen stone.

"You think something might be underneath it?" Olan asked. "I hope I'm not breaking any sacred or legal rules by moving this," he said, grunting as he picked up one end of the stone and moved it aside.

The ground was layered with rich, dark peat, formed over centuries of decayed grasses. Pucci took off her gloves and began to dig in the cold soil. Luckily it wasn't frozen solid. Olan leaned down and began to dig around as well.

Her fingers numb, she suddenly felt something smooth. "Olan, help me, there's something here."

They cleared away enough soil to reveal the edges of a glass bottle. The top had long since decayed, leaving it packed with earth. Olan gently lifted it from the ground, tilting it to see if anything remained inside besides hardened earth. Pucci's cipher around her neck started vibrating with excited energy. She covered it with her hand, it stopped.

"Olan, I think we found another piece of the cipher."

They set the center stone back in its place. Pucci carried the bottle reverently back to the car.

***

"I can't believe this!" Manier muttered, lowering the high-powered binoculars. From his vantage point near the roadside, he had a clear view of the distant stone circle. Pulling up the hood of his sweatshirt, he started the car, ready to move. "How the hell did they figure that out?" he said, slamming his hand on the steering wheel. "That bottle must contain the cipher that we were supposed to find. Bullocks! Now what . . . I've got to get that cipher. I'm sure Pirate will pay a lot to get his hands on it. And, I still have the one I stole off Oliver. The price just doubled."

Chapter 43

Morgan and Whiley

The television camera closed in on a tall, overweight, bald man leaving the courtroom in downtown Edinburgh with a ridiculous grin on his face.

"Whiley, bloody bastard," Morgan muttered, watching the news from the worn-out couch in his parents' cottage. He scrambled to turn up the volume on the TV, his stale sandwich and cheap whisky forgotten.

"A key suspect in a major blue diamond smuggling operation, John Whiley, has been released from custody due to insufficient evidence," the newsreader announced. "Scotland Yard brought Whiley back from South Africa for questioning after receiving undisclosed intelligence linking him to the S.A. Mine smuggling operation. Authorities confirm that while much of the smuggling network has been dismantled, a few individuals remain at large. The investigation is ongoing."

Morgan scrambled for his phone and called Whiley. He told him to meet him at the designated spot outside Old Town, Edinburgh. He hung up, seized his keys, and drunkenly departed the cottage. He stopped at the garage. Blood had pooled under Anya's legs. He kicked her in the ribs. No movement, no noise. She's dead. Good. He'd bury her later. Right now, there were bigger things at stake.

Whiley had the diamonds—his diamonds—and if Morgan didn't get to him first, the bastard would sell them off to the highest bidder.

He climbed into his car, the engine growling to life as he peeled onto the road, heading for Edinburgh. His grip tightened on the wheel, knuckles white. He would find Whiley and make him talk—make him cough up the location of those three raw blue diamonds.

Millions were on the line. And no one was getting in his way.

***

Connor had a gut feeling that trailing Whiley would pay off. The man was reckless, cocky—bound to slip up. And today, just a day after his release, he did. From across the street, behind a dumpster, Connor and Detective Ried watched as Whiley slipped through the rusted door of an abandoned building on the outskirts of Edinburgh's Old Town.

Ried let out a low chuckle. "What do you reckon he's going in there for, Davies?"

Connor narrowed his eyes. "Bloody good question. But look who just showed up."

A shadow moved at the alley's edge. Connor's jaw tightened as a second figure stepped into view—Morgan. He picked up his car radio, handed it to Ried. "Call for backup. I'm going in."

***

When Morgan looked around before entering the abandoned building, he didn't see the parked unmarked police car down the street behind the dumpster. He walked through the front door and called out, "Whiley?"

"How did you know I was back?" Whiley said, as he moved toward Morgan, his shoes crunching on broken glass in the large empty room.

"I saw you on the news. Got away with it, didn't you?" Morgan circled around a column, keeping Whiley in sight.

Outside, Connor crept up to a window, chancing a glance inside. He saw the two men, circling each other like vultures. He could hear the conversation through the window.

"Got away with what, exactly, Morgan?"

"Where is the final shipment? Where are the three large raw blues that you kept bragging about all these months?"

"Those are my ticket out of this mess. I'll never tell you, or Pirate, or anyone."

Morgan pulled out a gun. "You will, you'll tell me right now or you're a dead man."

Whiley stopped walking. "What the hell, Morgan. If you shoot me, you'll never find them, and I'm not telling you."

Bang! Whiley fell to the floor, his collar bone shattered from the bullet.

Connor called Ried from his cell phone. "Ried, I need you, now!" Connor half-whispered into the phone. He ran to the entrance and waited for Ried.

Morgan walked to the fallen Whiley. Pointing his gun at his head, he said, "Now, if you don't tell me, this is the last thing you'll ever see."

Whiley, staring at the gun barrel, "You're out of luck, Morgan," breathing heavily, wincing with pain. "I'll never tell you."

Morgan cocked the gun. Suddenly, Connor and Ried burst in with guns pointed at Morgan. Sirens screamed in the background.

"Drop it, Morgan. Don't even think about it," Connor yelled.

"You really are an idiot, Whiley. You were followed," said Morgan. He slowly turned, dropped the gun, and raised his hands. The detectives ran to him, cuffed him and called for an ambulance for Whiley.

Reid looked down. "We heard everything, Whiley. If you tell us where the diamonds are, you might get a lighter sentence."

"In your dreams," he said, and passed out.

Connor slammed the cuffed Morgan up against the wall. "Where is she, you bastard?"

"Who? Your undercover little snitch?"

"Where?!" Connor yelled an inch from Morgan's face.

"She's dead."

Connor's stomach clenched so hard, he almost doubled over. He released Morgan with a shove. "She better not be. Or so help me . . . "

"Detective Inspector, let it go. We'll find her," Ried said. He set a hand on Connor's arm as they watched Morgan being escorted out of the building.

Chapter 44

Olan and Pucci drove on an empty road back to Cat's place. His mind churned, trying to make sense of everything they had uncovered in the past few hours. Ciphers leading to an ancient treasure? Divination? The Knights Templar? It all spun in his head like a raging storm. Could a cipher really lead to an artifact that controlled evil spirits? No. There had to be a more logical angle—money. An artifact of King Solomon would be worth a fortune, and that made far more sense. He held on to that, on to the only world he truly understood—money, murder, smuggling—the tangible, the real.

But something was shifting in him. The visions were coming more frequently, especially when it came to Anya—flashes, sensations—just like the ones Pucci had described. Was it possible? Was he actually psychic? And then there was the energetic pull—the strange, electric connection he felt every time Pucci pulled the cipher from beneath her sweater. Maybe it was just his fantasy and jealousy of where that piece got to be next to, day in, day out. Her soft warm skin, the curve of her neck, flowing down to the curve of her . . .

"Olan, you missed Cat's driveway." Pucci's voice cut through his wandering thoughts.

His face flushed. "Oh, right, sorry."

At the B and B, they each went to their rooms to freshen up. Pucci was starving, too. Normally, for esoteric work, she wouldn't eat, but didn't think Olan could go another hour without food. They hid the ancient bottle in Olan's room, not wanting to rush unlocking its secrets.

They chose Port Charlotte Hotel bar and restaurant for food and hopefully a chat with Alasdair before it closed. After all, it was Wednesday. Pucci had not told Olan about the words on the chapel ceiling yet. She could feel his overwhelm. Maybe after she had a good Bowmore 15 year when they got to the bar.

Olan was on the phone to Connor getting an update as they drove to Port Charlotte. Whiley was now in critical condition and had been unconscious since they operated on him. Morgan wasn't talking. No update regarding Anya. They found and searched Morgan's van, and the Morris Minor he had drove to the building to meet Whiley. Lots of blood, but no Anya. He must have switched cars, that's why they couldn't find him the day he escaped.

After more long hours searching public records at Scotland Yard, Sara found a family cottage in Morgan's family name out toward Glasgow. Connor would send out a team there tomorrow.

Olan filled Pucci in as they drove the rest of the way to the hotel bar. While she listened, she tried to energetically connect with Anya. The vision was the same. Anya was lying in a cluttered room. Pucci extended her energy, sending a message of hope. *We'll find you, Anya. Hang on, please.* A tear dropped into her lap.

Olan looked over, took her hand and squeezed. "We'll find her."

They got out of the car and walked into the bar. There were a few open seats at the very small counter. The handful of tables held locals taking turns buying each other drams of whisky.

Pucci and Olan took seats on bar stools, marveling at the selection of upside-down bottles—for easy pouring—featuring every whisky made on Islay, alongside a few token upright bottles of alcohol that were rarely ordered: gins, vodka, brandy, and a few bottles of wine. Pucci ordered a beer, didn't want risk a whisky on an empty stomach. Olan ordered orange juice.

The bartender engaged Pucci, "Hi ya, American?"

She chuckled, "Yes, is it that obvious? I hadn't even opened my mouth."

"Aye, you have that look. How do you like our island?"

"I'm ready to move here! I'm staying at Catriona's."

"Aye."

"She told me to connect to Alasdair," she said, glancing around, unsure who she was even looking for. "She said he might be here tonight."

An old gray-haired gentleman with a tartan vest and sharp blue eyes answered, "And what would you be wanting with me, lass?"

"Oh, hello, Alasdair?" Turning to Olan, "I'll be right back."

Pucci got up and walked past a few barstools and stood next to him. She decided to jump right in. "My name is Pucci Riddle. I'm a journalist and blogger . . . " Alasdair pulled a face. "It's kind of an online journal. I'm doing a feature article on Islay and its whiskies. I have also been researching Gaelic, as it's so integral to your island. I found this saying in an old church. Cat translated it for me, but she suggested I get your translation as it might be slightly different. Would you mind?" Pucci asked, taking out her paper the Gaelic words were written on.

"Oh, aye, you're staying at Catriona's place? I'd love tae help. Any friend of Cat's is a friend tae me." Alasdair looked at the Gaelic words "Diomhaireachd na tha comasach," pronouncing out loud "Jee-a-vee-arach-k co-ma-sach. I bet a dram Cat translated this into 'the mystery of what is possible.'"

Pucci smiled, called the bartender over and ordered a dram from Kilchoman for Alasdair.

"Tapadh leat," pronouncing it tapa leht. "Thank you." He took a sip, savoring the moment. "May I ask, lass, where you got this saying?"

Pucci, not wanting to go into the whole story, just replied, "It's actually translated from Ogham, originally."

Taking a sip of his dram, he studied her with intensity. She felt his energy reach over and connect. His gray, unruly eyebrows raised in knowing. He didn't say anything. He gently removed the paper from Pucci's hands, asked for a pen, and wrote something below Cat's translation. He folded the paper and put it into her hand. "This is not for you tae look at . . . yet. You'll know when you need tae read this." He finished his dram, winked and walked out.

***

Pucci tucked the paper in her vest pocket, not looking at it as instructed. Olan was looking at her as she walked back over to him and sat down. "I know, I know, I haven't filled you in on all the details of my adventures. Let's order, get it to go, and eat at Cat's."

Pucci's phone rang. "Varv!" her heart swelled. "How are you? God, I miss you!"

"Pucci! So great to hear your voice! Oh my goodness! I have so much to catch you up on. But first things first. What was that text message about?"

"Oh, Varv . . . " Pucci signaled to Olan to order for her and walked outside to talk out of earshot of the village. Her cheeks burned with the cold after the warmth of the fireplace in the bar. She took a deep breath. "Varv, Anya is an undercover Scotland Yard detective."

"Wha . . . wait, what? Pucci, what are you saying?"

"It's true. Olan is here on Islay. He says she had been deep undercover infiltrating a diamond smuggling operation for years. She had been posing as one of Pirate's gang members to uncover the full scope of his operation. That's why she had been in Grand Cayman. Neither Connor nor Olan could let anyone know. They couldn't even acknowledge her to each other—for fear of being overheard or someone slipping up to the wrong people."

"She's been risking her life, undercover, this whole time?"

"Wow, Varv, when you put it like that . . . you're right. She's been risking her life." Pucci paused. "You know, when I think about this, some unusual things that we experienced on Grand Cayman start to make sense. Remember the protective wards, the energy shields I put in place so no evil could cross the threshold in the condo?" She heard Varv acknowledge. "Anya was not affected. And, now that I think about it, there was a moment on the boat, after we found Coop dead underwater, when Connor shared an energetic familiarity with Anya that caught my attention. I could never figure that out."

"Pucci, this is extraordinary. Is she back at Scotland Yard? Can we see her?"

"This is the bad news. She was kidnapped and shot when they raided the smugglers' headquarters in Edinburgh. The man who did this is now in jail, but he just keeps saying she's dead."

"Dear God. Pucci, no . . . "

"Wait, Varv—my psychic visions are showing me she's not dead—maybe. But, I can't find her. Listen, I'll need your energetic support tonight. I'm going to do a ritual to astral travel to see if I can find her."

"Anything, Pucci," Varv said, overwhelmed with this news.

"And, Varv, Olan and I think we found another piece of the cipher."

"For goodness sake! You are full of incredible surprises tonight! And when did you reconnect with Olan?"

"Long story."

"Pucci, I can't believe any of this! But, of course, I will meet you in the astral and offer any support you need. When are you going to do this?"

"Give me about an hour, Varv. Olan needs to eat. I'll eat after the ritual. And, one more thing. Will you call Randi and update her on the cipher? Our next stop is back at Rosslyn. I need you gals there with me!"

"You bet, my friend. Count me in! I'll connect with Randi and put her on alert. See you soon!"

Chapter 45

Buried within the soil and debris of the bottle, Pucci and Olan found it—a second piece of the jeweled cipher. A thrill shot through Pucci. Untouched for over five hundred years, the artifact was encrusted with dirt and decay, its surface dulled by soil. As they carefully removed each layer of earth, the unmistakable scent of peat filled the bathroom back at the B and B.

Olan handled the cleaning of the cipher with near reverence, as though consecrating something sacred with holy water. Slowly, the dirt gave way, revealing its brilliance—restored to its former glory, the cipher gleamed with a radiant, otherworldly light. It was even more magnificent than the one they already possessed. This piece bore a larger diamond, approximately two carats, set at the center and wrapped in delicate gold foil. Smaller diamonds traced an infinity shape around it, their arrangement hinting at something greater.

This cipher also had location tabs—small, deliberate facets along its edges. They were meant to fit together, to create something larger, something important. A message? A code? A key?

Pucci cleared a small space on the floor and sat down, steadied her breath as she lit the small candle she'd bought in Tarbert just days ago, preparing herself for the meditation. She had already slipped on her sacred ring—a talisman for protection, a link to her spirit guides. The scent of essential oils curled through the air as she inhaled deeply, grounding herself. An additional scent filled the room. Peat. Earthy, damp, ancient.

Olan watched as she set both pieces of the cipher in front of her on a satin handkerchief that she carried wherever she went to handle positive, or negatively, charged objects. She took one more deep breath, closed her eyes, and fell into a meditative state.

Pucci immediately felt Varv's presence and strength. It was a great comfort. First thing she wanted to do was to see if she could connect with Anya. Suddenly she opened her eyes. Anya was standing in the room, her energy flickering with the candle light.

"Pucci, help me," the words were mouthed more than spoken.

"Anya!"

Olan scanned the room. *Oh dear God, is Pucci seeing Anya's ghost?* "Pucci, what do you see? Is she here? Did we lose her?" Olan asked in desperation.

"Wait, Olan. I see her, she's asking for help. There's something off with her energy. Anya, please, where are you?"

Anya's voice, slightly louder came in and out like a badly tuned radio, "I don't know where I am. I think somewhere in the country." Her energy was fading.

"Can you tell me more? Anything? You don't feel like a ghost."

"I'm not dead ... yet. Please, Pucci, help. It looks like I'm in an old garage, or storage room." She was gone.

"Olan, what I just saw and heard, it felt like that was an astral projection." Pucci paused. "She's not dead, she's in a coma! Anya said she thinks she's somewhere in the country in an old garage or a storage room."

Olan was mobilized. He grabbed his cell phone and called Connor. "Get over to Morgan's family cottage, the one Sara found. Now, don't wait till the morning. Look for a garage or a storeroom. Anya is in there, in a coma. Have an ambulance follow you. NOW, Davies, GO!"

Pucci heard a faint but frantic, "Yes, chief," before Olan gave his last instruction.

"I want to know immediately when you find her."

***

Pucci's night was far from over. Olan had gone to his room to touch base with his superiors and let them know what was happening. He'd figure out how to explain how he knew where to find Anya, maybe use the old hunch excuse. Always worked in the past when Pucci was helping him.

Pucci calmed her rapid heartbeat with deep breaths. She wanted to focus on the jeweled ciphers to see if she could get any additional information from the spirit world regarding their significance. With two fingers on each of the ciphers, she felt herself slip into a trance, falling out of her physical body and floating in a room of some sort. She willed herself to touch down on the floor. Barefoot and robed in a deep purple garment, she walked toward stairs that led up to gigantic solid gold doors. She recognized this as the entrance to the Akashic Records. Believed to contain the soul's journey through all time—past, present, and future—the Akashic Records exist within the akasha, the Sanskrit word for astral light. This astral light is said to hold the thoughts, actions, and intentions of every living being—the collective knowledge of all life-forms and entities.

The entrance appeared always to Pucci as glorious, heavenly doors. She had heard that those who can access the Akashic Records experience the space and records in ways unique to them.

She hadn't asked for admission to the records in her intention before she went into the trance, so she was surprised to find herself in front of the doors. They opened for her. Bowing her head in reverence, with her palms together as if in prayer, she walked across a stone floor into an enormous room containing only one structure. A book and podium, both pure white, seemed to glow under a soft, radiant light. The pages, rustled faintly in an unseen breeze, delicate as breath, wafer-thin—nearly translucent, like ancient parchment, fragile yet enduring. Each sheet caught the light, the words casting ghostly shadows on the podium below.

The chamber filled with an ethereal presence. In her heart, she heard the words, "*What is your question, my child?*"

She stood in front of the book, the pages still moving without her touching them. She then felt what she needed to ask. "I would like to see the soul's past-life of the one that is currently known as Olan Lathen. He is somehow connected to ancient artifacts, a jeweled cipher that is associated with the Knights Templar and King Solomon."

"*We are aware. Your request is granted.*"

The pages started flipping backward at a rapid pace. Pucci could not see what was on any of the pages, until it stopped at one page. She leaned over and read. The language was not of the physical world, yet Pucci sensed its meaning. She interpreted it as best she could, feeling the words resonate through her heart chakra.

The soul known as Olan Lathen has lived many lives. In this one, he walks the path of a detective. Further back, he was a Master Mason. Guardian of the key. She went further back. "Oh my," Pucci exclaimed. "He was a Knights Templar—on Temple Mount—finder of King Solomon's artifacts and guardian. This would directly connect him with the ciphers and Solomon. No wonder he had a psychometric episode when he touch the cipher. He did see his past-lives!" She read one more line. *Only he and one other will be allowed to handle the artifacts, and only if the beings are in their true authentic power.*

The book closed as she pondered the last sentence. She felt the room changing into shimmering light all around her, indicating the session was over. She bowed her head in deep gratitude for the knowledge bestowed upon her, watching as the Akashic Records dissolved into the unknown.

Chapter 46

Pucci took a deep breath in her body. She slowly opened her eyes to the room on Islay. She was disoriented at first. The meditation had been deep. She reached for a pen and paper and began writing everything she experienced before forgetting. Astral travel was almost like dreamwork. She needed to write down everything she experienced immediately, before it faded.

Satisfied with what she wrote, she took a moment to close the session by thanking her spirit guides and the one who she serves in the light.

"Thank you, Adonai, Elohim, Shekhinah, and master of the light. Please protect us as we move forward. We will find and protect King Solomon's artifacts. Please guide me to where they are hidden." Bowing her head again, she looked at the ciphers and felt an energetic pull on her hands. She watched her hands pick up the two cipher pieces and easily connect them. Faint Hebrew letters glowed on each piece—letters that were invisible when the pieces were not connected. She couldn't quite make out what the letters were before they faded. Breathlessly she watched a holographic image of a third piece take shape, showing how the three pieces would fit together to form a triangle. Then, without Pucci touching them, the two ciphers broke apart.

***

Cat crept away from the closed door. What she just overheard confirmed their suspicions. She must contact the others. She dialed the phone back in her room.

"She's done it, my Lord. You were right."

***

As she marveled at the two pieces, contemplating the third piece, Pucci felt that familiar squeamish sensation in her stomach. She looked up, and there was Oliver. He looked at the ciphers. He looked forlorn, the regret on his face was evident.

"Oliver," Pucci said, not knowing what else to say.

"Ms. Riddle."

"Oliver, what happened to you? Who were you working for, and why were you in Scotland? Was it to find this piece?"

"Yes." Oliver's form faded slightly. "A man, Owen Nell, recruited me because of my expertise on distillery history, specifically whisky. Nell told me that another cipher—like the one he gave me—is hidden in an ancient whisky distillery on an island. But he didn't know where. Not very helpful in Scotland as there are hundreds of islands. Still, I had read in some history books about one of the oldest distilleries, supposedly on Islay—a rumor passed down through generations, shared in stories but never substantiated. I assumed it had to be near Bowmore, home to the island's oldest known distillery. He partnered me with a man called Manier. He never told me where he got the cipher, everything was very clandestine. We were supposed to use the cipher he gave us to help find the other cipher. I wasn't finding the ancient distillery where they believed the cipher was hidden fast enough for them, so Manier killed me and took the cipher back. When I was alive, I overheard Manier talking to Nell, and to someone else he seemed to call Pirate." Pucci blanched.

"Manier is on his way back to Edinburgh," said Oliver. "I overheard something about the key lying in Rosslyn. The rest you know. You found what I was supposed to find, Ms. Riddle."

"Please, call me Pucci."

He smiled. "How can you be so kind to me after all I did to you in life?"

"Oliver, you have to forgive yourself, otherwise dark spirits will prey on your soul. Besides—all your criticism made me be a better journalist. I had to up my game so you couldn't find anything wrong with my work."

"You're too good, Pucci."

"Oliver, you saved my life back in the distillery. If it wasn't for you yelling at me to watch out, I would have died."

"I had a little prodding from a friend of yours. He contacted me and told me you were in danger, and to fix it!" Oliver said, slightly embarrassed. "He said his name was JD Langer."

"JD? That's incredible, Oliver."

"You have a lot of friends over here, Pucci," he said, and was gone.

Chapter 47

Pucci was startled awake by loud knocking.

"Pucci, Pucci!" Olan was pounding on the door.

Pucci, bleary eyed with matted hair and crumpled pajamas, opened the door. Olan grabbed her and hugged her so hard she stopped breathing. He set her back down on the floor and took her face in his two hands, leaned down and kissed her.

Pucci, knowing she hadn't brushed her teeth yet, pulled back after a moment. "Olan, wha —what's going on?" She had never seen him so happy.

"Pucci, you did it! They rescued Anya!" He stepped back. "They found her in a garage on the back side of Morgan's family property. She was in a coma, almost dead, her vital signs extremely weak from loss of blood and no water or food. But, since the ambulance was already there, they administered lifesaving procedures all the way back to the hospital. The hospital operated on her wound and administered fluids. Connor is at the hospital."

Olan's phone rang. "Lathen. Connor, how is she? She just woke up?" he looked over at Pucci, his eyebrows raised. "That's grand news. And, Connor. Well done." He hung up.

Now it was Pucci's turn—running into Olan's arms, she hugged and kissed him, unbrushed teeth forgotten.

***

Pucci knew the path forward awaited her and Olan at Rosslyn Chapel. She emailed Randi and Varv. The email was somewhat cryptic as a precaution, just in case. It read, "Please come back to the Chapel. Be there on the full moon. We have come full circle, the game is afoot!" Sherlock Holmes was one of her favorites. The full moon was tonight. She hoped they'd both be able to come at such short notice.

They had tea and breakfast in Cat's kitchen to discuss next steps. Pucci noticed an unusual energy from Cat, who looked at Pucci with a strange expression on her face. Pucci couldn't quite get the feel of it. Maybe it was because she and Olan had just told Cat they would be leaving for Edinburgh today.

After Cat left the kitchen, Pucci filled Olan in about the night's meditation and Oliver's visit. She did not tell him everything she saw in the Akashic Records. She needed to have some time to digest this information and discuss it when they had more time and privacy.

When she relayed Oliver's message regarding 'the key lies in Rosslyn' they both agreed it could mean two different things. The cipher is a 'key' and it opens something in Rosslyn, or the key to this mystery, the answers, are in Rosslyn Chapel.

Olan packed and drove alone to the Islay police station to fill MacKay in on all the events. Olan wanted to let MacKay know the suspect in the murder of Williams-Tanaka had fled back to Edinburgh, and Scotland Yard will take if from here.

While Olan was at the station, he commissioned a charter flight to take Pucci and him directly to Edinburgh, as there were no direct commercial flights. He didn't want to waste time flying into Glasgow or Oban and taking a train.

While he was gone, Pucci packed with mixed emotions. She was excited to figure out the next piece of this riddle, but she was very sad leaving this extraordinary island. This land and her people had come to feel like home to her. She vowed to come back after her article was published to celebrate with everyone again.

She hauled her suitcases down the stairs. Pucci had left Cat the money for both rooms and walked out to the waiting taxi. The plane was leaving in an hour. Time was of the essence, no time for the ferry.

The taxi was putting the luggage into the boot. Cat suddenly appeared at Pucci's side and hugged her.

"Thank you for everything, Catriona. This was an incredible adventure! I'm so glad I got to say goodbye," Pucci said, welling with emotion. "Maybe I can come back after the article is published. We could have a little article launch party!"

"I'd like that," her smile was endearing. "Pucci, what an extraordinary person you are. Please . . . " she leaned in and whispered in her ear, "be careful."

Cat let go and walked inside. Pucci, slightly puzzled, got into the taxi and was off.

***

Pucci was disappointed that the clouds blocked any view of the island as they took off. She glanced across the narrow aisle, her gaze lingering on the man she'd spent seven years figuring out—and had never entirely succeeded. Their bond defied labels: moments when his touch felt like home, others when they bickered like siblings, but always a companionship as familiar to her as she'd ever known.

He sat upright, spine straight as a fence post, trench coat creased just so. His fedora—a recent replacement from the hat that was ruined by a bullet hole in Grand Cayman—balanced on his knee. Even with his eyes shut, his face carried the weight of a thought too heavy to lift. As she watched him, his energy changed to fear. At that moment, she saw the ghost that had been haunting him seven years ago and who she recently saw again at the bar in London. The ghost was cackling, willing Olan to relive a memory over and over. Recognizing what was happening, Pucci took the two jeweled ciphers from around her neck and put them around the neck of the sleeping Olan. The ghost's energy became incensed. Pucci woke Olan up whispering an incantation into his ear.

"Olan, I want you to say the following, 'Archangel Michael, protect me. Metatron, banish this spirit back to where he belongs, never to return.'"

Olan shook himself out of his nightmare of watching his love being shot over and over. Seeing the ciphers around his neck and hearing Pucci's voice, he leaned forward and commanded, "Archangel Michael, protect me. Metatron banish this spirit back to where he belongs, never to return, by the power authority of King Solomon, begone!" his last words shook the energy in the cabin.

Pucci was physically pushed back down in her seat at his last command. Where did that come from? How did he know to call on King Solomon? It must have been the ciphers around his neck connecting him to the past-life she had seen in the Akashic Records.

Olan looked down at the ciphers around his neck. When he uttered that command, he'd felt an energetic power surge through him. It seemed to be channeled through the ciphers into his being. He saw Pucci studying him with a strange look on her face.

Pucci's pulse quickened as a shimmering hologram of a Knights Templar slid into place over Olan, like a veil of time folding over the present. The spectral knight's presence felt so tangible, that Olan's form seemed to waver at the edges, almost vanishing beneath the centuries-old identity—though his glowing, emerald-green eyes remained constant. His features sharpened. A thick beard and unruly locks of hair shadowed his face, adding an otherworldly ruggedness, casting him as both warrior and enigma. The knight's white mantle draped over him with solemn grace, the blood-red cross emblazoned on it glinting with ancient purpose. He appeared as though resurrected from legend. The ghost that had been haunting him was banished for all eternity.

"Pucci? Are you alright?" Olan asked, handing back the ciphers as the image faded.

"Um . . . " she slowed her breathing, taking a moment. "Yes, yes, I'm alright. Are you? How do you feel? Did you see, or feel, what just happened?"

"Aye, I saw the ghost who's been haunting my dreams. I didn't realize he'd been manipulating me for the past year. Pucci, that's why I started drinking. I had to stop the nightmares somehow." He paused, glancing away before his eyes slowly found hers. "There's something I've never shared with you. I was engaged to a woman about ten years ago. Her name was Liana."

Pucci slightly surprised, asked, "What happened?"

"A ruthless killer I was tracking, found us one night. He warned me to stop investigating him and his gang. When I refused, he shot Liana. That's what I kept reliving in my nightmares—over and over again"

"Oh, Olan, I'm so sorry."

He exhaled, the weight of it pressing down. "I shot him dead in return. He's been haunting me ever since. But, I don't understand how he's been able to have this affect over me."

Pucci thought for a few moments. "Olan, when did the nightmares start?"

"Almost as soon as I returned from Grand Cayman."

"I have a theory. Maybe when you touched the original cipher, and had the psychometric episode in Georgetown, Grand Cayman, your energy opened—you became more receptive to otherworldly energies, but also more vulnerable. Without some sort of protection, like this cipher, or how I use my sacred ring, or even knowing how to call for protection, this ghost preyed on your greatest fears," she said, gently touching his hand.

"Believe it or not, that actually makes some sense to me. This is so new and different, it's hard for me to grasp. But, I can't deny what just happened, what I saw and felt. I also can't deny what's been happening to me since we've been on this, dare I say it—quest." They both smiled. "I feel such a strong connection to these pieces for some strange reason."

"Olan," Pucci hesitated, "I know why you're so connected."

"Please fasten your seatbelts, we'll be landing shortly," the pilot announced.

"I'll tell you later," Pucci said, almost relieved at the interruption.

With a quizzical look, Olan tightened his seatbelt, turned and looked out the window as Edinburgh airport came into view.

Chapter 48

They landed in Edinburgh in a sleet storm. Pucci felt the landing with a sour stomach. She needed food. She ran to a kiosk and grabbed protein bars and water for herself and Olan.

Connor was waiting at the curb outside. Pucci embraced him tightly, grateful for the moment, though uncertainty shadowed their reunion, neither of them could predict what lay ahead. Olan loaded the suitcases in the boot.

"Good to see you again, Pucci," said Connor, pulling away from the curb "What's happening, Chief? You didn't tell me what's going on when we spoke."

"I didn't want to speak openly on the phone, Connor. But first, how's Anya?"

"She's still recovering. It was touch-and-go for a while after she regained consciousness, it was a long night. But her vital signs are strengthening every moment. I think she's trying to get back out there to catch Pirate. She keeps mumbling his name, with a lot of expletives connected," Connor said, smiling at the memory.

"Thank God," Olan said. Pucci said a silent thanks to her spirit guides.

"Where are we going, Chief?"

"Rosslyn Chapel. I'll fill you in on the way."

As they drove south, Olan briefed Connor on the history of the ciphers, including the one they found in Grand Cayman and Pirate's involvement.

"I believe the ciphers are what has been their motivation all along. The smuggling operation was funding all of this," Olan said. "Clouding probably had Pirate kill Nell for the betrayal after Clouding discovered Nell stole their piece." Connor shook his head in disbelief. "It all comes down to these ciphers, which, when connected, are the key to some larger mystery."

Lastly, Olan filled Connor in on Manier's link to Nell and the murder of Oliver Williams-Tanaka on Islay.

"So you think this Manier is going to be at Rosslyn Chapel with the third cipher? Possibly with Pirate as well?" Connor asked, turning on the A720, skirting Edinburgh.

"Manier will for sure. I get the sense he's only in it for the money, not whatever the cipher is truly connected to. He might even try to ransom it to Pirate." Olan's gaze drifted to the scenery streaking past, his thoughts racing, never quite settling.

***

At that moment, that's precisely what Manier was planning as he walked around Rosslyn Chapel. He pulled down his hood, his gazed drifting up toward the ceiling's intricate stonework. Religion had never made sense to him. It was foolish—people clinging to something intangible. He only believed in one thing: money. And money meant freedom. His short, stocky frame moved toward the group of tourists and a tour guide. Maybe he could pick up something useful—some clue about the chapel, about what the ciphers were connected to, or what they were hiding. He absently ran a hand through his short blond hair, his eyes briefly settling on a cute Chinese tourist before his thoughts strayed back to the Riddle woman. He figured this was where she and the Scotland Yard detective were headed. They knew something Pirate didn't. That much was obvious. He had told Pirate to meet him here.

But Manier had arrived first—for a reason. He needed time to investigate, to determine the true value of the cipher in his possession. As for the other one? He had already ruled out trying to take it from the Riddle woman—not with a Scotland Yard detective by her side. He wasn't about to risk his life for Pirate. Yes, Pirate had taken care of him, even after the failure of the hoard heist. But Pirate had also ordered Valerie's death. The weight of the memory settled in his heart, silent, heavier than grief.

The tour group wandered toward the retrochoir at the east end of the chapel.

"Legends and names adorned these three pillars," the tour guide, dawning her official green tour guide vest was saying, pointing to the pillars immediately in front of the retrochoir.

"Each standing at a height of eight feet and carved in a distinct manner as you can see. The pillar on the far north is the Master Pillar, the middle one is the Journeyman Pillar, and at the southern end stands the legendary Apprentice Pillar—so named for the tale of the Master Mason who, consumed by jealousy, killed his apprentice after the young craftsman surpassed him by completing a pillar of extraordinary beauty. But, these are their Freemasonic names, which only existed from the late Georgian—early Victorian age—sometime around 1837. Prior to that, well, you'll just have to buy 'The History of Rosslyn Chapel' in the bookshop to find out what the pillars were originally called, on your way out!" she exclaimed, eliciting chuckles and groans from the little group.

Manier studied the Apprentice Pillar, looking to see if the piece he had in his pocket might fit somewhere into the carvings.

He bent down to examine one of the eight dragons at the base of the pillar when a sinister voice spoke.

"Get up, Manier. It's not there," Pirate hissed.

"How do you know? And what's not there?" Manier was incensed at Pirate's rude tone.

In a brief moment of honesty, Pirate replied, "I don't actually know what these pieces do and where they fit in this chapel."

"Clouding didn't know?"

"No."

"Then what the bloody hell are we doing, Pirate? The Riddle woman and the detective are on their way here. They must know something we don't." He stood up and was about to say something else when Pirate held up his hand for silence.

"May I have your attention, please? We need to close the chapel for the rest of the day," a voice called out from the north door. The people in the chapel turned to listen.

Pirate grabbed Manier and whispered, "Follow their directions, but once outside, hide so you can watch to see what's happening. Stay hidden, I think they're closing the chapel for Lathen, the Scotland Yard detective. I'm going to hide inside. Give me the piece you have from Nell. And don't even think about betraying me, Manier. You saw what I did to Nell for his betrayal." Manier blanched. "I'll text when I need you. GO!" Pirate shoved Manier toward the door after taking the cipher from him. The visitors were shuffling out.

"Don't worry, we will refund your money and give you a free day tomorrow. Thank you for your understanding," the women guide said, trying to sound upbeat amongst the grumblings.

Pirate ran down toward the sacristy, cloaking his energy. The sacristy was a small rectangular chamber, bare of any but the most minimal carvings, unlike the upper chapel. He hid in a small room off the east side of the sacristy, willing that no one would be looking that close.

He heard an employee come into the sacristy, take a cursory look around and call out, "All clear!"

**

Randi and Varv saw each other amongst the disgruntled crowd leaving the small visitor's center. They stepped off to the side to let everyone pass and shared a hug.

"It's so good to see you again, Varv!" Randi said, trying not to be distracted by all the people leaving.

"It's great to see you too, Randi. I'm so glad we could both come to support Pucci. What do you think is going on?" Varv watching the crowd.

"It seems like Pucci's detective requested the closure of the chapel. Luckily, it's almost closing time, anyway. But these folks aren't too happy about it."

"I bet you're right," Varv said, looking over at a car driving up. "I think that's Pucci!"

They ran over to the car as Pucci got out. The three hugged. Pucci thanked them over and over for coming. Olan and Connor watched with an English look of complete lack of emotion.

Connor patiently waited his turn, then scooped Varv up in his arms. "I've missed you."

"I've missed you, too. It's so good to see you." Varv said smiling.

As they walked toward the entrance, Connor went ahead to ask the staff for ladders in case they were needed. Varv said hello to Olan. Pucci introduced Randi to him.

"Nice to finally meet you, Chief Inspector. I've heard a lot about you," Randi said with a scrutinizing stare. She wanted to add, *and if you hurt my friend again, I'll kick ya till you're dead*, partially quoting a line from one of her favorite movies, *Moonstruck*, but kept it to herself, given the current situation and possible danger ahead.

As they made their way to the chapel, the staff were shutting down and departing. Manier watched from his hiding place outside as three women and two men approached the entrance. He texted Pirate the situation, then waited, sweating in his overcoat even though the temperature was dropping rapidly with the early twilight. He should have never given Pirate the piece, he thought. That was stupid. Now he had nothing to bargain with. His breathing grew more rapid with every angry moment. *Pirate isn't going to tell me what to do. I'm going to get what's owed to me.*

At that moment, Detective Connor Davies walked back outside. Manier's smile turned sinister as he took out his weapon.

Chapter 49

The five entered the chapel, standing just inside, in silent vigil. Once again, the magnificence of the carvings, the art and the energy were overwhelming.

Olan walked deeper into its interior. Something was off. "Connor, go back outside and keep an eye out. Something doesn't feel right."

Connor nodded.

Pucci, Varv, and Randi stood in the center of the chapel together. They looked around, then up at the ceiling, marveling at the ornate carvings of flowers, including roses and lilies, and a section of stars. Pucci realized she was gripping Varv's hand. She squeezed it and let go.

As Pucci removed her gaze from the sacred tiles on the ceiling, she looked down the center aisle toward the altar and the Lady Chapel behind.

In front of the three renowned pillars stood three grand arches, supported by fluted columns, framing the retrochoir. Above the central column, embedded in the wall, was a statue of Mary holding the Christ Child. Higher still, a breathtaking stained-glass window cast shimmering colors across the space.

Her heart swelled as a memory surfaced—something she'd seen in a book, or perhaps a diagram she'd once studied. Yes, that was it: *The Kabbalah of the Golden Dawn*. A diagram of the Garden of Eden, with three columns—Eve and Adam standing in the central column, much like Mary's placement now. Above them, Archangel Metatron radiated light from the top of the column, mirroring the glow now cast by the stained-glass window.

The resemblance was unmistakable.

She lingered on the thought. The architect and founder had been students of Kabbalah. Could the design be more than coincidence?

The ciphers began to softly vibrate.

Olan moved the tall ladder to the middle of the Lady Chapel to prepare for . . . what, he didn't know. But he just felt he should. After setting the ladder up near the Journeyman Pillar, he walked back over to the women.

Pucci pulled the two ciphers out from under her sweater.

"Varv, Randi, I'm going to open up my energy and channel it through these pieces to see if we can get any sort of message, or energetic pull, or something, anything, on what to do next." They nodded their heads and stood slightly away from her. Olan stood close to them.

Out of nowhere, a voice broke the silence.

"I'll be taking those, Ms. Riddle," Pirate smirked, approaching from the sacristy stairs, gun aimed at her heart.

Olan lunged toward Pirate.

Pirate turned the gun on him. "I wouldn't do that if I were you, Lathen."

The front door banged open. Pirate didn't flinch, still staring at Pucci. Connor stumbled in through the door, Manier holding a gun to his head. Varv screamed.

"Now, you see the situation, Lathen. Get the ciphers from your girlfriend and give them to me," Pirate said, waving the gun's barrel at Pucci. She could feel Pirate held the third cipher in his other hand.

Olan stepped toward Pucci, his movements slow, deliberate. His hand hovered, hesitating for just a breath before closing around the chain that held the ciphers still clenched in her grip. She didn't let go immediately. Their eyes locked, the weight of unspoken fears and unrelenting urgency pressing between them.

A charged silence stretched, crackling like a storm on the horizon.

If the legend was true, bringing the three ciphers together would lead to King Solomon's artifact—the one said to control evil spirits. If Pirate got to it first, he wouldn't just possess an ancient relic. He would have the power to unleash darkness upon the world. Failure wasn't an option. The fate of everything they knew hung by a thread, the cost too great to comprehend.

"Just toss the chain over, Lathen, and step away," Pirate called out. "Manier, bring Connor over and move everyone to the rear of the chapel."

Manier shoved Connor over to where the three women huddled together.

"You heard him. Start walking." They moved slowly toward the west door. "Now, sit. On the floor, hands where I can see them."

Pucci sat next to Varv and Randi. Olan sat near Connor after reluctantly tossing the ciphers to Pirate. They watched as Pirate removed the ciphers from the chain. He laid the pieces on the altar, adding the one he just received from Manier. Pucci could barely see what he was doing.

Pirate shifted the pieces. Finally. After years of searching, after hearing whispers of their existence for over a decade—he was the one chosen to unite them. Not Clouding. Him.

A sharp click echoed through the room, followed by a low hum as energy rippled through the air, tense and unsettling.

With a nod, the women wordlessly understood that they had all felt the same thing. Something ancient stirred in the chapel. Pucci could see energies flickering on the edges of her periphery vision. Her sacred ring on her right hand began to glow. Olan's eyes darted around. Connor's fists clenched.

"What's happening?" Olan whispered to Pucci.

"Shut up!" Manier yelled, physically shaking. He turned, "Pirate, what the bloody hell was that?"

Pirate didn't answer. The three cipher pieces fused into a perfect triangle. He closed his eyes, reaching into their energy, feeling the power humming beneath his fingertips.

The triangle began to glow, pulsing with an eerie, golden light. Carefully, he lifted it. Pain shot through his palm—a searing, unnatural heat. He cursed, dropping the triangle onto the altar with a clunk. Instantly, the glow vanished.

Gritting his teeth, Pirate pulled on a pair of gloves and picked it up again. He exhaled, adjusting his grip, then turned his attention to the Apprentice Pillar. Dragging the ladder closer, he prepared to find the place where ciphers belonged.

"I thought you said the ciphers won't fit into anything on that pillar," Manier yelled, turning his back to the group.

Pirate mumbled under his breath as he climbed up the ladder "It's not going to be on the bottom where everyone can reach it or see it you idiot."

Manier was losing control of himself. The gun by his side as he paced back and forth watching Pirate. Sweat beading on his upper lip, his breathing irregular.

Pucci wasn't paying attention to Pirate. Her focus had moved back to the columns in front of them at the far end of the chapel. Shifting to one side, she strained to see around the central column, the structure separating the retrochoir from the elegantly carved three famous pillars bordering the Lady Chapel. As her hands settled into her vest pockets, they brushed against the paper Alasdair had given her. His voice came to life in her mind, vivid and comforting. *You'll know when it's time to read this.* It was time.

She watched Manier as he paced. When he turned back to Pirate, she softly brought the crumpled piece of paper from her pocket. Shielding it from Manier, she read Alasdair's translated words she has seen in this very Chapel a little over a week ago. From the Ogham symbols to Gaelic, then to English, Alasdair's words: "The Secret of the Possible."

She studied the text for a few moments. She leaned to the side again to see the center pillar, the Journeyman Pillar.

While studying the chapel, she had discovered that before receiving their Freemasonic names, the three famous pillars had different designations. The Earl's Pillar was now known as the Master Pillar, the Shekhinah Pillar had become the Journeyman Pillar, and the Prince's Pillar was now the renowned Apprentice Pillar.

She looked down at the translation again. A sense of knowing overwhelmed her, filling her with warmth. In her study of Kabbalah, the Shekhinah **is** *The Secret of the Possible*, translating divine thought into life on earth. The ciphers are connected to the Shekhinah Pillar. Pirate was looking in the wrong place.

Varv looked at Randi. She was moving her right leg under a bench. Randi caught Varv's eye and slightly shook her head, signaling Varv not to bring attention to her. Varv nodded. She saw what Randi was doing. Randi was attempting to get to a thick black book from under the bench. She got her heel on it and slowly dragged it toward her, watching Manier the entire time. She grabbed it and handed it to Varv behind her back. Varv whispered to Pucci, showing her the book. Pucci nodded, waited for a moment when Manier turned away and took the book, handing it to Olan behind his back. He nodded, not looking at any of them.

Pucci watched Pirate climb to the top rung of the ladder. Manier, shifting into pure impatience and anger, yelled, "Pirate, I'm sick of this. One of them has to know something, I'm sure of it."

"Grab the Riddle woman and bring her here. Don't try anything stupid, Lathen, or we'll shoot her dead."

Suddenly the original Knights Templar ghost that was attached to the cipher appeared next to Pirate. He looked at Pucci, grinned, and nodded. In full poltergeist, he rammed into Pirate, titling the ladder at a dangerous angle.

Pucci yelled, "NOW, Olan." Olan hurled the book at Manier, knocking him in the head as he and Connor tackled him to the ground, struggling for his gun.

Pirate, tipping to one side, kept his balance. He reached for his gun. The ghost hit him again. Losing his balance, he desperately grabbed at the tipping ladder as it fell to the solid stone ground. The triangle of ciphers went flying, hit the stones, and broke apart.

The south entrance burst open. The Earl of Strathhammond, Braden MacNevin, and Mr. Anderson rushed in, just as Pirate, lying on his side, with his head bleeding, lifted his arm and aimed his gun at Pucci. Braden pressed his boot down on Pirate's wrist, pinning it to the ground. With a swift motion, he pried the weapon from Pirate's grip, yanking it away before he could fire.

Chapter 50

Pucci ran to Braden, embracing him for saving her life. Olan watched as she ran past him into another man's arms. He didn't know how he felt about this.

Connor had Manier in handcuffs, face crushed against the cold stone floor. He pulled out his cell and called for assistance. Mr. Anderson had Pirate in a full body hold on the ground. Olan cuffed Pirate, thanking Mr. Anderson.

Olan asked the man hugging Pucci, "Who are you?"

Pucci, still holding onto Braden, looked up at him, "Yeah . . . who are you guys, really? And how did you know we were here?"

Braden reluctantly let go of Pucci. He held out his hand to Olan. "Permit me to properly introduce myself. Braden MacNevin, Earl of Strathhammond, and one of the descendants of the Knights Templar. We are the current protectors of King Solomon's artifacts. We've never been able to find the ciphers, but, then again, we didn't want to look for them as they were safe where they were. But since Clouding's sect was after them, we needed to move carefully to protect them at all costs." Olan raised an eyebrow. "Aye, we're well aware of Clouding." He paused, studying the man in front of him. "We know who you are, Chief Inspector Olan Lathen, currently of Scotland Yard."

"Currently, sir?" Olan inquired at the peculiar turn of phrase.

"You are one of us, Chief Inspector."

Pucci's breath caught. The foray into the Akashic Records and the vision on the plane came flooding back into her consciousness: Olan's past-life as a Knights Templar, one of the original, on Temple Mount.

"And, Pucci. I felt you were special when I first met you on the plane. I could feel the energetic power kept in check, matted hair and all," Braden smiled. Pucci's cheeks burned. "When you were asking about all the intricate history tied to Rosslyn, especially your knowledge of Lady Davinia—who still haunts the halls, by the way—it made me wonder." A pause followed, then a soft nod. "Oh aye, I see her too, but I've never been able to speak with her. You have a rare gift, Pucci."

Randi and Varv stepped closer to Pucci, acknowledging Braden's comments.

"When I heard you were going to Islay, and your research regarding John, I contacted Catriona." Pucci's eyes widened, momentarily stunned. "Yes, she's one of us as well. She overheard you talking about a cipher and contacted me to let me know you'd be returning to Rosslyn. We have been following you ever since."

"Oh my God, the ciphers!" Pucci cried out. She bent down, along with Randi and Varv, searching for the three pieces. They each found one. They appeared unscathed.

At that moment, both the south and north doors opened to Edinburgh police storming in. Connor immediately took charge and called Detective Ried over for directions to his men. They picked both Manier and Pirate off the floor and escorted them out the door. Connor was on the phone to headquarters.

Pirate shrugged off the hands and lunged for Pucci.

"This isn't finished," he spat before multiple hands grabbed him and hurried him out the door.

Pucci shivered. Both Braden and Olan moved to comfort her. They stopped inches away from Pucci and stared at each other. An awkward silence fell as Pucci looked at Braden, then Olan.

"Thank you, gentlemen. I'm fine." They stepped back, slightly.

Pucci, Randi, and Varv walked to the altar and laid the three pieces down. They gazed in awe at the third and final cipher, a masterpiece of ancient craftsmanship. Like its counterparts, the table-cut diamonds caught the flickering candlelight, shimmering like liquid silver. The central marquise shaped diamond—about two carats—radiated an ethereal glow, flanked by four smaller diamonds, each glistening like celestial bodies. Above and below the marquise, two half-carat diamonds stood sentinel, their placement deliberate, their presence profound.

A hush settled over the room as Pucci's breath caught. The pattern was no accident. The arrangement, once obscured by the brilliance of the stones, now revealed its deeper truth. She exhaled, the revelation stirring something deep within her.

"As above, so below," she whispered, the words carrying the weight of centuries.

Her fingers traced the lines in reverence. It was more than just a pattern—it was a Star of David, an elongated six-pointed star, a symbol of divine harmony and cosmic balance.

Pucci saw immediately how they fit together. She moved them close to each other, connecting the location tabs. They heard the click and felt the energy pulse from the connected pieces that formed the triangle.

They all gathered around the sight of the connected ciphers. The beauty and mystical energy of the ancient pieces assembled left all of them breathless. Braden and Olan drew closer to the altar, marveling at the sight before them. Hidden Hebrew letters began to glow on each piece. Pucci reverently picked up the triangle. It was warm in her hands. She felt an energetic wind swirling around her. She gently laid the triangle back down.

Olan turned to Connor, "Connor, you and Mr. Anderson, stand watch outside."

Pucci looked at her friends and spoke. "Varv and Randi, remember the strange writing I saw on the ceiling when we were here? Varv, you found they were the ancient language of Ogham. From Ogham, they translated into a Gaelic saying. A gentleman on Islay helped me translate it from Gaelic to English. The English translation is 'The Secret of the Possible.'

"Through my previous studies of Kabbalah, I realized that this saying is the expression for the Shekhinah, the feminine aspect of God. Shekhinah is the field of all possibilities, spanning the upper and lower worlds. She translates divine thought into life on earth. It's also the original name of the center pillar of the three famous pillars, currently called the Journeyman Pillar. It's the least adorned of the three." She paused, looking over at the center pillar.

"Pirate was looking in the wrong place. He just assumed the ciphers had to be connected to the most famous pillar."

"Pucci, that's astonishing," Varv said as the three of them looked at the center pillar as well.

"Braden," Pucci turned to address him, "do you have any idea what we're going to find? Or, if this," pointing to the triangle, "is a key of some sort?"

"I don't actually know, Pucci. For centuries, legends have been whispered from one generation to the next, telling of a mysterious relic said to belong to King Solomon. It is believed that the Knights Templar unearthed this artifact during their excavation of Temple Mount, where Solomon's grand temple once stood. Between the years 1119 and 1129 AD, while the Knights laid their camp upon that sacred soil, they are said to have discovered nae just this powerful relic—but a host o' other artifacts imbued with ancient energies. I've tried to go back into my past-life to understand what is hidden and how to access it, but I do not have the authority to access the upper planes."

Pucci nodded in understanding. Only someone really skilled—an adept of great wisdom and power—may access the higher planes and the wisdom and knowledge it contains.

"What do you mean, Braden?" Randi asked.

He explained. "The astral plane itself is kind of a parallel world, a space where, consciousness can transcend the limitations of the body. Different traditions talk about it as this realm beyond the physical—a space where consciousness moves freely, unbound by the body."

Pucci added, "Some believe there are even higher realms beyond that—places only a true adept, or a Wizard can access."

"Aye," Braden gave Pucci an all-knowing smile. "According to ancient legend, King Solomon possessed not only great wisdom but the ability to access these higher planes of existence, through sacred rituals and magical artifacts, allowing him to command spirits and commune with divine intelligences."

"Olan, could you please pick up and move the ladder over to the center pillar?" Pucci requested.

As Olan did this, Randi asked, "Pucci, what happened to Pirate on the ladder? It looked as if he was pushed."

"That's exactly what happened, Randi. The Templar Knight ghost that I originally saw in Grand Cayman when Olan and I first discovered the cipher in the locket from the Cheapside Hoard has been keeping an eye on me and the cipher. He created a full poltergeist, an apparition powerful enough to affect the physical world, and threw himself at Pirate."

The folks in the chapel fell silent, mouths open, staring at Pucci.

"Seriously?" Randi exclaimed.

"Seriously. You all saw what happened. I saw why it happened," she smiled at the group.

Pucci walked over to the ladder beside the center pillar, the Shekhinah. She looked up at the five-pointed stars carved at the top of the pillar. She picked up the glowing triangle, warmth spread through her hand. Her sacred ring responded, it's light intensifying, forging a connection between the artifacts.

A memory surfaced as she studied the stars. The *Key of Solomon*—a sacred text and one of the most famous magical manuscripts—held wisdom and incantations for summoning spirits through King Solomon's ring, granting him power over demons. Pucci had studied its translated version, now published as *The Key of Solomon the King (Clavicula Salomonis)*. A Kabbalistic incantation of Solomon's came to mind: *Elohim, fight for me in the Name of Tetragrammaton.*

She climbed the ladder, reaching out to trace one of the intricately interwoven stars. She paused, feeling the moment. The Tetragrammaton, the sacred four-letter name of God—Y-H-V-H—was central in Kabbalistic tradition. She recalled that it was sometimes symbolized by a five-pointed star. Could the ciphers be connected to these stars on this pillar?

She looked down at the glowing Hebrew letters, one letter per piece, and one more forming at the top connection. "Braden," she called down, "do you know Hebrew?"

"A little," he said.

She climbed down and showed the Hebrew letters to him.

Reading right to left, starting at the bottom of the triangle: "It looks like Yodh, Heh, Waw, and Heh . . . *Yahweh*. The most sacred Name of God," he whispered. The triangle glowed brighter.

"Braden, look at the top of the pillar. It's the five pointed star, the metaphysical symbol . . . "

"For the Tetragrammaton," they said together.

Goosebumps appeared on all arms.

Chapter 51

"The Tetragrammaton," Pucci began, "is a Greek term that simply means 'the four lettered Name,' referring to the holiest name for God. In metaphysics traditions, the pentagram is believed to embody this sacred name and was even associated with King Solomon, who used both pentagrams and six-pointed stars as his seals. The five points of the pentagram represent the fundamental elements—Earth, Fire, Wind, Water, and Spirit—representing both divine energy and the natural world." She gently laid the connected ciphers back down on the altar.

"So, what you're saying, Pucci," Braden said, studying the top of the pillar, "these ciphers are a key of some sort, connected to the Shekhinah pillar. The Hebrew letters are guiding us to the stars on the top?"

"I believe so, Braden."

Varv's eyes lit up. "Pucci, if Shekhinah is the feminine aspect of God, then the five-pointed star makes total sense. It's also a symbol of Venus, goddess of love and beauty—the very essence of femininity. See? It all ties together."

Randi tilted her head thoughtfully. "You know, pentagrams can be found in Egyptian hieroglyphics as well. They're connected to the Goddess Sopdet, the goddess of fertility. They're also linked to the star Sirius." Sirius barked and wagged his tail at the recognition, though only Pucci could see. "But what now? Does this three part cipher fit into one of the carved pentagrams? If it does, then what?"

Olan reached out and picked up the triangle resting on the altar. He became very still. The triangle glowed brighter.

His current incarnation gave way to the thick-bearded knight with unruly locks of hair in a white mantle, embossed with the blood-red cross of the Templars. It was so powerful that Braden could practically see the shift in Olan, like Pucci did.

"What's happening, Pucci?" Randi asked. She and Varv felt an energetic vibration coming from the triangle and from Olan.

"When he touched the ciphers, Olan's past-life as a Knights Templar just emerged into this lifetime. I know he is directly attached to these pieces but had no idea this would happen!"

Olan began to climb the ladder.

As he got close to the top of the pillar, one of the stone-carved stars began to glow. Olan positioned the triangle so it overlaid part of the shape of the glowing pentacle. It clicked into place. Nothing happened.

"Maybe speak the name of Tetragrammaton," Braden offered.

Pucci climbed up next to Olan, still in a light trance-like state.

She spoke to the merged triangle and star, both still glowing with an ethereal light, "*Yahweh.*"

Nothing.

Olan's Templar persona watched, then smiled and turned toward the glowing pentacle and commanded, "By the authority vested in me by King Solomon, "Ee-y*ah*-hu-w*ah*," rhythmically emphasizing the two *ah* syllables, the most ancient pronunciation of the Name, the Tetragrammaton.

The pillar hummed with a deep, resonating vibration that seemed to pulse from its very core. As they watched in awe, the triangle—now revealed as a key—slowly rotated 180 degrees on its own before coming to a sudden halt. A collective breath was held in suspense. Then, a sharp click echoed through the air. In the negative space between one of the stars and a horizontal stone beam that divided them, a small, hidden chamber emerged like a spirit conjured awake after centuries of silence.

***

Almost to the top of the ladder, Pucci was the closest to the opening. She went up one more rung to peek inside, squeezing by Olan. There was a small pouch sequestered in the chamber. She slowly removed it, being extremely careful not to damage the fragile muslin material. She looked inside the opening once more in case anything was underneath the pouch. Empty. The chamber slid back into place. The cipher key rotated back into its original position and fell out into Pucci's hands. The pillar grew silent as a grave.

She slowly climbed down the ladder, helped at the end by Olan, now back in full chief inspector identity. He wasn't quite sure what just happened to him. He decided to ask Pucci about it later.

"My God, Pucci, you've done it. You've discovered what no one has been able to uncover since this great chapel was built, over five hundred years ago," Braden said. They all watched Pucci reverently set the pouch down on the altar, the ciphers next to it.

"Olan, I think you should do the honors," Pucci said, stepping aside and moving the pouch closer to him.

He nodded curtly. With careful hands, he slowly opened the pouch and tipped its contents onto the altar. A ring fell onto the satin-covered surface. They all leaned in, drawn by the quiet significance of the moment.

Its gold band, hammered into shape by an ancient hand, bore the weight of time in every mark and imperfection. It felt less like a ring and more like an artifact of power. Fused on top of the band rested a solid one-inch square of mysterious metal, each face, a little over a quarter-inch high, held carvings with ancient Hebraic script—four inscriptions, each different, each vibrating with an unseen energy. The engravings were impossibly clear, untouched by age, as though time itself had dared not erode them.

Atop the metallic block sat a striking, blood-red stone—triangular pyramid shape, and pulsing faintly at its core, as if alive. The color flickered in the light, shifting between deep crimson and something darker. More Hebraic letters encircled the gem, forming a continuous ring of symbols, their meanings lost to all but the most learned.

Within this circle, a perfectly arranged four-by-four grid of small squares was inscribed, each square containing yet more letters—too precise, too deliberate to be mere decoration.

Braden came closer, "It can't be . . . "

"What is it, Braden?" Varv asked, marveling at the antiquity, feeling it's power.

"Solomon's magic ring," he reverently whispered.

"Braden, it can't be." Pucci moved closer. "The one that's mentioned in Solomon's book of magic and incantations? The ring that was supposedly given to Solomon by an angel sent by God to give him power over demons?" Pucci exclaimed. "It's a myth!"

"You see it with your own eyes, Pucci," Braden said. "This looks like this is the seal," pointing to the top of the ring, "used for 'striking terror into the Spirits. Upon its being shown to them, they submit, and kneeling upon the earth before it, they obey,'" quoting from the *Key of Solomon*. "No wonder Clouding's sect wanted this. The consequences for humanity would have been catastrophic had the wrong individuals obtained this ring and understood how to wield its power."

Suddenly, Pucci saw the ghost of the Templar appear in front of her with look of desperation. Weak from his poltergeist experience that taxed his energy, he couldn't get out the words of warning.

Pucci cried out. "Something's wrong," before the door slammed open.

Clouding shoved an unconscious Mr. Anderson to the floor of the Chapel, gun pointed to his head.

"I'll take what's rightfully mine," he said, his voice eerily calm, stripped of all emotion. "Pirate told me to meet him here. Looks like I'll have to finish the job myself."

The warning gave Olan a split second to draw his gun from where it had been concealed beneath his jacket, keeping it out of Clouding's sight.

Pucci silently called upon her spirit guides for protection as she discreetly slipped Solomon's ring into her pocket.

"Step away from what's rightfully mine," Clouding commanded, his voice low and edged with menace, oblivious to the fact that Pucci had slipped it into her pocket.

"Where's Detective Davies?" Olan said as calmly as he could.

"Look outside, Lathen. You're lucky I didn't kill him. Now, I'll tell you again," pointing a gun at him, "step away from what's rightfully mine."

"Never!" Braden called out, moving in between Clouding and the altar.

Clouding cocked his gun. "Get out of the way." Suddenly, his hand shook as Sirius, in spirit form, bit down on his wrist. A shot rang out but missed Braden.

With split-second timing, Olan aimed his gun and shot him. Clouding's gun went flying. He gripped the wound, backed out of the door, and tried to flee the scene. Olan ran after him and tackled Clouding to the ground.

While Mr. Anderson was coming around, Braden grabbed his phone and called for an ambulance.

Varv ran to Connor just outside the Chapel. She sat next to him and checked his pulse. It was strong. She cradled his head, being careful not to touch the wound swelling on his left side. Willing him to wake up while she combed his short blond hair back, tears forming in her eyes.

"Varv, is he OK?" Randi put her hand on Varv's shoulder.

"I think so, I hope so," she said, letting a tear slip down her cheek.

Connor's eyes flicked open, then closed again. "It's going to be ok, Varv," said Pucci. "I already hear the sirens." Varv nodded her head, still gently combing his hair. Another tear fell.

"Here, Varv," Randi said, handing a tissue to Varv. "You're getting his face wet," she teased.

Varv smiled at Randi, "Thanks, you're right. I'm being silly."

"No, you're not. It's been a hell of a night," Randi exclaimed, while Pucci sat down next to them nodding and shaking her head at the same time.

Chapter 52

The ambulances came and went. Connor was still unconscious but his vitals were strong. Varv accompanied him to the hospital. They all agreed to meet there later. Clouding had passed out from the pain and loss of blood, but looked like he would survive. Mr. Anderson was nursing a nasty knot on his head, but he was on the mend.

Olan, Braden, Pucci, and Randi stepped back into the chapel, making their way toward the altar. With careful hands, Pucci retrieved the ring from her pocket and placed it on the altar once more.

Pucci hugged Randi. "Are you OK?"

"Remind me never to go on a relaxing vacation with you, Pucci!" Randi chuckled, releasing some of the adrenaline they were all feeling.

Olan turned to Braden, "That was an incredibly stupid thing to do, MacNevin. You could have been killed."

Braden answered, "I have sworn to protect Templar artifacts at all costs, including my life. Thank you for saving mine, Chief Inspector."

"Pucci, you never got a chance to tell me how you know these two gentleman," Olan said, acknowledging Mr. Anderson as well.

"Braden and I met on the plane from the States over to London and then I happened to be booked into his castle outside of Edinburgh for a few days. Total coincidence," she blushed slightly. She didn't believe in coincidence.

Olan raised an eyebrow, "Interesting. A castle, MacNevin?"

"It's been in my family for generations. I finally had to sell the ol' lass. It just got too much. It's a resort and spa now," he said sadly. "But I still conduct some of my affairs there."

They all three looked down at the ring, wondering what to do with it now and how to keep it safe from dark energy sects like Clouding's.

"I know what we need to do," Olan said as he began texting someone. "It belongs to the chapel."

"It belongs to the world," said Braden. "We should gift it to the Ashmolean or the British Museum. It will be heavily guarded."

"That decision is up to its owner to make. Plus, from a police procedure standpoint, it is the owner's property," Olan said.

After about half an hour, the west door opened, and a towering silver-haired gentleman strode in, his presence commanding the room before he even spoke. He was dressed in full Scottish regalia—save for the kilt—his tartan colors of pine green, red, gold, and blue interwoven in the wool jacket and bonnet he removed from his head as he entered the chapel. The air of authority around him was unmistakable. Alongside him, three other individuals entered, bustling around him, some on their phones, some holding notepads.

He exuded a commanding presence, even more so when he spoke in a booming voice.

"Ye better not have soiled my chapel, Lathen!" With a genuine smile, he formed a heartfelt connection with Olan through a distinct handshake and an embrace.

Pucci noticed the handshake. *Masonic?* she wondered.

Olan whispered in his ear, and the tall, distinguished looking man asked his entourage to step back out of the chapel. With puzzled looks, they nodded, turned and walked back out.

"The fewer people know about this, the better, Sir," Olan addressed the man.

"Aye." To Braden, he said, "Good to see you, my Lord."

"Good to see you, Sir," Braden acknowledged.

Pucci and Randi were transfixed, captivated by the presence of these three distinguished Scottish gentlemen. Pucci found herself unable to decide who was the most handsome among them. Randi was equally entranced, her gaze full of admiration. Their eyes met, and they shared a quiet, amused glance, stifling a giggle.

"This must be the infamous, Ms. Riddle," the gentleman said, taking Pucci's hand and bringing it to his lips.

Pucci, momentarily stunned that he knew her name, felt a flush creep up her neck. Blushing furiously, she once again had the absurd urge to curtsy.

Olan spoke, "Yes. May I present Pucci Riddle? And this is Randi Baklen." Randi grinned as he took her hand as well. "They, together with Varvada Conti, solved the ancient riddle of the jeweled ciphers I informed you about a year ago. They—and MacNevin—sacrificed their lives to keep the key, and ultimately the ring, from falling into Clouding's possession."

Pucci was astonished that this distinguished gentleman had heard of her—let alone with the level of detail Olan seemed to assume he knew.

She spoke, "Sir, did you know Solomon's ring was in this chapel?"

"I was aware of the legends and certain facts that were handed down by my ancestors. But, to be honest, I never believed an ancient magical artifact of King Solomon's was somewhere in this chapel."

Pucci smiled, looking at the Shekhinah Pillar. "Your chapel is truly a reliquary structure. Housing one of the most sacred artifacts in the history of humanity."

He acknowledged this with a smile and a slight bow before reverently picking up the ring.

"I, and the world, owe you all a debt of gratitude. Thank you." He turned the ring slowly between his thumb and finger, his voice solemn. "I know exactly where this belongs—back with my ancestors, here in Rosslyn. No one will know, except my son, when it's time to tell him. Maybe one day, when there isn't a threat from evil, we'll give it back to the world." He placed the ring back in its pouch, formally bowed to the ladies, nodded a thank you to Olan and Braden, turned and walked out.

Chapter 53

"So that's it then," Braden said to the group standing in front of Rosslyn Chapel's visitor center entrance. Mr. Anderson went to retrieve the car.

Olan, Pucci, and Randi turned to face the sunrise, their movements synchronized as if drawn by an invisible force. The first rays of sunlight crept over the horizon, soft and golden. It was the winter solstice, the shortest day of the year, a sacred turning point, when the world begins to breathe in the promise of returning light.

Olan called the hospital and headquarters.

Braden pulled Pucci aside.

"I don't know what to say, Pucci. I want to take you in my arms and never let you go," he grinned like a schoolboy. "But I believe your heart lies with another." He glanced over to Olan.

Pucci, aware she might never see Braden again, reached up and gently touched his cheek. "You've always been an extraordinary man, across lifetimes. I believe we've finally fulfilled an ancient agreement by recovering and guarding Solomon's ring from the forces of darkness. Perhaps that was our true purpose, not to unite as lovers in this life, but to protect humanity. Our connection transcends time, Braden. I hope we see each other again."

With a gentle kiss and a bow, the Earl of Strathhamond bade Pucci farewell and drove away in his waiting car.

Randi put her arm around her softly crying friend. "I have a feeling you'll see him again."

"Do you, really, Randi?"
"I do. Now, let's get some food! I'm starving!"

***

A police car arrived to transport Olan, Pucci, and Randi to the hospital. In the back seat, Pucci pulled out the protein bars she'd purchased to hold them over till they got to the hospital. Although they were exhausted and hungry, they were all anxious to see how Connor and Anya were doing.

As soon as they entered the hospital lobby, Varv was there. She ran to Pucci and Randi. They hugged.

"Connor is OK, the head injury wasn't serious," Varv said. "They're keeping him overnight."

Pucci asked, "Have you seen Anya yet?"

"No, they haven't let her see any visitors. But now you're here, Chief Inspector, I hope they'll let us in to see her," Varv said as they walked to the elevator.

Connor and Anya were on the same floor. Olan showed the staff his badge and asked after Connor. They let him know it was a mild concussion. They were keeping him overnight. He'll be fine in the morning.

"We'd like to see Anya Hesch," Olan said.

"Aye, but ye can only stay a short while," the nurse said as she led them to her room.

"I'd like to go in first, without all of you," Olan said. "I need to ask some questions before she gets distracted by you lot." He walked in.

Anya's color was returning. Olan said a silent prayer once again that she had survived.

"Hello, Anya, how are you feeling?"

"Hi, chief. No worse for the wear," smiling and grimacing at the same time. She took a breath. "Chief, I remembered a conversation I overheard. Pirate and Morgan mentioned an informant in Scotland Yard . . . "

Olan could feel her anxiety, draining her energy. He lifted a hand, signaling her to stop. "We found him, Anya. Actually, Sara figured it out. She told Davies that Sergeant Tress had been hanging around her more and more. She thought he was flirting, in a creepy sort of way, but she realized he kept asking her about her research on Clouding's operations. At one point, she gave him false information, then followed him outside the station. She overheard him relaying the same information to someone over the phone. She alerted Davies. He's been arrested."

Anya's jaw muscles relaxed. "Sara . . . I knew she was good. I hope you give her the recognition she deserves."

"Aye, we already have." Olan grinned. "I have a surprise for you."

Olan opened the door for Pucci and Varv. Randi stayed in the hall since she didn't know Anya and didn't want to overwhelm her.

Anya's face lit up when she saw her friends. "Oh my God!" Anya exclaimed. "Oh my . . . Varv! Pucci!"

They hurried to her bedside and embraced her as best they could, despite the tubes in her arms.

Tears formed in Anya's eyes. "You're here. I can't believe you would want to see me after what I put you all through. Pucci, I almost got you killed."

"Anya, from the moment we met, I sensed goodness in you. Deep down, I knew there was no way you could ever be aligned with something so evil. When Olan told me you were working undercover, it all fell into place," Pucci said.

"And Varv. I'm so sorry. You were such a good friend to me. I hated deceiving you all those months. Please forgive me."

"You are already forgiven, my friend," Varv said, tearing up.

Olan cleared his throat, "Och, OK, enough, she needs to rest." He turned to Anya, "We'll fill you in on the rest of our adventures later."

"Chief, by the way. Did you ever find the three, ten-carat blue diamonds Whiley was smuggling out?" Anya asked.

"What? We just thought those were a rumor. We still checked everywhere, but you're saying he actually had three of them? Bloody hell, those are worth about five million pounds each!" Olan exclaimed. "I'll let the mine know to keep searching. We know Whiley didn't get them out." He paused, seeing her energy draining. "Thank you, Anya. Now get some rest."

The women said their goodbyes. Anya promised to be well enough to be at the Cheapside Hoard's museum debut opening in a few days.

***

The three women and Olan found a nearby restaurant in Edinburgh. They were all exhausted but also exhilarated about solving the riddle of the jeweled ciphers. Waiting for their food, Randi overheard Olan talking to the S.A. Mine regarding the continued search for the three blue diamonds.

He got off the phone.

"You know, Chief Inspector," Randi began, "I'm familiar with mining operations. We installed a generator set in one of the mines in the U.S.—a job I had before I got into shipbuilding. I received a tour of the entire operation, even underground. Everyone is searched when they come out of the mine, even me. I was especially fascinated by the front loaders that are down in the mine removing earth in large quantities. They only bring them up out of the mine a couple times a year for maintenance. If I was going to smuggle something out, I'd put it somewhere in the loader."

All three were staring at Randi, amazed.

"Randi, only you would be fascinated by a bunch of equipment! Did you even get to see some of the diamonds?" Varv asked jokingly.

"Oh, yes, Varv. They were amazing too! Did you know the largest blue diamond found so far is 122.5 carats from the Petra mine in South Africa?"

Olan spoke up, "We did search the loader, Randi. Good call but we didn't find anything anywhere."

Randi chewed her food contemplating. "Did you check the hydraulic reservoir, Chief Inspector? That would be a wonderful place to hide them. The stones would just be bathing in hydraulic fluid until removed."

Olan stared at her for a moment, then excused himself to make a phone call to the team still searching at the mine.

Meanwhile, Pucci let Varv and Randi know what happened with Braden. Varv agreed with Randi, she felt they would see each other again.

The women had finished their coffee and dessert and were preparing to pay the bill, wondering where Olan had gone. They were just discussing where to stay in Edinburgh before heading to London for the opening of the Cheapside Hoard exhibit when Olan returned, standing beside Randi's chair.

"Randi, please stand up," he said.

Puzzled, Randi stood next to him.

"Randi Baklen, by the power vested in me by the commissioner of police of the metropolis, the head of Scotland Yard, I hereby award you an Honorary Commendation for Meritorious Service," he said, with as much pomp and circumstance as he could muster. "The three blue diamonds were exactly where you said they'd be. If we weren't together this entire time, I'd arrest you on suspicion of smuggling!" He laughed.

They all laughed and cheered.

"I'll let Anya know that her friends, old and new, solved the mystery!" Olan exclaimed. "Thank you, Randi, that was a stroke of genius."

Pucci and Varv beamed with pride, their faces illuminated by the satisfaction of their achievement. *What an extraordinary team we are*, Pucci mused, her heart swelling with admiration for what they had accomplished together.

Chapter 54

Pucci, Randi and Varv all splurged on evening dresses for the big event of the Cheapside Hoard opening night exhibit at the Museum of London. Pucci and Varv were special honored guests for helping to retrieve "the greatest hoard of its kind ever recovered on British soil."

Pucci's deep-purple sequined gown shimmered with every step she took, casting a soft, dazzling glow around her. The multi-colored sapphire turtle necklace the women had bought together in Grand Cayman rested on her heart chakra. Varv, graceful and alluring, wore an off-the-shoulder silk dress in a rich shade of pink, complemented by a black shawl adorned with delicate floral patterns that draped elegantly over her tall, slender frame. She also wore the emerald encrusted turtle necklace from their previous trip. Randi exuded classic elegance in a flawlessly tailored little black dress, with small blue diamond earrings, a gift from the S.A. Mine.

Brent Nash came hurrying up to them, his familiar khaki pants traded for the sharp lines of a tuxedo that hinted at the importance of the evening. He looked every bit the polished curator, appointed by the museum in recognition of his leadership over the now-renowned exhibit. They exchanged warm hugs and introduced Randi.

"Brent," Pucci said, pulling him aside. "Remember the reliquary locket you researched for JD? I think I saw it in one of the display cases."

"Yes, of course, Pucci. That's what started this whole adventure for me. Did you ever get it to open?" Brent saw Pucci's grin. "You did! Did it contain anything?"

She removed three small velvet pouches from her purse. Opening the purple one, she took out the jeweled cipher that had once been sequestered inside the locket. She reverently handed it to Brent. As he gently inspected it, Pucci continued. "There is a very long and intriguing story that accompanies that piece."

"It's a cipher... these are extremely rare. I wonder what it connects to?" he said still entranced by the piece. He didn't notice her open two more pouches.

"It connects to these."

"Oh my God. Pucci, do you know what you have here? Where did you get these?"

She interrupted before more questions came. "Again, long story, Brent. The chief inspector and I are donating these to the museum. When joined, they form a beautiful triangle." She left it at that. The magic had faded from the triangle, but not the magnificence. "Take care, Brent," she said, watching as he carefully tucked the three pouches into his inside jacket pocket.

He bowed his head. "Thank you, Pucci. One day, I hope to hear the 'long story.'" He straightened his jacket and dashed off. He moved with practiced ease, heading toward a group that exuded elegance and importance—what appeared to be British royalty, the tailored suit and a glittering tiara catching the light as they entered.

Pucci's gaze drifted toward the entrance where Olan was gently guiding Anya's wheelchair through the doorway. A wave of love and admiration washed over her, catching her off guard with its intensity. His unwavering strength and the quiet depth of his care stirred something deep within her. There was power in his presence, but also a rare, quiet tenderness—an effortless balance of strength and compassion that filled her with quiet reverence.

Olan saw a vision of beauty coming toward him. Pucci's hair, pulled back into a beautiful butterfly hair clip, showed off her sparkling tanzanite earrings. Her eyes looked alight with energy and fire. As she embraced Anya, he caught a light sensuous scent of Frankincense. At that moment, the last few days caught up to him. He slowed his mind and took her in. This remarkable women, so humble and unassuming, had just saved humanity—and yes, she had saved him. He moved toward her but Varv interrupted.

"Anya, you look beautiful," Varv said, leaning down and hugging her. Anya wore a soft lavender layered silk pantsuit that accentuated her baby blue eyes and long blond hair, now flowing down over the wheelchair's back. Anya admired Pucci's and Varv's turtle necklaces.

Pucci removed a small jewelry box from her purse. "I've been carrying this around this entire trip, not knowing if I'd ever see you again, Anya. Varv and I want to give you a gift."

Anya gently accepted the black velvet box from Pucci's hand. She opened it to find a jeweled turtle of moonstones, the one she had wanted so desperately in the jewelry store in Georgetown. She didn't want to cry and ruin her makeup, but she couldn't help it. Tears ran down her cheek.

"I . . . I don't know what to say. You two have shown me friendship that I've never known. I . . . thank you. Thank you, both."

They squeezed her free hand. Varv put the necklace around her neck.

"We need a picture! Randi, get over here with your blue diamonds!" Varv said. Everyone laughed. Pucci looked over, and who was photo-bombing? None other than the ghost of J.D. Langer. Pucci smiled and mouthed *hey*. He laughed and disappeared.

She found Connor and Olan, deep in conversation. "You look fully recovered, Detective Inspector."

"Thank you, Pucci. I feel fine—except for the news the chief just told me." Turning back to Olan, Connor, incensed, said, "I can't believe that. Clouding is out of hospital? And out of custody already? How can that be?"

"Friends in very high places. And I have to answer as to why I shot him," Olan said, disgusted. "I am being investigated by DPS. That's internal affairs to you, Pucci. Let's hope they don't drag you into it, Connor. Don't worry, I'll protect you."

At that moment, Pucci heard a sinister voice in her ear.

"This isn't over," it hissed, and was gone.

She whirled around looking for the source, champagne flying. No one was there. Chills crept up her spine. Clouding was alive and free. She'd have to be vigilant in this and the spirit realm. She knew his powers were great.

Pucci accepted another glass of champagne and took a moment to look around the room and breathe, calming her nerves. As she admired the emerald and diamond salamander brooch behind the glass display, a petite Japanese woman approached her. She was dressed in a red kimono-style dress with yellow and white birds adorning one side. Her short black hair gleamed under the lighting from the display cases. Pucci immediately recognized her as Naoko Cordary, famous artist and chef. She had her own cooking channel that Pucci watched regularly, wishing she could cook like Naoko.

"Are you Pucci Riddle?" Naoko asked.

"I am. How did you know, Ms. Cordary?"

"I have friends on the other side, too. Please, call me Naoko. They told me to contact you. I need your help."

An apparition came into focus next to Naoko.

"I see what you mean, Naoko. Oy vey."

Author's Note

The story of the pink bunny underwear is true. This was confirmed by my friend, who had lost her husband and did not remember the gift. Later, she went to her drawer and, to her surprise, found the pink bunny underwear. This is an example of evidence-based paranormal communication.

The story of The Lady on the Stairs is inspired by the apparition of Lady Catherine, known as the "Grey Lady" of Dalhousie Castle. Strathhammond Castle is based on my own stay at Dalhousie, where I had a conversation with the Grey Lady. She asked me, "What are you doing in my house?" I asked her, "Why are you still here?" She replied, "Why are you still here, in my house?" She had no interest in crossing over—she was staying. I later described her to an employee at the castle, noting the enormous hat she wore. He later showed me a picture of her—wearing the exact same hat!

According to extensive online research conducted by the author and the *Official Guidebook for Rosslyn Chapel*, written by The Earl of Rosslyn; Sir William St. Clair, the Earl of Orkney and Caithness was appointed Patron and Protector of the Freemasons of Scotland in 1441 by King James II.

The description of Sir William St. Clair is based on both the guidebook and *Rosslyn Chapel Decoded* by Alan Butler and John Ritchie, referencing Sir William's collection of books now housed in the Bodleian Library.

The history of Robert the Bruce and his connection to the St. Clair family is drawn from the guidebook and additional research by the author.

The story of Angus Óg fighting alongside Robert the Bruce and his sons is historically accurate. John, the son of Angus Óg, received Islay in the early 14th century. His son, John II, remained on Islay until about 1493. However, the story of the early distillery that John and Callum founded is the author's creation.

Mhurachaidh Distillery is fictional. It is inspired by one of the last illicit distillers on Islay, Baldy Mhurachaidh, who made whisky in a cave near Proaig (*Tales of Islay* by Peggy Earl).

The passage on the language of the trees is drawn from *The Green Man Tree Oracle* by John Matthews and Will Worthington. It references the Ogam alphabet, also known as the Ogham alphabet.

The story of Bessie Williamson is historically accurate. She was the first female distiller and distillery owner, according to Laphroaig's history. Unfortunately, she did not speak to me at the distillery—our conversation is purely from the author's imagination.

The shop in Tarbert is inspired by *Zing Organics*—a marvelous shop. Check them out at www.zingorganics.co.uk.

The Shekhinah is described as "The Secret of the Possible, receiving the emanation from above and engendering the varieties of life below." (*The Essential Kabbalah: The Heart of Jewish Mysticism* by Daniel C. Matt).

"Shekhinah is the field of all possibilities, spanning the upper and lower worlds. She translates divine thought into life on earth." — Direct quote from *The Book of Mirrors: Sefer Mar'ot ha-Tsove'ot* by David ben Judah he-Hasid.

"Ee-ya*h*-hu-wa*h*," rhythmically emphasizing the two *ah* syllables as the most ancient pronunciation of the Name of God, is referenced from *The Secret Doctrine of the Kabbalah: Recovering the Key to Hebraic Sacred Science* by Leonora Leet.

The Gaelic translations and pronunciation were provided by Iain MacGillivray, an exceptional piper and fiddle player, and Scotland's youngest Clan leader. Iain is a fluent Gaelic speaker, and I had the pleasure of meeting him when *The Tannahill Weavers* performed in Albuquerque. Their music is incredible!

Find out more at ljaldon.com and check out Pucci's blog—Spirits by Pucci! On Instagram @ljaldon and @pucciriddle

About the Author

Lisa Aldon is the author of Pucci Riddle Mystery series, *Riddle of the Haunted Hoard*, the first novel in the series and her earlier work of non-fiction *Transcendent Leadership and the Evolution of Consciousness*. She currently lives in Albuquerque, New Mexico, where she also works part time as an engineer and consciousness leadership consultant. Her passions are helping the planet evolve, her family, and her dog, Luna. Visit Lisa at LJAldon.com.

About the Publisher

The Sager Group was founded in 1984. In 2012 it was chartered as a multimedia content brand, with the intent of empowering those who create art—an umbrella beneath which makers can pursue, and profit from, their craft directly, without gatekeepers. TSG publishes books; ministers to artists and provides modest grants; and produces documentary, feature, and commercial films. By harnessing the means of production, The Sager Group helps artists help themselves. For more information, please see www.TheSagerGroup.net.

More from The Sager Group

The Swamp: Deceit and Corruption in the CIA
An Elizabeth Petrov Thriller (Book 1)
by Jeff Grant

Eat Wheaties: A Novel
by Michael Kun

#MeAsWell: A Novel
by Peter Mehlman

Death Came Swiftly: Novel About the Tay Bridge Disaster of 1879
by Bill Abrams

High Tolerance: A Novel of Sex, Race, Celebrity, Murder... and Marijuana
by Mike Sager

Miss Havilland: A Novel
by Gay Daly

The Orphan's Daughter: A Novel
by Jan Cherubin

Lifeboat No. 8: Surviving the Titanic
by Elizabeth Kaye

Into the River of Angels: A Novel
by George R. Wolfe

Goodbye, Sweetberry Park: A Novel of City Life,
Creeping Gentrification and Flesh-eating Snakes
by Josh Green

See our entire library at TheSagerGroup.net

THE SAGER GROUP

Artifex Te Adiuva